COLONEL SUN

'After the death of Bond's creator, Ian Fleming, in August 1964, Bond devotees feared this would be the end of the super secret agent but, as in all his adventures, 007 survives to embark on another thrilling assignment. Mr Kingsley Amis, under the pseudonym of Robert Markham, takes over where Fleming left off and the story takes our intrepid hero to the Greek Islands on yet another death-defying mission . . . Three years ago, Mr Amis himself studied Bond in great depth for *The James Bond Dossier*. He is also a Bond fan and has been since he discovered the first paperback, *Casino Royale*, on a railway bookstall . . . Because of his knowledge of the character, Kingsley Amis seemed the obvious successor to Fleming. But is Amis's Bond (or, more accurately, Markham's) the same as Fleming's Bond?'

The Times Educational Supplement

'It is as indistinguishable from the real thing as butter is from butter . . . Markham has done an extremely efficient job of resurrection . . . .Bond is dead. Long live Bond.'
Harper's Bazaar

ROBERT MARKHAM

COLONEL SUN

UNABRIDGED

PAN BOOKS LTD : LONDON

First published 1968 by Jonathan Cape Ltd.
This edition published 1970 by Pan Books Ltd,
33 Tothill Street, London, S.W.1

330 02304 7

Printed in Great Britain by
Cox & Wyman Ltd,
London, Reading and Fakenham

CONTENTS

To the memory of
IAN FLEMING

AUTHOR'S NOTE

Two methods of indicating dialogue are used in this book.

Dialogue *given in English translation* from Russian or Greek, following Continental practice, is introduced by a dash; for example,

—Good morning, Comrade General.

Dialogue *in English* is enclosed in the normal inverted commas; for example,

'He was hit in the back, I think.'

Chapter 1

A Man in Sunglasses

JAMES BOND stood at the middle tees of the eighteenth on the Sunningdale New Course, enjoying the tranquil normality of a sunny English afternoon in early September. The Old Course, he considered, with its clumps of majestic oak and pine, was charmingly landscaped, but something in his nature responded to the austerity of the New: more lightly wooded, open to the sky, patches of heather and thin scrub on the sandy soil – and, less subjectively, a more testing series of holes. Bond was feeling mildly pleased with himself for having taken no more than a four at the notoriously tricky dogleg sixth, where a touch of slice in the drive was likely to land you in a devilish morass of bushes and marshy hummocks. He had managed a clear two hundred and fifty yards straight down the middle, a shot that had demanded every ounce of effort without (blessed relief) the slightest complaint from the area where, last summer, Scaramanga's Derringer slug had torn through his abdomen.

Near by, waiting for the four ahead of them to move on to the green, was Bond's opponent and incidentally his best friend in the Secret Service: Bill Tanner, M's Chief of Staff. Noticing the deep lines of strain round Tanner's eyes, his almost alarming pallor, Bond had taken the opportunity of an unusually quiet morning at Headquarters to talk him into a trip down to this sleepy corner of Surrey. They had lunched first at Scott's in Coventry Street, beginning with a dozen each of the new season's Whitstable oysters and going on to cold silverside of beef and potato salad, accompanied by a well-chilled bottle of Anjou rosé. Not perhaps the ideal prelude to a round of golf, even a little self-indulgent. But Bond had recently heard that the whole north side of the street was doomed to demolition, and counted every meal taken in those severe but comfortable panelled rooms as a tiny victory over the new, hateful London of steel-and-glass-matchbox architecture, flyovers and underpasses, and the endless hysterical clamour of pneumatic drills.

The last of the four, caddie in attendance, was plodding up to the green. Tanner stepped to his trolley – having some minor Service shop to exchange, they were transporting their clubs themselves – and pulled out the new Ben Hogan driver he had been yearning for weeks to try out. Then, with characteristic deliberation, he squared up to his ball. Nothing beyond a nominal fiver hung on this game, but it was not Bill Tanner's way to pursue any objective with less than the maximum of his ability – a trait that had made him the best Number Two in the business.

The sun beat down. Insects were droning in the little belt of brambles, rowans and silver birch saplings to their left. Bond's gaze shifted from the lean, intent figure of the Chief of Staff to the putting green a quarter of a mile away, the famous, ancient oak by the eighteenth green of the Old Course, the motionless line of parked cars. Was this the right sort of life ? – an unexacting game of golf with a friend, to be followed in due time by a leisurely drive back to London (avoiding the M4), a light dinner alone in the flat, a few hands of piquet with another friend – 016 of Station B, home from West Berlin on ten days' leave – and bed at eleven thirty. It was certainly a far more sensible and grown-up routine than the round of gin and tranquillizers he had been trapped in only a couple of years back, before his nightmare odyssey through Japan and the USSR. He should be patting himself on the back for having come through that sticky patch. And yet . . .

With the sound of a plunging sabre, Bill Tanner's driver flashed through the still, warm air and his ball, after seeming to pass out of existence for an instant, reappeared on its soaring arc, a beautiful tall shot sufficiently drawn to take him well to the left of the clump of Scotch pines that had brought many a promising score to grief at the last minute. As things stood he had only to halve the hole to win.

'It looks like your fiver, I'm sorry to say, Bill.'

'About time I took one off you.'

As James Bond stepped forward in his turn, the thought crossed his mind that there might be a worse sin than the cardinal one of boredom. Complacency. Satisfaction with the second-rate. Going soft without knowing it.

* * *

The man wearing the rather unusually large and opaque sunglasses had had no difficulty, as he sauntered past the open windows of the club lounge towards the putting-green, in identifying the tall figure now shaping up to drive off the eighteenth tee. He had had plenty of practice in identifying it over the past few weeks, at greater distances than this. And at the moment his vision was sharpened by urgency.

If any member had marked out the man in sunglasses as a stranger and approached him with inquiring offers of help, he would have been answered courteously in a faintly non-British accent – not foreign exactly, perhaps South African – to the effect that no help was needed. Any moment now, the stranger would have explained, he expected to be joined by Mr John Donald to discuss with him the possibilities of being put up for membership. (Mr John Donald was in fact in Paris, as a couple of carefully placed telephone calls had established earlier that day.) But, as it turned out, nobody went near the man in sunglasses. Nobody so much as noticed him. This was not so surprising, because a long course of training, costing a large sum of money, had seen to it that he was very good at not being noticed.

The man strolled across the putting-green and seemed to be examining, with exactly average interest, the magnificent display flower-bed and its thick ranks of red-hot pokers and early chrysanthemums. His demeanour was perfectly relaxed, his face quite expressionless, as the eyes behind the glasses looked in the direction of the flowers. His mind, however, was racing. Today's operation had been set up three times already, before being abandoned at the eleventh hour. There was a date schedule on it so tight that further postponement might mean the cancellation of the entire scheme. This would have greatly displeased him. He very much wanted the operation to go through, not for any fancy idealistic or political reason, but simply out of professional pride. What was being undertaken would, if all went well, end up as the most staggeringly audacious piece of lawlessness he had ever heard of. To be associated with the success of such a project would certainly bring him advancement from his employers. Whereas to be associated with its failure . . .

The man in sunglasses drew his arms in to his sides for a moment, as if the approach of evening had brought a stray gust of air that suddenly struck chill. The moment passed. He had no trouble making himself relax again. He considered dispassionately the undeniable fact that the time schedule he was working to was even tighter than the date schedule, and was showing signs of coming apart. Events were running half an hour late. The man Bond and his companion had lingered hoggishly over their lunch in the rich aristocrats' restaurant. It would be very awkward if they lingered over the drinks these people felt bound to consume around this hour.

A casual glance showed that the two Englishmen had finished their round of infantile play and were approaching the club house. The man in sunglasses, his eyes invisible behind the dark lenses, watched sidelong until, laughing inanely together, they had passed out of sight. No further delay had occurred. Although he had not looked at his watch for half an hour, and did not do so now, he knew the correct time to within a minute.

A pause. Silence but for a few distant voices, an engine being started in the car park, a jet aircraft in a distant corner of the sky. Somewhere a clock struck. The man went through a tiny underplayed pantomime of somebody deciding regretfully that he really cannot be kept waiting any longer. Then he walked off at an easy pace towards the entrance. As he neared the road he took off his sunglasses and slipped them carefully into the top jacket pocket of his anonymous light-grey suit. His eyes, of a washed-out blue that went oddly with his dead black hair, had the controlled interestedness of a sniper's as he reaches for his rifle.

* * *

'Do you think I'm going soft, Bill?' asked Bond twenty minutes later as they stood at the bar.

Bill Tanner grinned. 'Still sore about ending up two down?' (Bond had missed a four-foot putt on the last green.)

'It isn't that, it's . . . Look, to start with I'm under-employed. What have I done this year? One trip to the States, on what turns out to be a sort of discourtesy visit, and then that miserable flop out East back in June.'

Bond had been sent to Hong Kong to supervise the conveying to the Red mainland of a certain Chinese and a number of unusual stores. The man had gone missing about the time of Bond's arrival and had been found two days later in an alley off the waterfront with his head almost severed from his body. After another three days, memorable chiefly for a violent and prolonged typhoon, the plan had been cancelled and Bond recalled.

'It wasn't your fault that our rep. went sick before you turned up,' said Tanner, falling automatically into the standard Service jargon for use in public.

'No.' Bond stared into his gin and tonic. 'But what worries me is that I didn't seem to mind much. In fact I was quite relieved at being spared the exertion. There's something wrong somewhere.'

'Not physically, anyway. You're in better shape than I've seen you for years.'

Bond looked round the unpretentious room with its comfortable benches in dark-blue leather, its decorous little groups of business and professional men – quiet men, decent men, men who had never behaved violently or treacherously in their lives. Admirable men: but the thought of becoming indistinguishable from them was suddenly repugnant.

'It's ceasing to be an individual that's deadly,' said Bond thoughtfully. 'Becoming a creature of habit. Since I got back

I've been coming down here about three Tuesdays out of four, arriving at the same sort of time, going round with one or other of the same three friends, leaving at six thirty or so, driving home each time for the same sort of evening. And seeing nothing wrong with it. A man in my line of business shouldn't work to a time-table. You understand that.'

It is true that a secret agent on an assignment must never fall into any kind of routine that will enable the opposition to predict his movements, but it was not until later that Bill Tanner was to appreciate the curious unintentional significance of what Bond was saying.

'I don't quite follow, James. It doesn't apply to your life in England, surely,' said Tanner, speaking with equally unintentional irony.

'I was thinking of the picture as a whole. My existence is falling into a pattern. I must find some way of breaking out of it.'

'In my experience that sort of shake-up comes along of its own accord when the time is ripe. No need to do anything about it yourself.'

'Fate or something?'

Tanner shrugged. 'Call it what you like.'

For a moment there was an odd silence between the two men. Then Tanner glanced at the clock, drained his glass and said briskly, 'Well, I suppose you'll want to be getting along.'

On the point of agreeing, Bond checked himself. 'To hell with it,' he said. 'If I'm going to get myself disorganized I might as well start now.' He turned to the barmaid. 'Let's have those again, Dot.'

'Won't you be late for M?' asked Tanner.

'He'll just have to possess his soul in patience. He doesn't dine till eight fifteen, and half an hour or so of his company is quite enough these days.'

'Don't I know it,' said Tanner feelingly. 'I still can't get near him at the office. We've taken to doing most of our confabulating over the intercom and that suits me fine. I've only to say it looks like rain for him to shout at me to stop fussing round him like a confounded old woman.'

It was a life-like imitation and Bond laughed, but he was serious enough when he said, 'It's only natural. Sailors hate being ill.'

The previous winter M had developed a distressing cough which he had testily refused to do anything about, saying that the damn thing would clear up when the warmer weather came. But the spring and early summer had brought rain and humidity as well as warmth, and the cough had not cleared up. One morning in July Miss Moneypenny had taken in a sheaf of signals to find M sprawled semi-conscious over his desk, grey in the face and fighting for breath. She had summoned Bond from his fifth-floor office and, at the angry insistence of the headquarters MO, M had been bundled half by force into his old Silver Wraith Rolls and escorted home. After three weeks in bed under the devoted care of ex-Chief Petty Officer Hammond and his wife, M had largely recovered from his bronchial congestion, though his temper – as Bond had amply discovered on his periodic visits – looked like taking longer to heal. . . . Since then, Bond had taken to breaking his weekly return journey from Sunningdale by looking in at Quarterdeck, the beautiful little Regency manor-house on the edge of Windsor Park, ostensibly for an informal chat about the affairs of the Service but really to keep an eye on M's health, to have a sly word with the Hammonds and find out whether the old man was following the MO's orders, getting plenty of rest and, in particular, laying off his pipe and his daily couple of poisonous black cheroots. He had been prepared for a characteristic explosion from M when he suggested the first of these visits, but as it was, M had growled an immediate, if surly, assent. Bond suspected he felt rather cut off from the world by being, among other things, temporarily condemned to a three-day working week. (The MO had only won that concession by threatening to send him on a cruise unless he agreed.)

Bond now said, 'Why don't you come along too, Bill? Then I could give you a lift back to London.'

Tanner hesitated. 'I don't think I will, James, thanks all the same. There's a rather important call from Station L coming through to the office later on which I'd like to take personally.'

'What's the Duty Officer for? You're doing the best part of two men's work as it is.'

'Well ... it isn't only that. I'll give M a miss anyway. There's something about that house of his that gives me the creeps.'

A quarter of an hour later, having dropped the Chief of Staff at the railway station, Bond swung the long bonnet of his Continental Bentley left off the A30. Ahead of him was the pleasant, leisurely drive of ten minutes or so that would bring him, via twisting minor roads, to Quarterdeck.

The man who had been watching Bond earlier sat in a stolen Ford Zephyr, unobtrusively parked fifty yards from the turning. He now spoke a single word into his Hitachi solid-state transceiver. Four and a half miles away, another man acknowledged with a monosyllable, switched off his own instrument, and emerged with his two companions from the dense woodland thicket where they had been lying for the past two hours.

The occupant of the Zephyr sat quite still for another minute. It was his nature to avoid unnecessary movement, even at moments like the present when he was as tense as he ever allowed himself to become. The time-table of the operation was now fifty minutes in arrears. One more major delay would entail, not merely cancellation, but disaster, for the step his radio signal had just initiated was as irreversible as it was violent. But there would not be another delay. None was inherently present in the situation. His training told him so.

At the end of the minute, calculated after careful research as the optimum interval for following in the wake of the Bentley, he put the Zephyr in gear and started for the turning.

Bond crossed the county boundary into Berkshire and made his unhurried way among the ugly rash of modern housing – half-heartedly mock-Tudor villas, bungalows and two-storey boxes with a senseless variegation of planking, brick and crazy paving on the front of each and the inevitable TV aerial sprouting from every roof. Once through Silwood village and across the A329 these signs of affluence were behind him and the Bentley thrummed down a gentle slope between pine-woods. Soon there were lush open farmlands on his left and the forest established in force on his right. Places like this would last longest as memorials of what England had once been. As if to contradict this idea, there appeared ahead of him a B E A Trident newly taken off from London Airport, full of tourists bearing their fish-and-chip culture to the Spanish resorts, to Portugal's lovely Algarve province, and now, as the range of development schemes grew ever wider, as far as Morocco. But it was churlish to resent all this and the rising wage-levels that made it possible. Forget it. Concentrate on cheering M up. And on tonight's piquet session. Raise the stakes and gamble in earnest. Or scrub it altogether. A couple of telephone calls and a night out for four. Break free of the pattern . . .

These thoughts ran in Bond's head as he carried out almost mechanically all the minute drills of good driving, including, of course, an occasional glance at his rear-view mirror. Not once did the Zephyr appear there. Bond would have paid no particular attention if it had. He had never seen it before and would not have recognized its driver even if brought face to face with him. Although he had been under close surveillance for over six weeks, Bond had noticed nothing out of the ordinary. When not on an assignment abroad, a secret agent does not expect to be watched. It is also much easier to watch a man who keeps regular hours and has a fixed domicile and place of business. Thus, for instance, it had not been necessary to set up any kind of checkpoint at Bond's flat off the King's Road, nor to follow him between there and Service headquarters in Regent's Park. More important, the operation involving him was regarded by its planners as of the highest priority. This meant a lavish budget, which meant in turn that an unusually large number of agents could be employed. And that meant that watchers and followers could be changed frequently, before the repeated presence of any one of them had had time to register on that almost subconscious alarm system which years of secret work had developed in Bond's mind.

The Bentley slid across the Windsor–Bagshot road. The familiar landmarks came up on the left: the *Squirrel* public house, the stables of the Arabian stud, the Lurex thread factory (often a focal point of M's indignation). Now, on the right, the modest stone gateway of Quarterdeck, the short, beautifully kept gravel drive, and the house itself, a plain rectangle of Bath stone weathered to a faintly greenish grey, luminous under the evening sun, shadowed in parts by the dense plantation of pine, beech, silver birch and young oak that grew on three sides of it. An ancient wistaria straggled up to and beyond the tiny first-floor balcony on to which the windows of M's bedroom opened. As he slammed the car door and moved towards the shallow portico, Bond fancied he caught a flicker of movement behind those windows: Mrs Hammond, no doubt, turning down the bed.

Under Bond's hand, the hanging brass bell of a long-defunct ship of the line pealed out sharply in the stillness. Silence followed, unbroken by the least rustle of air through the tree-tops. Bond pictured Mrs Hammond still busy upstairs, Hammond himself in the act of fetching a bottle of M's favourite Algerian wine – the aptly named 'Infuriator' – from the cellar. The front door of Quarterdeck was never latched between sunrise and sunset. It yielded at once to Bond's touch.

Every house has its own normally imperceptible background noise, compounded it may be of distant voices, footfalls, kitchen sounds, all the muted bustle of human beings about their business. James Bond was hardly across the threshold when his trained senses warned him of the total absence of any such noise. Suddenly taut, he pushed open the solid Spanish mahogany door of the study, where M habitually received company.

The empty room gazed bleakly at Bond. As always, everything was meticulously in its place, the lines of naval prints exactly horizontal on the walls, water-colour materials laid out as if for inspection on the painting-table up against the window. It all had a weirdly artificial, detached air, like part of a museum where the furniture and effects of some historical figure are preserved just as they were in his lifetime.

Before Bond could do more than look, listen and wonder, the door of the dining-room across the hall, which had been standing ajar, was thrown briskly open and a man emerged. Pointing a long-barrelled automatic in the direction of Bond's knees, he said in a clear voice:

'Stay right there, Bond. And don't make any sudden movements. If you do I shall maim you very painfully.'

Chapter 2

Into the Wood

IN THE course of his career, James Bond had been held up and threatened in this sort of way literally dozens of times – often, as now, by a total stranger. The first step towards effective counter-measures was to play for a little time and analyse what information was immediately available.

Bond set aside as profitless all speculation about the enemy's objective and what might have happened to M and the Hammonds. He concentrated instead on the enemy's gun. This was recognizable straight away as a silenced 9-mm. Luger. The impact of a bullet of such a calibre, weighing nearly half an ounce and travelling at the speed of sound, is tremendous. Bond knew that to be struck by one at the present range, even in a limb, would hurl him to the floor and probably shock him unconscious. If it hit anywhere near the knee, where the weapon was now aimed, he would almost certainly never walk again. All in all a professional's armament.

The man himself had a thin, bony face and a narrow mouth. He was wearing a lightweight dark-blue suit and well-polished brogues. You might have taken him for a promising junior executive in advertising or television, with a taste for women. What Bond chiefly noticed about his looks was that he was as tall as himself, but slighter in build. Perhaps vulnerable in a physical tussle, then, if one could be engineered. What made him disquieting was the economy and force of the words he had just used and the businesslike tone in which they had been uttered, devoid of vulgar menace or triumph, above all without the faintest hint of that affected nonchalance which would have marked him down as an amateur and therefore a potential bungler. This was the surest possible guarantee that he knew how to use his gun and would do so at once if he felt it to be advisable.

All this passed through Bond's mind in three seconds or so. Before they were quite up, he heard a car turn into the drive and felt a flicker of hope. But the man with the Luger did not even turn his head. The new arrival was clearly going to lengthen the odds, not shorten them. Rapid footsteps now sounded on gravel and another man entered by the front door. He hardly bothered to glance at Bond, who had a fleeting impression of washed-out blue eyes. Smoothing his crop of black hair, the man drew what looked like an identical Luger from just behind his right hip; then, moving as if to some carefully worked-out and practised drill, he passed outside and well clear of his companion to the foot of the stairs.

'Out here and up, slowly,' said the first man in the same tone as before.

However difficult it may be to escape from a ground-floor room in the presence of armed enemies, the problem becomes virtually hopeless when the scene is shifted upstairs and there is a guard on the landing or in the hall. Bond appreciated this at once, but simply did as he was told and moved forward. When he was three yards off, the thin-faced man backed away, preserving the distance between them. The second man, the one with black hair, was on the half-landing, his Luger grasped firmly in front of his belly and pointed at Bond's legs. These two were professionals all right.

Bond glanced round the incongruous normality of Quarterdeck's hall – the gleaming pine panels, the 1/144 scale model of M's last ship, the battle-cruiser *Repulse*, M's own antiquated ulster thrown carelessly on to the old-fashioned hall-stand. This thing was bad and big. Bad on all counts, not least his lack of any weapon: British agents do not go armed off duty in their own country. Big in that to be prepared to maim, probably even to kill, in such circumstances was unknown in peacetime – except for frighteningly high stakes. Not to know what these stakes might be was like an intolerable physical thirst.

James Bond's feet mounted mechanically on the worn old

olive-green Axminster stair-carpet. The two gunmen preceded and followed him at the same safe distance. Despite their total competence they were obvious employees, non-commissioned material. The officer in charge of whatever operation this might be would no doubt be revealed in a moment.

'In.'

This time the black-haired man spoke. The other waited on the stairs. Bond crossed the threshold of M's bedroom, that tall, airy room with the brocade curtains drawn back from the shut balcony windows, and came face to face with M himself.

A gasp of horror tore at Bond's throat.

M sat in a high-backed Chippendale chair by his own bed-side. His shoulders were hunched as if he had aged ten years, and his hands hung loosely between his knees. After a moment he looked up slowly and his eyes fastened on Bond. There was no recognition in them, no expression at all; their habitual frosty clarity was gone. From his open mouth came a curious wordless sound, perhaps of wonder, or of inquiry, or of warning, perhaps of all three.

Adrenalin is produced by the adrenal glands, two small bodies situated on the upper surface of the kidneys. Because of the circumstances which cause its release into the circula-tion, and its effects on the body, it is sometimes known as the drug of fright, fight and flight. Now, at the sight of M, Bond's adrenals fell to their primeval work, pumping their secretion into his bloodstream and thus quickening respiration to fill his blood with oxygen, speeding up the heart's action to improve the blood-supply to the muscles, closing the smaller blood-vessels near the skin to minimize loss in case of wound-ing, even causing the hair on his scalp to lift minutely, in memory of the age when man's primitive ancestors had been made to look more terrible to their adversaries by the raising and spreading of their furry crests. And while Bond still stared appalled at M, there came to him from somewhere or other, perhaps from the adrenalin itself, a strange exultation. He knew instantly that he had *not* gone soft, that at need he was the same efficient fighting machine as ever.

A voice spoke. It was a neutral sort of voice with a neutral accent, and it used the same practical, colourless tone as the earlier voices had done. It said sharply, but without hurry, 'You need not be distressed, Bond. Your chief has not been damaged in any way. He has merely been drugged in order to render him amenable. When the drug wears off he will be fully himself again. You are now about to receive an injection of the same drug. If you resist, my associate here has orders to shoot you through the kneecap. This, as you know, would render you utterly helpless at once. The injection is painless. Keep your feet quite still and lower your trousers.'

The speaker was a burly man in his forties, pale, hook-nosed, nearly bald, at first glance as unremarkable as his subordinates. A second glance would have shown there to be something wrong about the eyes, or rather the eyelids, which seemed a size too large. Their owner was certainly conscious of them, for he continually raised and lowered them as he spoke. Instead of looking affected, the mannerism was oddly disturbing. If Bond's mind had been open to such reflections, he might have been reminded of the Black Stone in Buchan's *Thirty-Nine Steps*, the man who could hood his eyes like a hawk and who had haunted Bond's daydreams as a boy. But Bond's thoughts were racing all out in a more practical direction.

He had registered purely subsconsciously the positions of his adversaries: one gunman facing him, the other somewhere on landing or stairs covering the door, the man who was doing the talking stationed with his back to the windows that gave on to the balcony, a fourth man, a doctor of some sort, physically negligible, standing at the foot of the bed with a hypodermic in his hand. So much for that. What clamoured for solution were two problems, which Bond knew to be vital without understanding why. Where was the fallacy in what the man by the windows had just finished saying? And what was the tiny unimportant fact about those windows that none of these four would know and Bond did and could use – if only he could remember it?

'Move.'

The lids closed imperiously over the eyes and lifted again. The voice had not been raised in volume or pitch.

Bond waited.

'You will gain nothing by this. You have five seconds in which to begin carrying out my instructions. Should you not have done so, you will be disabled and then given the injection at our leisure.'

Bond did not waste any of his attention on the countdown. Before it was over he had the solution to the first of his two problems. He had found something contradictory in what was proposed. There is no point in giving an already helpless man an injection designed to render him helpless. Why not maim him immediately, which as things stood would be quick, certain and without risk, and forget about the injection, which was already turning out to be troublesome? So they wanted him not merely helpless, but helpless *and undamaged*. The chances were high that the gun threat was just bluff. If it were not, if there were some extra factor Bond had failed to spot, the penalty would be dreadful. But there was no alternative.

The voice had finished counting and Bond had not moved. In the silence M made another small inarticulate sound. Then—

'Take.'

Bond's arms were seized from behind and jerked backwards – he had not heard the approach of the thin-faced gunman from outside the room. Before the nelson grip was complete Bond had lashed backwards with his heel and made contact. One arm came free. It was instantly seized by the black-haired gunman.

The struggle that followed, though two-to-one, was almost on equal terms, for Bond was full of the exultation of having his guess proved right and thus winning the first point, not to speak of his joyful recovery of confidence in his fighting abilities. And he could hurt them in ways they must not hurt him. But he was up against one man who was his equal in build and another who, though slighter, had a genius for throwing on the most painful available nerve-hold as soon as the one before it had been broken.

An elbow-jab that just missed the groin brought the top of Bond's body forward. Before he could recover, ten fingers that felt like steel bolts had sunk into the ganglia at the base of his neck. The muscles of his upper arms seemed to turn into thin streams of cold mud. Again he tried to bring his heel back and up, but this time his legs were grabbed from the front and held. A wrench, a heave, and Bond hit the floor. He lay face down, one body across his shoulders, the other immobilizing his lower half, relaxed, not struggling uselessly, thinking, thinking about the windows, if he ever reached them, the windows . . .

'Jab.'

Bond felt the arrival of the third man, the doctor, above him, and gathered himself for a supreme effort. In the next minute he proved how difficult it is even for two strong, skilful and determined men to render a third equally powerful man completely helpless if they are not allowed to inflict anything really violent and ruthless upon him. Bond used that minute. As he strove and sweated, with no objective beyond not allowing any favourable area of his body to become available to the hypodermic, dimly aware that some sort of argument was going on between the man with the hooded eyes and the doctor, he remembered what he had to remember. The windows, though closed, could not be fastened. The catch was broken. Hammond had mentioned it the previous week and M, tetchy as ever, had said he would be damned if he was going to let some carpenter johnny turn the room into a shambles – it could wait a couple of weeks, until the time of M's annual salmon-fishing holiday on the Test. So a sharp shove where the windows met would . . .

Perhaps the triumph of remembering this snatch of talk – to which Bond had not been consciously listening at all – made him relax for an instant. Perhaps one gunman or the other found an extra ounce of strength. Anyway, Bond's wrist was caught and held and the next instant he felt the prick of the needle in his left forearm. He drove off a wave of despair and loathing, asked himself how long the stuff was supposed to take before it worked, experimentally let himself go limp, found the pressure on him relaxing slightly but significantly, and moved.

In that one possible split second he was able to twist himself partly free. He arched his back and drove out with both feet. The thin-faced man screamed. Blood spurted from his nose. He fell heavily. The other man chopped at the back of Bond's neck, but too late. Bond's elbow took him almost exactly on the windpipe. The man with the hooded eyes swung a foot as Bond came up off the floor, but he was not in time either. All he did was lay open Bond's path to the windows. The two halves flew apart with beautiful readiness as his shoulder struck them. One hand on the low stone balustrade, over, down to a perfectly balanced four-point landing, up and away into the nearest trees.

Those first scattered pines seemed to move past him only slowly, run as hard as he might. Now there were more of them. And brambles and wild rhododendrons. Making the going difficult. Very important not to fall. Not to slow down either. Keep up speed. Why? Get away from them. Who? Men. Man with eyes like a hawk's. Man who has done terrible things to M. Must save M. Go back and save M? No. Go on. Save M by running away from him? Yes. Go on. Where? Far. Go on far. How far? Far . . .

Bond really was hardly more than a machine now. Soon he had forgotten everything but the necessity to take the next stride, and the next, and the next. When there was nothing left of his mind at all his body ran on, as fast as before but without sense of direction, for perhaps another minute. After that it slowed and stopped. It stood where it was for a further minute, panting with slack mouth, the arms hanging loosely by the sides. The eyes were open, but they saw nothing. Then, impelled by some last flicker of intelligence or will, the body of James Bond took a dozen more steps, dropped, and lay full length in a patch of long coarse grass between two dwarf poplars, virtually invisible to anybody passing more than five yards away.

In fact, nobody came as close as that. The pursuit was hopeless from the start. The thin-faced man, bleeding thickly from a smashed nose, was over the balcony and round the corner of the house nearly – though not quite – in time to see Bond disappearing among the pines, but it was ten or twelve more seconds before he was joined by his fellow and by the man with the hooded eyes, who was not accustomed to jumping from balconies and had had to descend by the stairs. If the thin-faced man had been working for an organization that encouraged initiative, he would have made without delay for the edge of the woods, listened, and been able to give effective chase. As it was, Bond was just out of earshot by the time the trio reached the first trees. They moved in the obvious, and indeed in the right, direction for a time, but time was the very thing they were short of. It was not very long before the leader looked at his watch and called a halt.

'Back.'

Before they turned away, the speaker unhooded his eyes and looked with a peculiar intentness at the thin-faced man. That face lost some of its colour. Then the three moved off. By the final irony in a day of ironies, another sixty or seventy yards advance would have brought them straight to where Bond lay.

More time passed. The shadows in the wood lengthened, began to fade into the blur of dusk. The hum of insects fell to a murmur. Once a blackbird called. No other sound. If Bond had been able to strain his ears to their limit, he might just have heard a distant scream, abruptly cut off, and then, a little later, a car being started and driven away. But he heard nothing. He was nothing.

*　　　*　　　*

The room was small, but it was still not possible to decide what was in it or where it was, and there seemed no point in trying. Those men, two of them probably, or three, were talking again, first one, then another. Their voices were muffled by long tangled strips of grey stuff, vague and smoky at the edges, that hung in the air in front of them. The same grey strips made their faces hard to see. Or did they just make it hard to want to see their faces? What was really there?

Did it matter? There was something, something like a book or a man or a secret or a telephone, that said it did matter, something a long time ago, round hundreds of corners, thousands of slow difficult paces back, that said there was no giving up, ever. Try. Want to try. Try to want to try. Want to try to . . .

Another man, much nearer. Face very close. Doing something with eye. Holding wrist. Doing more with eye. Grunting. Talking. Going away. Coming back. Doing more – what? Pulling, helping up from chair. Something with jacket. Something with shirt-sleeve. Little pain. Gone. Back in chair again.

'Well, doctor?'

'He's been given a massive dose of some drug or other, I couldn't say which at this stage. Could be hyoscine. I've given him something that should help him come round.'

'Drug addict, is he, then?'

'Possibly. I doubt it. We'll have to wait and see. How did you get hold of him?'

'A motorist brought him in getting on for half an hour ago. Said he found him wandering about in the road near one of the entrances to the Great Park. Of course, we thought he was tight at first.'

'There's a similarity. The quiet kind of drunk. I can't think of any better way of making a man docile. You know, sergeant, there's something nasty about this, whatever it is. Who is our friend?'

'Name of Bond, James Bond. Business address in London, Regent's Park somewhere. I gave 'em a ring on the off-chance and they said to hold him and not let anyone but a doctor see him and they'd send a man down right away. The Inspector should be here soon, too. Went off just about two minutes before this chap arrived. Pile-up on the M4. It's getting to be quite a night.'

'Indeed . . . Ah, I think we may get something now . . . Mr Bond? Mr Bond, you're quite safe and in a very few minutes you'll be completely yourself again. I'm Doctor Allison and these officers are Sergeant Hassett and Constable

Wragg. They are only here for your protection. You're in a police station but you've done nothing wrong. All you need do is rest a little.'

James Bond looked up slowly. There was nothing left of the grey tangle that had obscured his vision and hearing. He saw a very English face with an inquisitive pointed nose and dependable dark eyes, eyes that at the moment were puzzled and concerned. In the background were two solid-looking men in dark-blue uniform, a battered desk with a telephone, filing cabinets, wall maps and charts, a poster announcing a Police Ball: recognizable, everyday, real.

Bond swallowed and cleared his throat. It was very important that he should get exactly right what he knew he had to say, the more so since he was not as yet quite sure what all of it meant or why he had to say it.

'Put your feet up for a bit, Mr Bond. Bring that chair over, Wragg, will you? Could you organize a cup of tea?'

Now take it slowly, word by word. 'I want,' said Bond in a thick voice, 'I want a car. And four men. Armed. To come with me. As quickly as possible.'

'Mind wandering, poor chap,' said the sergeant.

The doctor frowned. 'I doubt it. You'd get confusion all right, but not actual fantasy.' He leant down and put his hands firmly on Bond's shoulders. 'You must tell us more, Mr Bond. We're all listening. We're trying to understand.'

'Admiral Sir Miles Messervy,' said Bond distinctly, and saw the sergeant react. Bond's mind was clearing fast now. 'There's been some trouble along at his place. I'm afraid he's been kidnapped.'

'Go on, please, sir,' said the sergeant, who had picked up the telephone before Bond had finished speaking.

'There were four men. They'd given him a shot of the same stuff as me. I don't quite know how I got away.'

'You wouldn't,' said Dr Allison, offering Bond a cigarette and a light.

Bond drew the life-giving smoke deep into his lungs and exhaled luxuriously. He began quickly and coolly to consider, analyse, predict. The immediate conclusion he arrived at appalled him. He jumped to his feet. At the same moment the sergeant put down the telephone.

'Number unobtainable,' he said grimly.

'Naturally,' said Bond. 'Give me that thing.' When the police operator answered he said, unconsciously clenching his fist, 'London Airport. Priority. I'll hang on.'

The sergeant looked at him once and left the room at a run.

While Bond was rattling off descriptions of M and the four enemy agents to his friend Spence, the Security Officer at the airport, the Inspector arrived, followed a minute later by Bill Tanner. Bond finished talking, hung up, drew in his breath to start explaining the position to Tanner, but just then the sergeant returned. His round, good-natured face was pale. He addressed himself to Bond.

'I got a patrol car up to the house, sir,' he said, swallowing. 'They've just come through. I'm afraid it's too late for your armed men now. But we shall need you, Doctor. Not that you'll be able to do very much, either.'

Chapter 3

Aftermath

THE BODY of the thin-faced man lay on its back in the hall at Quarterdeck. There was not much left of the face. Parts of it and what had been situated behind it could be seen here and there on walls and floor. The Luger bullet was half an inch deep in one of the panels.

Ex-Chief Petty Officer Hammond had been shot twice, once in the chest and again, to take no chances, in the back of the neck. It was assumed that he had been disposed of immediately on answering the front door, and that the use of a small-calibre weapon in his case had been dictated by the necessity of not leaving any traces in the hall that would have alerted Bond on his arrival. The corpse had been dumped in a heap in the kitchen, where the third body was also found.

Mrs Hammond at least could have known nothing of what happened to her. The killer, using the same light gun, had got her with a single well-aimed shot through the back of the head as she stood at the stove or the sink. She was lying close to where her husband had been dropped, so close that the back of his outflung hand rested against her shoulder. It was as if he had tried to reassure her that he had not left her, that he was near by, as he had been for twenty years. Since Hammond had been demobilized just after the war and had come with his wife to serve M, the two of them had not spent a night apart.

Bond thought of this as he stood beside Tanner and the Inspector and looked down on what was left of the Hammonds. He found himself beset by the irrelevant wish that he had listened more appreciatively to Hammond's anecdotes about pre-war naval life at the Pacific Station, that he had had the time and the kindness to thank and encourage Mrs Hammond for her self-dedication to M during his illness. Bond made a muffled sound between a sob and a snarl. This act, this casual sweeping aside of two lives just to save trouble – there were half a dozen ways in which the Hammonds could have been neutralized with the minimum of violence and without risk to the enemy – was not to be endured. The men who had done it were going to die.

'It's a good job you didn't fall in with my suggestion about coming along here tonight, Bill,' said Bond.

Tanner nodded without speaking. Then the two turned away and left the bodies to the doctor and the police experts. Not that any of them was expected to add to what was already known or self-evident. The Hammonds' fate was an open book. There remained, of course, the question of the shooting of the thin-faced man.

In M's study a minute later, Bond and Tanner decided to start with that. Each tacitly avoiding the straight-backed Hepplewhite armchair where M habitually sat, they had settled themselves on either side of the low stone fireplace that was bare and swept clean at this time of the year.

'Perhaps his boss had him knocked off in a fit of rage,' suggested Tanner. 'By what you told me on the way here our dead friend didn't handle himself too cleverly in the scrap upstairs. Could be considered to have helped to let you escape, anyway. But then these people don't sound as if they're given to fits of rage. Of course, a man with a bloody nose is to a certain extent conspicuous. Would that have been enough to earn him a bullet ? Rather frightening if it was.'

Before replying, Bond picked up his Scotch and soda from the silver tray that sat on a low table between the two men. He had had to harden his heart to bring in the tray from the kitchen, where Hammond, as on previous Tuesdays, had had it ready for his arrival.

'That would fit the airport theory.' Bond drank deeply and gratefully. 'It would be a big risk already to walk M through Immigration, passing him off if necessary as under the weather or whatever they had lined up. Presumably it would have been a still bigger risk if they'd managed to persuade me to join the party. Or would it? Anyway, we can leave that for now. The point is that, whatever the risk, it was one they'd been able to prepare for to the nth degree. But here was something they couldn't have taken into account. A man who'd clearly just been in some sort of serious fight would be just the thing to arouse that fatal flicker of official curiosity. Yes, it fits. And yet . . .'

Tanner glanced at him mutely and fumbled for a cigarette.

'I can't help feeling there's something else to it. Some added point. After all, why leave him here? That's making us a present of God knows how much information. You'd have expected them at least to try to hide the body.'

'They hadn't time,' said Tanner, looking at his watch. 'This must all have been planned to the minute. And talking of time, when are they going to get that damned telephone repaired? We'd better start looking for—'

'No rush there. I wish there were. With the shifts changed an hour or more ago Spence's job won't be easy. He's having to rout out the people who were on duty earlier on. And that Security staff is tiny. They'll be up to their eyebrows pushing the descriptions out to all the other airports. And in any case . . .'

A police constable in shirt-sleeves knocked and entered. 'Phone's in order, sir,' he said. 'And London Airport Security informed as you requested.'

'Thank you.' When the man had gone, Bill Tanner put his glass of Scotch down with a slam. 'It's all hopeless anyway,' he said with sudden violence. 'Let's get moving, James. Every sort of important person has got to be collected and told about this, and fast. What are we hanging about here for?'

'If we move we're off the telephone. And we've got to be sure there's nothing more this end. The police will find it if there is. That Inspector Crawford's a competent chap. What do you mean anyway, hopeless? With a call gone out to the seaports and —'

'Look, James.' Tanner got up and began pacing the faded Axminster rug. He studied his watch again. 'They've had something like four hours start now. . .'

Bond drew in his breath and bit his lip hard. 'Christ, you don't know how I wish . . .'

'Don't be a fool, man. Nobody could have done more than you did. Pull yourself together and listen to me.'

'Sorry, Bill.'

'That's better. Now. Four hours. They wouldn't have counted on much more whatever had happened. They'll have cut it as fine as they dared in the first phase. If they took him out by aeroplane, then with the airport not much more than down the road from here they'd have been in the air in well under an hour. Another hour at the most to Orly or Amsterdam, or these days as far as Marseilles – and they *must* have gone somewhere comparatively near, they wouldn't have dared spend six or eight hours in transit and risk being met by the wrong people at the far end. . . . Well then. That's two hours. Another half hour at the outside for Customs and Immigration. By now they could be, what, seventy, eighty miles from their touchdown? Or out at sea?'

'What makes you think they aren't in East Berlin?' asked Bond flatly. 'Or most of the way to Moscow?'

'I don't know.' With shaking fingers, Tanner chain-lit another cigarette and thrust his hand through his thinning grey hair. 'It doesn't sound like that lot. Too grown-up these days. That's what I think, anyway. Perhaps it's only what I hope.'

Bond had nothing to say.

'Perhaps they haven't taken him out at all. That might be their best bet. Hole up with him in Westmorland or somewhere and operate their plot from a derelict cottage. Whatever the hell their plot may be. No doubt we shall find out in their own good time. We've had it, James. We've lost him.'

The telephone rang noisily from its alcove in the hall (M would not have the hated instrument where he could see it). Tanner jumped up.

'I'll take it. You relax.'

Bond lay back in his chair, half-listening to the intermittent drone of Tanner's voice in the alcove. The muffled noises of the police at work, their deliberate footsteps, sounded false, out of key. The study where Bond sat – he noticed for the first time M's old briar pipe lying in a copper ashtray – looked even more museum-like than earlier. It was as if M had left not hours before, but weeks or months. A derelict stage-set rather than a museum. Bond had the uneasy fancy that if he got up and pushed his hand at the wall, what was supposed to be stone would belly inwards, like canvas.

Tanner's abrupt return brought Bond out of his daze – evidently traces of the drug still lingered in his system. His friend's face was tightly drawn at the forehead and cheekbones. He looked ghastly.

'Well, James, I was nearly right. A great consolation.' Tanner went back to pacing the rug. 'Shannon. They went off on Aer Lingus flight 147A at twenty to nine. The fellows on duty remember them all right. The whole thing was stage-managed down to the last detail – pattern of previous trips by supposedly the same four people, a diversion timed to the second, the lot. I wonder what they had lined up for you and our pal in the hall. Anyhow . . .

'They landed at Shannon at half-past nine or so. That's . . . nearly two and a half hours ago, while you were still wandering about in that wood. So they're away. Met by car at Shannon and driven off to God knows what remote inlet, any one of hundreds. I know that coast a bit. It must be the most deserted in the whole of Western Europe. After that . . . you can bloody well take your choice. Boat out to ship, or to submarine for all I know – this thing looks as if it's on that kind of scale. Rendezvous with flying-boat a hundred miles out in the Atlantic. Then anywhere in the wide world.

'So that's that,' Tanner finished. 'We'll pass the word to the Irish coastguards and navy. Tell 'em to keep a special lookout. Very useful that'll be. And we'll get a man over there tonight. He'll be a great help, too. Then there are various parties in London we can at least tell to foregather. Come on, James, let's go and do a bit of telephoning. There's nothing more for us round this place. It always did give me the creeps.'

Inspector Crawford, a tall saturnine man in his forties whom Bond had immediately taken to, came up as they finished the last of three calls. He carried a large unsealed manilla envelope.

'We're about through here, gentlemen. If you want to get away I think you'll find all you'll really want in this.' He handed Tanner the envelope, then gestured without looking at the body on the floor. 'Contents of the man's pockets. Rather a surprise that there were any, I suppose. You'd have expected them to try to cover up his identity. Clothing labels, all standard, I'm afraid. No laundry tags. Three pretty good photographs of what there is of him, and a set of fingerprints. Height and approximate weight. Distinguishing marks, none. If he's on your files at all, though, I reckon you should be able to turn him up in no time without any of this clobber, Mr Bond having had a good look at him. Oh, and doctor's preliminary report, just for completeness. That's the lot. I'll have to ask you to sign for the dead man's effects, sir. And we'll be wanting them back when you've finished with them.'

Tanner scrawled on the proffered slip. 'Thank you, Inspector. I'm afraid we must ask you to accompany us to London right away, to attend a meeting that may go on for the rest of the night. Most of it won't be your concern but somebody's certain to complain if you don't turn up to give the complete police picture. I expect you understand.'

Crawford nodded impassively. 'I expect so, sir. Now if you'll just give me two minutes I'll be at your disposal.'

'You realize of course that there's a complete black-out on this business? Tell the GPO to put the telephone out of order again as soon as everybody's out of here. Thank you for all you and your men have done. We'll see you outside when you're ready to go.'

As they moved off, Bond glanced down at the corpse of the man whose death he had unwittingly brought about. It lay there waiting to be removed and disposed of according to routine, a piece of debris, totally insignificant. Bond hated and feared the half-unrevealed purpose that had brought the man to this house, but he could not repress a twinge of pity at the thought of the casual chance that had led to this summary removal. Was this how James Bond would end, shot in the head and flung aside like a heap of unwanted clothing to smooth out a kink in somebody's plan?

The immense blaze of starlight in the velvety late-summer sky outside drove away these thoughts. Good flying weather. Where were they taking M? Never mind that for now: no point in guessing in a vacuum. There was a faint chill in the night air and Bond realized he was hungry. Never mind that either. There would be nothing to eat before London, if then.

At Tanner's side, Bond passed the dark bulks of the two police cars and made for his Bentley, still where he had parked it an age ago. Tanner put a hand on his shoulder.

'No, James. You're riding with me. I'll see about your car tomorrow.'

'Nonsense, I'm perfectly all right.'

'And we can't be sure the thing isn't booby-trapped.'

'That's nonsense too, Bill. They wanted me alive and uninjured.'

'Then they did. Nobody knows what they might want now.'

Chapter 4

Love from Paris

SIR RANALD Rideout, the Minister concerned, was not best pleased at being abruptly summoned from the late stages of a dinner-party given by an Austrian princess whose circle he had been trying to infiltrate for years. The telephone message stressed the magnitude of the matter requiring his attention without revealing anything about what it was. The underling who spoke to him had rung off before Sir Ranald had had the chance to protest at the impropriety of his being allowed no say in the arrangements for this meeting or conference or whatever. So he was to present himself at the offices of the Transworld Consortium, i.e. the headquarters of the Secret Service, was he? That confounded old admiral, notorious for his obstinate resistance to political guidance, was in trouble, then. The fellow should have been given the push long ago. It was a more than mildly irritated Sir Ranald who, at the horrid hour of one twenty in the morning, trotted up the steps of the big grey building that overlooks Regent's Park, an agile little figure of sixty in perfect condition, this as a result not of any self-discipline but of that indifference to food and drink which so often accompanies interest in power.

The facts were baldly laid before him. He looked about with angry incredulity at the faces ranged round the battered oak table: the Permanent Under-Secretary to his Ministry, Assistant Commissioner Vallance from Scotland Yard, the man whose office this was and whose insignificance was shown clearly enough by the condition of its furnishings, the spy called Bond who seemed responsible for the mess, and some policeman or other from Windsor.

'Well, gentlemen, really.' Sir Ranald inflated his cheeks and blew out long and noisily. 'A pretty kettle of fish, I must say. This will have to go to the Prime Minister. I hope you realize that.'

'I'm glad to find you agree with us, sir,' said Tanner in level tones. 'But, as you know, the Prime Minister flew to Washington today – yesterday. He can't do anything about this from there, and I doubt if he'll be able to cut short his stay. So it looks as if we must push ahead ourselves.'

'Of course we must.' This time Sir Ranald sniffed emphatically. 'Of course we must. The question is where. Push ahead where? You people seem to have nothing at all that can be called information. Extraordinary. Take this man you found shot. Not the servant, the gangster or whatever he was. All you appear to know about him is that he met his death by a bullet shattering his skull. Most helpful. Is that really as much as anybody can say? Surely something must have been found on him?'

Inspector Crawford spoke up at once and Sir Ranald frowned slightly. One might have expected the least important man present to satisfy himself that none of the comparatively senior people wanted to answer, before pushing himself forward. At least, one might once have expected that.

'Oddly enough there were some belongings, sir,' the Inspector was saying. He nodded towards the small heap of miscellaneous objects that Vallance was turning over. 'But they don't tell us much. Except— '

'Do they tell us anything about who the man was?'

'Not in my view, sir.'

Vallance, dapper as ever in the small hours, glanced over at Crawford and shook his head in agreement.

'Then may I take leave to ask my question again? Who was he? Assistant Commissioner?'

'Our fingerprint files are being gone over now, Sir Ranald,' said Vallance, his direct gaze on the Minister's face. 'And of course it's conceivable that this chap will be on them. We're also checking abroad, with Interpol and so on, but it'll be a couple of days at least before all the returns are in. And I feel strongly that we shan't learn anything useful from anywhere.

To my way of thinking, the mere fact that he was left behind like that, just as he was, proves that knowing his identity wouldn't help us.'

'I agree with Vallance,' said Tanner. 'We're in the same position here exactly and I'm sure we shall get the same results, or lack of them. No, sir – this chap'll turn out to be one of a comparatively new type of international criminal who's been turning up in rather frighteningly large numbers in the sabotage game, terrorism and so on. They're people without a traceable history of any sort, probably white Africans with a grudge, various fringe Americans – but that's all supposition because they turn up out of thin air. The lads in Records here call them men from nowhere. Damn silly twopenny-blood sort of name but it does describe them. What I'm saying, sir, is that it's a waste of time trying to find who this fellow was, because in a sense he wasn't anybody.'

'You're guessing, aren't you, Tanner?' said Sir Ranald, crinkling up his eyes as he spoke to show he wasn't being personally offensive yet. 'Just guessing. Educated guess-work no doubt you'd call it but that's a matter of taste. I'm afraid I was trained to observe carefully, impartially and thoroughly before venturing on any theorizing. Now ... Bond,' the Minister went on with a momentary expression of distaste, as if he found the name unaesthetic in some way, 'you at any rate saw this man when he was alive. What could you say about him that might help?'

'Almost nothing, sir, I'm afraid. He seemed completely ordinary apart from his skill in unarmed combat, and he could have learnt that anywhere in the world. So ...'

'What about his voice? Anything there?'

Bond was tired out. His head throbbed and there was a metallic taste in his mouth. The parts of his body on which the dead man had worked were aching. The ham sandwich and coffee he had grabbed in the canteen were hardly a memory. Even so, he would not have answered as he did if he had not been repelled by the politician's air of superiority in the presence of men worth twenty of him.

'Well, he addressed me in English, sir,' said Bond judicially.

'By my standards correct English. I listened carefully, of course, for any traces of a Russian or Albanian or Chinese accent but could detect none. However, he spoke no more than about twenty words in my hearing, which may have been too small a sample upon which to base any certain conclusions.'

At the other end of the table, Vallance went into a mild attack of coughing.

Sir Ranald appeared not in the least put out. He flicked his eyes once at Vallance and spoke to Bond in a gentle tone. 'Yes, you weren't about the place very long, were you? You were anxious to be off. I congratulate you on your escape. No doubt you would have considered it ridiculously old-fashioned to have stayed and fought to save your superior from whatever fate was in store for him.'

The Under-Secretary turned away suddenly and stared into an empty corner of the room. Inspector Crawford, sitting opposite Bond, went red and shuffled his feet.

'Mr Bond showed great courage and resource, sir,' he said loudly. 'I've never heard of anybody who could hope to subdue four able-bodied men single-handed and unarmed let alone being full of a drug that incapacitated him a few minutes later. If Mr Bond hadn't escaped, the enemy's plans would be going ahead *in toto*. As it is, they'll have to be modified, they may even be fatally damaged.'

'Possibly.' Sir Ranald beat the air with his hand. With another grimace of displeasure, he said to his Under-Secretary, 'Bushnell, get a window open, will you? The air in here isn't fit to breathe with three people chain-smoking.

While the Under-Secretary hastened to obey, Bond was hiding a grin at the memory of having read somewhere that hatred of tobacco was a common psychopathic symptom, from which Hitler among others had been a notable sufferer.

Rubbing his hands briskly, as if he had won an important point, Sir Ranald hurried on. 'Now just one matter that's been bothering me. There doesn't seem to have been any guard or watch on Sir Miles's residence. Was that normal, or had somebody slipped up?'

'It was normal, sir,' said Tanner, who had started to redden

in his turn. 'This is peacetime. What happened is unprecedented.'

'Indeed. You agree perhaps that it's the unprecedented that
particularly needs to be guarded against?'

'Yes, sir.' Tanner's voice was quite colourless.

'Good. Now have we any idea of who's behind this business
and what its purpose is? Let's have some educated guesses
on that.'

'An enemy Secret Service is at any rate the obvious one.
As regards purpose, I think we can rule out a straight ransom
job, if only because they could have operated that from inside
the country and so avoided the immense risk of getting out
with Sir Miles, and presumably Mr Bond too if they'd managed to hold on to him. And why hold two people to ransom?
The same sort of reasoning counts against the idea of interrogation or brainwashing or anything of that sort. No, it's something more ... original than that, I'm certain.'

Sir Ranald sniffed again. 'Well? What sort of thing?'

'No bid, sir. There's nothing to go on.'

'Mm. And presumably we're in a similar state of non-infor-
mation about where this scheme, whatever it is, whoever's
running it, is going to be mounted. Any reports of unusual
activity from any of your stations abroad?'

'No, sir. Of course, I've asked for a special watch to be kept.'

'Yes, yes. So we know nothing. It looks as if we have merely
to wait until the other side makes a move. Thank you, all of
you, for your help. I'm sure none of you could have done
more than you have. I'm sorry if I may have seemed to suggest
that you, Mr Bond, could have acted in any other way. I spoke
without thinking. Your escape is the one redeeming feature of
this whole affair.'

The Minister spoke with what sounded very much like
simple sincerity. The thought had occurred to him – belatedly,
but then he had always been prone to let his impatience with
lower-echelon muddle run away with him – that although he
was not in fairness accountable for the abduction of the head
of the Secret Service, his Cabinet colleagues as a whole held
the view of fairness common to politicians. In other words,

this business could be turned into a most useful weapon in the hands of anybody who might want to get him pushed out. Envy, spite, ambition were everywhere around him. These people here might not be the most satisfactory or effective allies, but they were the only ones immediately available. He turned to Vallance, whom he had several times in the past dismissed as an over-dressed popinjay, and said in a humble tone, unconsciously smoothing the front of his own frilled azure evening shirt as he spoke, 'In the meantime, Assistant Commissioner, what about the Press? A "D" notice, do you suppose? I'm more than content to be guided by you.'

Vallance did not dare glance at Bond or Tanner. 'I think not a black-out, sir. The Admiral has plenty of connections and we don't want them turning inquisitive. I suggest a short tucked-away paragraph saying his indisposition continues and he's been advised to take a thorough rest.'

'Excellent. I'll leave that in your hands, then. Now – any more suggestions? However tentative. Anybody . . . ?'

Crawford stirred. 'Well, sir, if I may just . . .'

'Go on, Inspector. Please go on.' Sir Ranald crinkled his eyelids. 'Most welcome.'

'It's this piece of paper with the names and numbers which we all had a look at earlier. We found it crumpled up in a corner of the man's wallet. I understand the cipher people are working on a copy of it still but are just about sure it's a waste of time, there being so little of it. I wondered whether we might perhaps take another look at it ourselves. Have we considered the possibility that these are telephone numbers?'

'I'm afraid there's nothing in that, Inspector,' said Tanner, rubbing his eyes wearily. ' "Christiana" looks like Christiania in Norway, of course, and "Vasso" might be Vassy in north-eastern France, and we all know where Paris is, but it didn't take us ten minutes to establish that these numbers aren't possible for the exchanges at those three places, any more than, say, Whitehall 123 would be for London. If they are telephone numbers they're probably coded on some substitution system we've no means of cracking, so we're back where we were. Sorry to disappoint you.'

'Might they be map references?' put in the Under-Secretary.

Tanner shook his head. 'Wrong number of figures.'

'Actually, sir,' the Inspector went on with quiet persistence, 'I wasn't really meaning it quite like that. Take the one we haven't mentioned – Antigone. What does that suggest to people?'

'Greek play,' said Tanner. 'Sophocles, isn't it? Code word for God knows what.'

'That is possible, sir. But Antigone isn't only a Greek play, is it? It's also a Greek name. A woman's name. I don't know whether it's still in use there, but I do know a lot of these classical names are. Now Christiana. Doesn't that sound like a woman's name too, on the lines of Christine and Christina and so on? Christiana might be the Greek form. And Paris, of course, is another Greek name.'

Abruptly, Bill Tanner got to his feet and hurried to a telephone that stood on an ink-stained and cigarette-burned trestle table by the wall.

'As regards Vasso, I'm afraid I don't—'

'What are you leading up to, Inspector?' broke in Sir Ranald, with a return to his earlier manner.

'That our man was going to Greece and had got some telephone numbers off somebody so that he could fix himself up with some female company if he felt inclined. That these are telephone numbers on the same unstated exchange. A large one, presumably. Athens, as it might be. Or at least that that's what we were supposed to think, sir.'

Sir Ranald frowned. 'But Paris is a man's name. I hardly—'

'Quite so, sir, the abductor of Helen of Troy, the man who started the Trojan War. But if you'll just take another look . . .'

Crawford passed over the small creased sheet of cheap lined paper. The Minister, still frowning, hitched over his ears a pair of spectacles with heavy black frames and peered at the ballpoint scrawl. He sniffed. 'Well?'

'Immediately above "Paris" there, sir . . . It's not at all clear, but it looks to me like "If supplies fail' or "fall". If Antigone and the other two were away or he didn't like them or something then Paris was going to be able to fix him up.'

'Mm.' Sir Ranald took the spectacles off again and chewed at the earpiece. His eyes darted briefly to Tanner, who was still telephoning. 'What did you say about our being supposed to think this?'

'To me this looks planted, sir. If it's genuine it got into our hands as a result of at least three oversights. Not removing the body. Not emptying the pockets. Not at any rate searching the pockets. Well, now . . .'

'You mean it's a red herring?'

'No, sir, quite the contrary. It's a straightforward pointer to Greece, clear enough but not too clear.'

Tanner rang off and returned to his chair. He glanced over at Crawford with heightened respect.

'All four are perfectly possible modern Greek first names, according to Mary Kyris at the Embassy. And the figure groups could be telephone numbers in Athens, Salonika and a couple of other cities.'

'We're on to something, gentlemen,' said Sir Ranald, his eyes almost disappearing in crinkles. 'We're on to something.'

'And we know exactly what we're on to.'

James Bond's head had been sunk in his hands since he had last spoken a quarter of an hour earlier. He had seemed half asleep. In fact he had been striving to keep his exhausted brain ceaselessly analysing and evaluating the course of the discussion. Now, as his voice sounded through the low-ceilinged, smoke-laden room, he sat up in his chair and gazed at Tanner.

'Inspector Crawford is right. This is a plant. Or let's call it a lure. They were very anxious to include me in their plans. Clearly they still are. The names and numbers on that paper are a brilliant piece of improvisation designed to get me following in their track at full speed. Which of course I'll have to do. As far as that goes they could have written GREECE on that bit of paper and left it at that.'

Tanner nodded slowly. 'Where would you start?'

'Anywhere,' said Bond. 'Let's say Athens. It doesn't really matter, because I shan't need to look for them. They'll find me.'

Chapter 5

Sun at Night

THE ISLAND of Vrakonisi lies midway between the coasts of southern Greece and southern Turkey; more precisely, near the middle of the triangle formed by the three larger islands of Naxos, Ios and Paros. Like its more distant neighbour, Santorini, thirty miles to the south-west, Vrakonisi is volcanic in origin. It is what remains of the crater walls of an immense volcano extinct since prehistoric times. Ancient upheavals and subsidences have given it a ragged profile, with a misshapen semicircular backbone of hills rising in places to twelve hundred feet. From the air, Vrakonisi looks like the blade of a sickle drawn by a very drunk man. The tip of the blade has broken off, so that a hundred shallow yards of the Aegean lie between the main body of the island and a tiny unnamed islet off its northern end. The islet is inhabited, but apart from a couple of fishermen's cottages there is only a single house, a long low structure in brilliantly white-washed stone situated among palm and cactus at the farthest corner. The owner, a Piraeus yacht-builder, lets it to foreign visitors in the summer months.

This particular summer month the house had been occupied by two men whose passports said they were French; morose, taciturn men, their complexions suggesting little acquaintance with life in the sun. Their behaviour suggested the same thing. Pallid and uncomfortable-looking in gaudy bathing-shorts, they could sometimes be seen sprawled in canvas chairs above the little private anchorage (empty throughout their stay so far) or splashing grimly and very briefly across it. For long periods they were not to be seen at all. They had the air of men filling in the time until they could start to do whatever they had come all this way to do.

Their identity and purpose, and very much more, were well known to Colonel Sun Liang-tan of the Special Activities Committee, People's Liberation Army. The two men on the islet were out of sight of the colonel as he sat at the window of a smaller and even less accessible house than theirs, situated on the main body of the island. For even the chance of a look at them he would have had to go outside, make his way up an overgrown hillside to a point perhaps two hundred and fifty feet above sea level, and look down across the farther slopes, the stretch of water and the eighty-yard length of the islet, about a kilometre in all. But, ever since arriving here by water the previous night, Colonel Sun had not gone outside for a moment. The immediately recognizable Oriental facial type has in itself seriously hindered the expansion of Chinese infiltration and espionage in the Western countries, except for those, like the United States and Great Britain, where Orientals are not uncommonly seen. They are excessively rare in the Greek islands. Nobody on Vrakonisi, nobody outside China, come to that, must even have cause to wonder whether a Chinese might not be present here and now.

And nobody catching a glimpse of the colonel would have had to wonder about his origin. He was tall for a Chinese, nearly six foot, one of the northern types akin to the Khamba Tibetan, big-boned and long-headed. But the skin-colour was the familiar flat light yellow, the hair blue-black and dead straight, the epicanthic eye-fold notably conspicuous. It was only when you looked Sun straight in the eyes that he seemed less than totally Chinese. The irises were of an unusual and very beautiful pewter-grey like the eyes of the newborn, the legacy perhaps of some medieval invader from Kirgiz or Naiman. But then not many people did look Sun straight in the eyes. Not twice, anyway.

The colonel continued to sit on his hard wooden chair while darkness fell outside. Normally he was a voracious reader, but tonight he was attuning his mind and feelings for what lay ahead. Twice he smoked a cigarette, not inhaling, allowing it to burn away between his lips. They were British cigarettes, Benson & Hedges. Sun did not share his colleagues' often-expressed contempt – in some cases, he suspected, routine rather than sincere – for everything British. He was fond of many aspects of their culture and considered it regrettable in some ways that that culture had such a short time left.

The men themselves (he had met none of their women) had often aroused his admiration. He had first encountered the British in September 1951, at a prisoner-of-war centre near Pyongyang in North Korea. There, as a twenty-one-year-old subaltern attached, in the capacity of Assistant Consultant on Interrogations, to Major Pak of the North Korean Army, he had had the opportunity of getting to know the British soldier intimately. After September 1953, when the last of them had been repatriated, his experience of Westerners had been confined almost entirely to Frenchmen, Australians, Americans: interesting types in many cases, but not up to the British – 'his' British, as he mentally referred to them. He had had to content himself with the odd spy captured inside China and the occasional US Army prisoner taken in South Vietnam who turned out to be a recent immigrant from the 'Old Country'. Fortunately, his reputation, as an expert on, and interrogator of, the British was well known to his Service superiors and had even reached the ears of the Central Committee, so it was rare indeed that any British captive was not passed over to him. But the last of these occasions had been nearly six months ago. The colonel could not repress a gentle thrill of anticipation at the thought of tonight's reunion with his British and of the seventy-two hours of uninterrupted contact which were to follow. In the darkness, the pewter-coloured eyes grew fixed.

There was a tentative knock at the door. Sun called amiably in English, 'Yes, please come in.'

The opening door let in a shaft of light which illuminated the outline of a girl. Also tentatively, also in English, a naturally harsh but not loud voice said, 'May I put on the light, Comrade Colonel?'

'Just let me close the shutters. . . . Good.'

The instant blaze of the unshaded bulb fell on a stone floor without covering, four whitewashed walls, a cheap nondescript table and an equally cheap and nondescript unoccupied chair. The interrogation-room atmosphere soothed the colonel, and at a time like this put him on his mettle too.

Now his eyes blinked neither at the sudden glare nor at the sight of the girl, which, although he had seen her a dozen times since arriving, they might well have done.

The Albanians, as a race, are not noted for their beauty. They are, of course, much less a race than the end-product of successive admixtures with the native stock – Latin, Slavonic, Greek, Turco-Tatar. Now and then this cocktail of heredities produces an individual physically remarkable even by the high standards of the eastern Mediterranean. Doni Madan, aged 23, citizen of Korçe in south-eastern Albania, strictly temporary holder of a Greek passport (forged in Tiranë with unusual competence, thanks to Chinese supervision), was physically remarkable.

She wore a pair of serpent-green Thai-silk trousers, close-fitting and low-cut, with a plain turquoise jacket of the same material and Ferragamo slippers in embroidered leather. Nothing else: even within twenty yards of the open sea, fine September nights in these latitudes can be hot and humid. Although this outfit had been selected purely to do its part in proclaiming Doni to be one of a standard house-party of well-off cosmopolitan holidaymakers, it did more for her than that.

She was above middle height, within a couple of inches of Sun, but slender and light of frame, narrow in the waist, richly rounded above and below. Her wide hips and ever-so-slightly protuberant belly strained at the stuff of the pants; the swell of her breasts made the casually-buttoned jacket fall straight, well clear of her midriff. Asia was in her cheek-bones and the strong planes of her jaw, Asia Minor in the all-but-black brown of her eyes, Venice in the straight but fully-moulded mouth. The light brown of her hair, cut in a simple bell, made an odd and exciting contrast with the delicate swarthiness of her skin. She stood there in the door-way of the bare room in an attitude of meek unconscious provocation that took no account of Sun as a man.

Anything more overt would certainly have been wasted.

Sun Liang-tan was unmoved by women, though if challenged on the point he would have replied, rather mechanically, that he respected them as wives, mothers, and the bringers of comfort to men. He glanced somewhere in Doni's direction and said simply, 'Yes?'

'I am wondering if you wish any food,' said the quiet harsh voice.

Doni's Italian, Serbo-Croat and Greek were idiomatic and relatively accentless. Her English was neither, but she had no other means of communication with her temporary master. Being forced to use the enemy's language in order to work with European agents is a habitual source of irritation to Chinese subversives, but the mild irritation Sun now showed sprang from an opposite feeling.

He laced his fingers behind his long head and leant back as far as his chair allowed, making a curious semi-Westernized figure in his white tee-shirt and uncoloured cotton trousers. 'I was wondering,' he said slowly, 'if you wanted any food. If you would like, if you would care for something to eat. If you'd like me to rustle up – no, that's American – if you fancy a snack. Do try not to be a peasant in everything you say and do, my dear. And in any case, no. No thank you. Not just now. Let's hang on for a bit until our chums join us, shall we? They shouldn't be long.'

The colonel's English was correct enough – he had studied the language for two years at Hong Kong University – but his pronunciation would have been a joy to any phonetician. His quick ear and passionate desire to learn, allied to a total ignorance of the British dialectal pattern, had issued in a kind of verbal salad of regional peculiarities. The tones of Manchester, Glasgow, Liverpool, Belfast, Newcastle, Cardiff and several sorts of London worked in successive syllables against those of the governing class. The result might have sounded merely bizarre, even ridiculous, from another mouth than Sun's, accompanied by a different kind of gaze.

Doni looked to one side of him. 'I'm sorry, Comrade Colonel,' she said humbly. 'I know my English not good.'

'Better than the other one's, anyway,' said Sun with a

tolerant smile. His lips were dark, the colour of dried blood, his teeth pointing slightly inwards from the gums. He went on: 'But enough of the Comrade Colonel. You sound like somebody in a progressive youth play. Call me Colonel Sun. It's more friendly. And enough of solitude – let's be sociable, eh? Where are the others?'

Followed by Doni, he walked out of the room, across a stone-flagged corridor, and into the main sitting-room of the house, a high-ceilinged, airy place with a cobbled floor that sloped gently and splendid shapely furniture of olive-wood, made in the island. The brightly-patterned modern rugs and cushions, the pair of run-of-the-mill abstracts on the rough-cast wall, were incongruous. Open double doors gave on to a narrow terrace with folding chairs and a low table, and beyond there was nothing but the sea, flat calm and so brilliantly lit by a fast-rising full moon that it seemed both infinitely liquid and impossibly shallow, a sheet of water one molecule thick stretching out to the edge of the sky. Invisible wavelets made tiny hushing sounds on the stretch of pebbles between the two stubby moles of the anchorage.

Sun stood for a moment by the doors, keeping well into the shadow, and gazed out. He had not seen the sea for fifteen years, and the sight still fascinated him. It was the British element, on which the men of those cold islands had ventured out, long ago, to bring a quarter of the world under their sway. A perfect setting, thought Sun with a full heart, then turned back to the room.

The girl stretched out on the square-cut day-bed looked up quickly. She was Doni's height, had the same near-black eyes, wore the same kind of outfit (black pants, white jacket in her case), but her slimness made the other girl appear almost lumpish. Long-legged and high-breasted, with an exquisitely-shaped small dark head cut short in a boyish style, Luisa Tartini was Italian in more than her name. Like Doni, however, she was Albanian by nationality, carrying a similar passport. But she had none of her companion's docility of manner, and her glance at Sun now was edged with resentment and fear.

It seemed that Sun did not notice. He said pleasantly, 'What a lovely evening. And how very decorative you look, my dear.'

'Is boring,' said Luisa sulkily, shifting her slender legs so that Doni could sit beside her. 'What we doing here?'

'Your main function, as I told you, is to give our little party the appearance of a group of friends on holiday. Not very exacting. But tonight your duties will be, er, enlarged. You and Doni will put yourselves at the disposal of some men who will be arriving soon. That may prove rather more exacting.'

'Which men?' Luisa sat up so that her shoulder touched Doni's. 'How many?'

'Six in all. Two are reactionaries and needn't concern you. The other four are fighters for peace who have been on a dangerous mission. You must give them all the comfort in your power, both of you.'

The two girls looked at each other. Luisa shrugged. Doni gave a sleepy smile and put a brown arm round Luisa's waist.

'And now . . . Ah, right on time, Evgeny. What a very good servant you are. You should take it up professionally!'

The fourth member of the household, a stocky, bullet-headed Russian, was edging his way into the room with a tray of drinks. Evgeny Ryumin had considered himself underpaid and without prospects at the Soviet Embassy in Peking and had defected without fuss ten years earlier. His new masters had found him unimaginative but capable, also quite ruthless. These qualities, and his being European, suited him admirably to act as the man-of-all-work in Sun's group. He put the tray down on a sturdy round table and cocked his close-cropped head at the girls.

The colonel watched with a tolerant smile as Luisa was handed a vodka on the rocks and Doni a Fix beer, refused a drink himself, gestured genially for the Russian to take whatever he wanted.

Hands in pockets, Sun turned away and strolled towards the open doors. Then he halted, stood quite still for a moment, and glanced at his watch, a steel-cased Longines WD pattern which he had had for nearly fifteen years. Its former owner, a captain in the Gloucestershire Regiment, had died under interrogation as bravely as anyone Sun had ever met. The watch was a precious possession, a memento, not a trophy.

Sun called sharply over his shoulder, 'Evgeny. The lights. All of them.'

Ryumin put down the Fix he had just tasted. 'All?'

'All. What can't be concealed should be flaunted. This is the remainder of our little house-party arriving.'

Just below the crest of the hillside above the house, the two men from the islet lay under a stunted fig-tree and saw the terrace and anchorage spring into bright illumination. They watched the slow approach of the motor-boat, and waited without moving or speaking while lines were thrown and secured, laughter and cries of greeting were borne faintly to their ears, and three men came ashore, one of them needing some assistance, the other two springing forward to be embraced by the two women from the house. The servant dealt with some suitcases. The party retired indoors. The boat, its engine popping gently, slid out from the shore and turned west, no doubt preparing to circumnavigate the islet and make for the public anchorage in the middle of the inner curve of Vrakonisi.

On the hillside, one man looked at the other and spread his palms. The two got up and resumed their arduous and ineffective patrol. They had eleven more houses to check on tonight.

In the house, Sun Liang-tan sat and surveyed the three new arrivals. He said nothing.

The black-haired gunman, he who had followed James Bond from Sunningdale to Quarterdeck thirty hours earlier, spoke. 'Bond,' he started to say, but his throat was dry and he had to clear it. 'Bond got away from us in England.'

Sun nodded, perfectly expressionless.

'But steps have been taken to retrieve the error and there is every reason to hope that he will be in our hands within twenty-four hours,' the man said woodenly, as if repeating what he had learnt by heart.

Sun nodded again.

'HNC-16 only takes effect at once when administered intravenously,' put in the second man. 'He was struggling so much that I could only manage an intramuscular injection, which meant he could—'

He stopped with the last word half bitten off at a tiny gesture from Sun, a mere raising of one yellow hand from the wrist.

'He escaped after damaging Doyle's face severely enough to attract attention,' the first man went on as before. 'So Doyle was eliminated on the spot. After that everything proceeded according to plan. The double diversionary tactics at the airport were successful in—'

Again the hand came up.

'Quantz brilliantly improvised a clue which he left on Doyle's body,' the recital continued, 'and which he estimates cannot fail to lure Bond to Athens in search of his chief. The details are in here,' said the gunman in a hurry, as if to forestall another flick of the hand, and passed Sun a sealed envelope. 'By now Quantz is in Athens himself. We put the flying-boat down off Cape Sounion and he set out for the shore in the rubber dinghy. He will contact our friends in Athens. Should Bond fail to appear after all, Quantz will arrange for the abduction of one of the regular British agents there and will transport him to this island. Quantz estimates that even in that event the operation will succeed in its main object.'

Sun sat on in silence for half a minute, tapping the envelope gently against his knee. Sweat showing on their faces, the two men stood before him in awkward attitudes. Luisa sat on the day-bed and furtively watched Sun; Doni, at her side, looked from one man to the other.

At last the colonel looked up, and the purple lips parted in a smile. Tension relaxed; somebody exhaled sharply.

Turning to the gunman, Sun said, 'Well, De Graaf, you certainly seem to have had the most damnable bad luck. But I must say it looks as if you've done everything in your power to put things right.' Sun was a fair-minded man. Further, that obsession of the Chinese secret services, the splitting-up of every team project into independent units directed from the top, had seen to it that his responsibility started and finished with the Vrakonisi end of the plan. And, although bitterly disappointed at the non-arrival of Bond, he could not consider betraying any such emotion in the presence of Westerners.

'But now you'll want to relax,' he went on. 'Full discussion in the morning. Help yourselves to a drink. Evgeny will prepare a meal to your requests. These girls are called Doni and Luisa. They've been instructed to please you in every way and at any time. Oh, and finally . . .'

Rising unhurriedly to his feet, Sun went over to the third of the newcomers, who had remained slumped in a chair since entering the room.

'Good evening, Admiral. I am Colonel Sun Liang-tan of the People's Liberation Army. How are you feeling, sir?'

M raised his head. Some of the old sharpness had returned to his grey eyes. He spoke firmly.

'I shan't be answering any of your other questions, you yellow-faced bandit, so I might as well make a start by not answering that one. Save your breath.'

'The main reason for your presence here, Western filth, is not the answering of questions. But answer them you will when the time comes. Rest assured of that.'

Sun's tone was as equable as ever. He continued, 'Now, Lohmann, take your patient away and put him to bed with a shot of something that'll give him a good night's sleep. Evgeny will show you where.'

The doctor, a bald, under-sized man in his forties, did as he was told.

Holding a tumbler half-full of vodka, De Graaf sauntered over to the day-bed. He looked each girl up and down in the manner of a farmer at a cattle-market. Finally he pointed at Luisa.

'The colonel said any time,' he murmured. 'So now.'

Luisa glanced at Doni, who talked emphatic Albanian for almost half a minute. At the end of it, Luisa shrugged, then nodded. Doni fixed her eyes on De Graaf.

'I like you to take me also. The other man disgusting. No hairs on his head and too little and hands like a bird. You take me also. We did this before. We do many things for you. You enjoy it.'

'Suits me,' said De Graaf, draining his glass and grinning. 'Lead on, my dears.'

Left alone, Sun Liang-tan strode to the terrace and spat as hard as he could towards the Aegean.

Chapter 6

The Shrine of Athene

JAMES BOND sat in the bar of the Hotel Grande Bretagne in Athens and waited for something to happen.

There was no alternative, no active policy in the least pursuable. Hours of four-cornered discussion between Bond, Bill Tanner, Head of Section G in London and, from time to time, Head of Station G in Athens over the radio link had finally produced something that, for want of a better word, had to be called a plan. Bond ran over the points in his mind as Tanner had scrawled them down on the back of a message-form in the office.

1. Ideally, 007 should identify the enemy agents entrusted with his abduction, evade capture and tail them to the next higher echelon with a view to locating M.

2. This can be ruled out as a practical proposition. 007 will be unable to identify these agents in advance, and the degree of practical efficiency displayed in the Quarterdeck operation strongly suggests that they will render evasion of capture impossible.

3. Therefore, 007 must invite capture and depend on the following safeguards:

(a) Operatives of Station G will keep 007 under surveillance at all times and trace the movements of the abduction party with a view to intervention in force.

(b) A midget homing-transmitter will await 007 on arrival in Athens for installation in his clothing.

(c) Escape devices in clothing.

(a) and (b): Head of Station G for action.

(b) and (c): Head of Q Branch for action.

Bond smiled thinly to himself. Station G was famous throughout the Service; its Head, a mild-looking Welshman called Stuart Thomas, had served long and valiantly as 005 before an eye defect had begun to impair his ability with firearms, since when he had run the Athens unit with unsurpassed skill and imagination. But even Thomas could not be expected to produce the kind of supermen demanded by Bill Tanner's 3(a), which the enemy must have taken into account and would surely guard against. While as for 3(b) and 3(c) . . .

A packet containing the midget transmitter had been awaiting Bond when he checked in at the hotel, and he had duly installed it in the compartment Q Branch had made for it in the heel of his left shoe. A miniature pick-lock was fitted into the right heel, and two wafer-thin tungsten steel hacksaw blades, hardly less pliable than the cloth itself, in the lapels of his charcoal-green mohair suit. Such devices grew more sophisticated every year; their possible hiding-places remained constant. Men like the ones who had planned and carried out the Quarterdeck operation would be unlikely to overlook any of them. Bond realized grimly that, on this assignment as on all his previous ones, the tools he basically had to depend on were invisible, intangible, within himself. They would be tested to the utmost by what lay ahead. Everything else was uncertain.

He had a look around the crowded, decorously noisy bar. Perhaps, merely for curiosity's sake, he would be able to pick out the local agents whose job it was to keep him under their eye. (Standard Service procedure, aimed at minimizing the possibility of betrayal under torture, dictates that no agent shall have any knowledge of his co-agents that is not absolutely necessary.) The place seemed full of conventional business and professional types and their women, Athenian bankers, ship-owners from the islands, politicians from Salonika, less readily classifiable visitors from Istanbul, Sofia, Bucharest – not forgetting the tourists – all with the appearance of solid respectability.

Bond had chosen to stay at the Grande Bretagne because it was public in the way he wanted and because he had always responded to its slightly seedy grandeur, inter-war in period with a thin veneer of modernism. He enjoyed the lofty foyer with its stained glass, green marble pillars and handsome Gobelin tapestry, a good copy of the original in the Louvre, depicting Alexander the Great entering Babylon on a fat, crafty-looking horse, a dignified figure at the head of his retinue but gone a bit blowzy, more like Cleopatra than a Macedonian prince. Bond accepted too the rather Frenchified style of the bar, all broken pediments, terracotta friezes and heavy, expensive silk curtains, plus the very un-French sedate courtesy of the waiters.

It was ten o'clock, the hour when fashionable Athens considers where it will dine. Bond was hungry. Arrival at the hot, crowded little airport under Mount Hymettus early that afternoon had found him too tired to eat. He had dropped his bags at the Grande Bretagne and gone straight to a pavement café in the square. A quick carafe of cheap wine in the sun had been an ideal prelude to seven hours of wallowing sleep in the comfortable bed of the room he always asked for, 706 on the top floor, far from quiet, but with a fine view of the Acropolis and a glimpse of the sea.

By now the enemy would have confirmed Bond's arrival, finalized his own plans and moved his units into position. Time to go. Bond signalled to the waiter. Almost simultaneously, a man sitting not far away, his back half-turned to Bond, made the same bill-summoning gesture. He looked the most comfortably bourgeois of all the bar's customers, and had been sitting chatting quietly with his companions, a replica of himself and two handsome but unglamorized women. Thomas's sort of people. No pairs of silent toughs in dark suits for him. It would be interesting to see whether . . .

Bond's bill came. He was reaching for his money when his eye was caught by a sudden movement at the little table on his other side. A tubby, swarthy man with a thick moustache, a Turk by the look of him, had seized the bare upper arm of the girl next to him, pulled her close and was talking into her ear in something between a whisper and a snarl. She was young and strikingly pretty, with the delicate features, full breasts and tobacco-blonde hair of the most attractive physical type in this region. Now she was straining away from the Turk's heavy head and writhing red mouth, trying to undo his hand, her tan-coloured eyes wide with what looked like shock and fright. Their glance fell on Bond, who was only a few yards off and the nearest unattached male.

'Please,' she called in English, not loudly but urgently. 'Please do something.'

Bond weighed it up briefly. He could perfectly well pay and leave. The waiters could deal quite adequately with the man if he persisted. On the other hand, Bond's instinct told him, as just now, that here was something relevant, something that stuck out from the innocently busy social scene round him. And the girl certainly was a beauty. ... And there was nothing to be lost. He made his decision.

'Bring it to me in a moment, please,' he told the waiter, walked across and sat down next to the Turk on the corner of the green plush bench. 'Now what is all this?'

'He's annoying me,' said the girl with much resentment. 'He says awful, obscene things to me. I beg you to get rid of him.'

Bond's Greek was small but well-chosen. He leant close to the man, who was staring at him contemptuously, and said in his deadliest tone, '*Fíye apo tho, málaka.*'

This, though probably as obscene as anything the man had been saying to the girl, is a standard Greek insult. What made it effective was Bond's air of determination and his sudden grip on the man's nearer arm. There was a pause while the two men stared at each other and Bond tightened his grip, noticing half-consciously that the arm was distinctly harder than its owner's general corpulence would have suggested. Then the Turk quickly and quite calmly let go the girl, waited for his own arm to be released, rose to his feet, adjusted his jacket, and walked out of the bar. His departure did not go unnoticed by the two couples Bond had picked out earlier.

'Thank you,' said the girl in excellent American English. 'I'm sorry about that. I could see no other way without a public disturbance. You dealt with him very competently.'

She chuckled suddenly, a warm-hearted, gay sound that showed remarkably quick recovery from the fear she had been displaying. 'You must have had practice.'

'Shall we have a drink?' asked Bond, raising his hand. 'Yes, I rescue girls from obscenity-spouting Turks all the time.'

'Thank you. Tzimas isn't a Turk. He just behaves like one. But he is obscene. My family have been pushing me at him – he has a good carpet-manufacturing business here. After this tonight my mother will talk to my father and there'll be no more pushing in that direction. Are you married?'

Bond smiled. 'No. I sometimes think I never will be. What will you have?'

'Ouzo and ice,' said the girl, glancing up at the waiter. 'Not that Sans Rival stuff you serve all the time. Have you Boutari?'

'Certainly, madam. And for you, sir?'

'The same. Plenty of ice.'

'You know ouzo?' The girl looked at Bond consideringly. 'You know Greece well?'

'Greece I know a little and love what I know. Ouzo I know much better: a Greek version of Pernod with a much more sinister smell but similar effects. Love would be too starry-eyed a word to use there.'

'That's a slander. And not accurate. The French took it from us and flavoured it with aniseed and dyed it green. Horrible! My name is Ariadne Alexandrou.'

'Mine is Bond, James Bond. How did you know just now that I spoke English?'

The girl laughed again. 'Most people do. And you look English, Mr Bond. Nobody could mistake you, not even for an American.'

'As a matter of fact I'm not strictly English at all. Half Scottish, half Swiss.'

'The English have swallowed you, then. What are you doing in Athens? Business or pleasure?'

'Business, but I hope to get some pleasure in while I'm here.'

Ariadne Alexandrou returned Bond's gaze for a moment without reacting to it, then turned away to observe critically as the two small tumblers of cloudy drink – the cloudiness curling whitely outwards from the ice-cubes like liquid smoke – were set in front of them and as much again of water added. Bond watched her lovely profile, very Greek yet totally unlike the overrated, beaky, 'classical' look one associates with old coins, a carefully-finished sculpture overlaid with the softest tints of tan and white and olive and rose. The effect was set off by earrings in an ancient style, small thick hoops of beaten gold.

No doubt it was for her splendid appearance and obvious quickness of mind that she had been picked by the enemy – of whose presence behind the events of the past five minutes Bond was no longer in the smallest doubt. All the girl's apparent confidence and warmth had not been able to disguise the patness and predictability of the way she had established acquaintance with him. He guessed that, left to herself, she would have stage-managed things with more imagination. Some plodding middle-echelon spymaster had come up with that amorous-Turk routine. Encouraging: the other side were getting lazy. Bond brushed aside the thought that they could afford to.

The girl Ariadne had raised her glass and was looking at him with a kind of down-turning smile that might have been ugly on anyone else, but in her case only emphasized the marvellously delicate yet firm lines of her lips.

'I know the sort of thing you expect me to say now.' The smile turned upward. ' "In Greece, when we drink to someone, we say *ees iyían*, your health, or colloquially *yássou*." Well, sometimes we do, but half the time it's "cheers" and "here's looking at you" these days.' The smile faded. 'Greece isn't very Greek any more. Every year less. I'm being a little conservative and sentimental just by asking for ouzo. The newest people want vodkatini, or Scotch and soda. Are you free for dinner, Mr Bond? Shall we go out somewhere together?'

Despite himself, Bond smiled in his turn. He was beginning to enjoy the girl's tactic of wandering away from the point

THE SHRINE OF ATHENE 63

and then jumping back to it with a direct question. But the other half of his mind was cursing. Why hadn't he taken the simple, obvious precaution of getting something under his belt before allowing the enemy to make contact? He could visualize, as clearly as if it had already happened, the deserted street where she would lead him, the men closing in, the car, the long drive to and across the Bulgarian frontier, and then. . . . Bad enough on a full stomach, he thought wryly. Was there another way?

Bond sipped the deceptively mild drink, its flavour reminding him as always of the paregoric cough-sweets he had sucked as a child, before he answered. 'Splendid, I'd love to do that. But why don't we eat in the hotel? I've done a lot of travelling today and—'

'Oh, but nobody dines at the Grande Bretagne unless they have to. It's not exciting. I'll take you somewhere where they have real Greek food. You like that?'

'Yes.' Perhaps he should come part-way into the open. 'It's just that I should hate to be prevented from getting to grips with it. I've never liked being sent to bed without any supper.'

A flicker of alarm showed in the light-brown eyes, to be instantly followed by blankness. 'I don't know what you mean. All the good restaurants stay open late. What they have they will give you. The Greeks have the oldest tradition of hospitality in Europe. And that's not tourist-bureau talk. You'll see.'

The hell with it, thought Bond savagely – what could he do but play along? It was far too early to start trying to capture the initiative. He decided to give in gracefully.

'Forgive me,' he said. 'I'm too used to England, where you have to choose between dining early and reasonably well, and late and badly – if at all. I'm in your hands,' he added. And meant it.

Three minutes later they stood on the steps of the hotel between the Ionic columns. Constitution Square was ablaze with light: the BEA offices, Olympic Airlines, TWA on the far side beyond the rows of trees, American Express to the right, the gentler illumination of the Tomb of the Unknown Soldier to the left. What Ariadne Alexandrou had said about the decreasing Greekness of Greece came to Bond's mind. In thirty years, he reflected, perhaps sooner, there would be one vast undifferentiated culture, one complex of super-highways, hot-dog stands and neon, interrupted only by the Atlantic, stretching from Los Angeles to Jerusalem; possibly, by then, as far as Calcutta, three-quarters of the way round the world. Where there had been Americans and British and French and Italians and Greeks and the rest, there would be only citizens of the West, uniformly affluent, uniformly ridden by guilt and neurosis, uniformly alcoholic and suicidal, uniformly everything. But was that prospect so hopelessly bad? Bond asked himself. Even at the worst, not as bad as all that was offered by the East, where conformity did not simply arise as if by accident, but was consciously imposed to the hilt by the unopposed power of the State. There were still two sides: a doubtfully, conditionally right and an un-conditionally, unchangeably wrong.

The grey-uniformed commissionaire blew his whistle and a taxi, to all appearance innocently cruising, swung in to the kerb. Bond laid his fingers on Ariadne's upper arm as he walked her over. The flesh was firm and the skin deliciously cool. She spoke briefly to the driver, an elderly, paunchy type who, again, looked the soul of innocence, and they were away.

Ariadne studied Bond's profile. As always, her employers' instructions had been confined to essentials. She had been told only to induce the Englishman to go with her to a desig-nated area where fellow-workers would take over the operation from her. What would happen to him afterwards was no concern of hers – officially. But, more and more, the question bothered her as a woman, a woman who had learnt to recognize on sight the kind of man who knew how to love. Bond was such a man. She was certain, too, that he found her desirable. She had always been a loyal servant of her cause, and not for a moment did she seriously contemplate disobeying orders, allowing Bond to take her home after dinner and do with her whatever he wanted. Ariadne only wished, passionately, that it had been possible. That mouth was made to give her brutal kisses, not to become distorted in a grimace of agony; those hands existed to caress her body, not to be stamped on by the torturer's boot. These images were so painfully vivid that she could find almost nothing to say as the taxi approached the slopes of the Acropolis.

At her side, Bond mistook her silence for that of tension. The next stage of the plan must surely be imminent. At each intersection he was ready for the sudden lurching acceleration to left or right that would bring them to the dark alley and the pick-up team he had imagined earlier. Automatically he began ticking off possible counter-measures in his mind before he remembered, sickly, that this time there must be no counter-measures, that capture was not the danger but the aim. And then, quite suddenly it seemed, the street widened, the shadows receded, the taxi, slowing, began to pull in towards a low incline at the top of which glittered the lights of an open-air restaurant. The driver stopped, switched off his engine and simply sat there.

Paying the man off, Bond resolved quite coolly to behave as if this were what it appeared to be, an encounter between an English visitor and a beautiful Greek girl anxious to entertain him in any way he wished. As they walked towards a narrow flight of steps that led up the incline, their shoulders touched for a moment. Bond laid his arm round Ariadne's waist and murmured, 'We're going to enjoy our dinner tonight. Nobody can stop that.'

She half-turned towards him, her back arching in what might have been either nervousness or desire, so that the swell of one firm breast brushed his arm. There was light enough for him to see an expression of defiant determination animate her lips and eyes. Her hand grasped his in an oddly warm, confiding gesture.

'Nobody shall,' she said. 'Nobody shall spoil it – James. It's all right for me to call you James? You must call me Ariadne, if you can manage it.'

'Ariadne. Easy. Four pretty syllables.'

'The original Ariadne was supposed to have been the

girl friend of King Theseus of Athens. She helped him to kill the Minotaur – you know, that guy with the bull's head who lived in the maze. But then Theseus went and dumped her on the island of Naxos so that he could go and . . .'

She stopped speaking so abruptly that Bond gave her a quick glance. 'Go and do what ?'

'Oh, I forget what came next. I suppose he went off and hunted the Calydonian boar or something. Anyway, Ariadne wasn't on her own for long. The wine-god Dionysus happened to be passing at the time and she latched on to him. Which is a funny coincidence because this restaurant's named after him. Well, what do you think ? It's lovely, isn't it ?'

From the top of the steps they looked over at the platform of the Acropolis, an enormous flat-topped chunk of rock adorned with temples of Athens's golden age, the lights of the theatre of Herodes Atticus showing near its base. Dominating everything was the moonlit length of the Parthenon, the temple which Bond had heard called the most beautiful building in the world. He could see it was beautiful, but was half distracted by the tiny teasing incident of a minute before. Ariadne Alexandrou had chopped off what she was saying exactly in the manner of somebody just not quite blurting out an important secret. But what could be either important or secret about which mythical exploit a legendary hero undertook after a former mythical exploit ?

Bond gave up the problem. He felt a pang of tenderness at Ariadne's obvious anxiety that he should be impressed. 'I've never seen a view like it,' he said rather lamely.

'I'm glad it pleases you, because it's the main attraction here.' She began to move on. 'The food is rather pretentious and expensive, though you can have a reasonable meal if you know what to order. Will you leave this to me ?'

'Gladly.'

Their table, set among cactus-beds, gave them a clear view of the Acropolis and also of the restaurant entrance, through which, a minute later, came the two couples Bond had decided were Thomas's people, talking as animatedly as before. He ignored them, not simply as an obvious precaution but because they brought with them an unpleasant reminder of reality. Fantasy was so much more attractive – the fantasy that he and Ariadne were destined to become lovers that night. He imagined what it would be like to slip the low-cut white piqué dress off those graceful shoulders and inhale the odour of the warm bared skin. Their eyes caught and held at that moment and Bond was certain she knew his mind, knew it and responded. But she too must be aware that what they both desired must remain a fantasy.

They began their meal with tender young crayfish, moist in the mouth and well set off by freshly-made mayonnaise. Bond savoured the scents of exotic foods, the pure warm East Mediterranean air, the surrounding atmosphere of relaxed, respectable enjoyment, the calm permanence of the ancient buildings in the middle distance, above all the girl opposite him, eating unfussily and with enjoyment.

She looked up and smiled. 'But you really like this food.'

'Of course. It's made of genuine materials and it tastes of them. What more could one ask?'

'Many of your countrymen ask for something different. Steaks, eggs and bacon, French fries.'

'The English call them chips.'

'Not here, not any more. It's French fries for years now. But you don't seem very English. Not English at all. I'm told it was the same with your Lord Byron.'

'I'm sure you mean to be kind,' said Bond, grinning at her, 'but I don't really enjoy being compared with Byron. As a poet he was affected and pretentious, he ran to fat early and had to go on the most savage diets, his taste in women was appalling, and as a fighter for liberty he never got started.'

Ariadne's mouth had set in a stern line. She spoke now in an even, measured tone, reasonable and yet forceful, the kind of tone which (Bond guessed) had been considered proper for ideological discussion in whatever political indoctrination centre had trained her. But her femininity triumphed over the propounders of Marx and Lenin, turning what might have been a schoolmarmy earnestness into a young and touching

solemnity. Bond did not often find himself wishing so hard
that the game was only a game.

'It's not proper for you to talk so lightly of one of your
greatest compatriots,' said the severe voice. 'Lord Byron was
a founder of the romantic movement in your literature. His
exile from England was a victory of bourgeois morality. It
was a tragedy that he died before he could lead his troops into
battle against the oppressor.'

(Lesson 1, thought Bond sardonically. Emergence of the
Greek nation. The War of Independence. Defeat of the Turks.)

'But his support of the Greek cause with money and influence was. . . .' Ariadne faltered, as if she had momentarily
lost her place in the script, and went on with something much
nearer her normal warm eagerness, 'Well, no Greek can ever
forget it, that's all. Whether he deserved it or not, he's a
national hero, and you ought to be proud of him.'

'I'll try to be. I suppose I had him rammed down my throat
too much at school. Childe Harold. Not a very lively chap, I
thought.'

Ariadne was silent for a moment. Then she said quietly,
'It wasn't only him, of course. The English have helped us in
many ways. Some time ago, not recently. But we haven't
forgotten. In spite of Cyprus, in spite of . . . so much, we
still—'

Bond could not resist it. 'In spite of our having helped your
government to put down the Communists after the war ?'

'If you like.' The light-brown gaze was candid and troubled.
'That was a terrible thing, all that fighting. For everybody.
History can be very cruel. If only one could re-make the past.'

A faint flicker of hope, the first in this whole affair, arose in
Bond's mind. However determined the enemy in general might
be, this particular enemy was not whole-hearted. He had
found someone who, given a massive dose of luck, could conceivably be turned into an ally.

This thought stayed with him while they talked lightly and
with an enjoyable shared malice about the Greek rich set and
the cavortings of shipping millionaires. Ariadne showed some
inside knowledge, confirming Bond's impression that she

must have come to Communism as a way of revolting against some sort of moneyed upbringing, rather than by local and family conviction, as an embittered child of the middle classes, not a militant ex-villager. Another point in his favour. Bond felt almost relaxed, finding the charcoal-grilled lamb cutlets with bitter local spinach very acceptable, enjoying the tang of retsina, the white wine infused with resin which some palates find musty or metallic, but which had always seemed to him the essence of Greece in liquor: sunshine-coloured, scented with warm pine-groves, faintly touched by the salt of the Aegean.

Then reality returned in short order. As they sipped the delicious, smoky-tasting Turkish coffee, Ariadne said quickly, 'James. I want to ask you something. It's eleven thirty. Tonight it's full moon and the Acropolis stays open late. If we leave now we can go and have a look at it. You must see it like this. It's indescribable. And I've a wish to see it again myself. With you. Will you take me? Afterwards . . . we can do anything you want.'

God! Bond's gorge rose at the vulgarity of it, the confident obviousness, the touch of footling melodrama in the choice of pick-up point. But he fought down his disgust and said with as good a grace as he could muster, 'Of course. I don't seem to have any alternative.'

Chapter 7

Not-So-Safe-House

THERE IS something to be said for the view that the Parthenon is best seen from a distance. Certainly the place was badly knocked about in an otherwise forgotten war of the seventeenth century. The restoration work, such as it is, is mainly incompetent, far less competent than could be expected from Germans, say, or Americans, who would have produced a reconstruction faultlessly in accord with the theories of the most respectable historians – and faultlessly dead. But by moonlight, with the bad joinery hidden and the outside world at a proper distance, those tall columns can seem much more than rows of battered antique marble. A dead world lives in them.

Even James Bond was not untouched by such feelings as he paced the southern aisle at Ariadne's side and waited for what must happen. The rocky, windy hilltop was thinly scattered with figures in ones and twos, late visitors, tourists or lovers, catching the final few minutes before the gates of the site were closed. Among them, of course, must be a party who were neither tourists nor lovers. Bond wasted no energy in trying to pick them out. They would come when it was time.

Quite soon it was time. Bond was watching Ariadne's face and saw its expression change. She turned to him and his heart filled with longing and despair.

'James,' she said. '*Khrisi mou*. Darling. Kiss me.'

He took her in his arms and her body strained against him and her firm dry lips opened under his. When they drew apart she looked into his eyes.

'Forgive me,' she whispered.

Her glance moved over his shoulder and she frowned. In a few more seconds they were there. Two of them. Both tallish, one plump, the other average build. Each had a hand in his jacket pocket. They took up positions either side of Bond. The plump one spoke to him in Greek, ordering him to come with them and adding something else he couldn't follow. The girl asked the other man a rapid question. An instant's hesitation, an equally rapid reply. Ariadne Alexandrou gave a satisfied nod, stepped close to Bond and spat in his face.

He barely had time to recoil before she followed up with her hands, no little-girl slaps but stinging blows that rocked his head. A stream of Greek insults, of which 'English pig' was the most ladylike, burst from her snarling mouth. Apart from the physical pain he felt only sadness. He caught a glimpse of the plump man's face split in an embarrassed grin.

Then, still hitting him, she switched to English. She used just the same abusive tone as before, so that she seemed to be cursing him in his own language. But what she said was:

'Listen to me. These men . . . are enemies.' Slap! 'We must get away. I'll take the fat one. You take' – slap! – 'the other. Then . . . follow me.'

She stopped, moved laughing towards the plump man, cracked her knee into his crotch and drove her stiffened fingers at his eyes. He squealed thinly. Without conscious thought Bond went for the other man, who had involuntarily half-turned, and chopped him cruelly at the side of the neck. The plump man was doubled up with his hands over his face. Bond brought his joined fists down on the base of the squat skull, grabbed Ariadne and ran.

Straight along the empty, shadowed colonnade to the western end, off the marble pavement on to the ground, uneven and awkward with its tussocks of slippery grass, past a pair of willowy youths with Germany written all over them, towards the entrance. . . . But Ariadne pulled him away to the left. Yes – danger of more men at the main gate. But was there another way out? He couldn't remember. Where were they going? No questions: he had instinctively chosen to stick to

the girl and must continue to. Covering distance without
falling took enough attention. He ran on.

Now a shout from behind them; another couple of aston-
ished faces; the edge of a cliff too high to jump from, too sheer
to clamber down in a hurry. But a stretch of wall joins the cliff
at an angle, and in the angle a bunch of thick electric cables
runs down. Down, then, down a face of irregular, almost
vertical rock hanging on to the cables, the girl following. A
gentler slope close to the wall, a final slither down more wall,
helped by a single cable running horizontally. Run together
across bumpy rock and earth – a yard away a jet of earth
springing into the air. No report: silencer. Above them the
sounds of scrambling and cursing. Now another drop, off the
roof of some hut built into the hillside, a curving, descending
path, a metal fence, and people ahead and below, hundreds of
people. Easy to get over the fence, help the girl over, and join
them.

At Bond's side, Ariadne laughed shakily. 'Theatre of
Herodes Atticus. Performance ending. In all senses, I hope.'

Bond's glance was full of admiration. Whatever her motives
might be, the girl had shown herself to be speedy, resourceful
and determined: a valuable ally indeed. He said easily, 'It
was clever of you to know about that alternative exit.'

'Oh, we plan carefully. I could draw a map of the Acropolis
blindfold.'

'Who are "we"?'

'Maybe I'll tell you later. Right now it's your job to push
us through this crowd, get us out to the street and grab the
first taxi, by force if necessary. Show me how rough and rude
and un-English you can be.'

The next few minutes were a hell of struggling and shoving.
Bond felt the sweat running down his chest and back. The
departing audience were cheerful, talkative, in no hurry, not
in a mood to resent being jostled, not heeding it much either.
Twice the two of them were separated, but at last reached the
street together. There was a brief scuffle by a taxi, Ariadne
keeping up a stream of indignant Greek about the airport and
her husband's sick father, and they were in and driving off.

Ariadne lolled against Bond's shoulder, trembling violently, and her lips shook as she kissed his cheek. He put his arm round her shoulders and drew her close. She had fully earned her moment of reaction, of temporary collapse after the extreme and varied time of stress she had just gone through. He murmured softly to her.

'I'm sorry I spat at you,' she whispered jerkily, brushing her cheek with her hand. 'But I thought I had to do it. And then all those mean things I said. I kept hoping you weren't understanding. And you can't think I meant—'

'You were brilliant, absolutely brilliant. I don't know anybody who could have made a plan as fast as that and then carried it out so skilfully. You made fools of the pair of them. But now . . . I've got to ask you some questions. Haven't I ?'

Her face was against his shoulder and he felt her nod.

'You were to decoy me to the Acropolis where I was to be picked up by two of your men. Correct ?'

She began in a muffled voice: 'But I didn't want to—'

'We'll save that for now. Well, when the men appeared you realized they were the wrong men. How ?'

Ariadne swallowed and pulled herself upright. 'We . . . there was to be a recognition signal just before they moved in. A thing with a handkerchief. They didn't give it. So I told them I was informed Legakis and Papadogonas were going to do the job. Then the guy said they'd been called away to another assignment. But as far as I know there's nobody named Legakis or Papadogonas who's working for us. So then I just gambled that they won't know enough English. And here we are. Can I have a cigarette ?'

'Of course.'

Bond gave her a Xanthi, the pungent Macedonian blend he always smoked in Greece, lit one himself and inhaled deeply. He felt charged-up, almost exhilarated. Whatever lay immediately ahead the expected gloomy pattern of abduction and captivity had been broken. He was still free and the initiative was not all on the other side – or sides.

'Ariadne, who are you working for ? You said you'd tell me.'

When she spoke she was herself again, quick and assured.

'I said maybe. It's still maybe. For the moment I can't tell you anything. And there's so much I don't know myself. Who were those men? It's frightening. The whole situation must have changed in the last few hours. It could be it isn't you we want after all. I don't see how it can be, now that this . . .'

She was thinking aloud, but her voice died away before she had done much more than express confusion. By now Bond had arrived at his own views about the scene on the Acropolis. For the moment he must follow through and put what faith he could in the midget transmitter in his shoe and the efficiency of Thomas's men. He said dryly, 'Where are you taking me?'

'To see my chief. He must talk with you. Obviously I can't force you to come with me. You can stop the driver now and get out and walk away. But please don't. We have to talk. Can you trust me?'

'Trust doesn't enter into it. I've got to come with you.'

'I don't understand that. Like most things about this.' Ariadne turned and gripped his hands. 'But I do have one reason for feeling happy. Oh, not happy, but less miserable than a quarter of an hour ago, when I thought I'd never see you again. We're still together. Sure, you've no reason to trust me on anything else, but you do believe me about this, don't you, James? That I want us to go on being together?'

'Yes.' Bond spoke as he felt. 'I believe you, Ariadne.'

They kissed, and for a moment left the world of enmity, violence and treachery in which they worked. Just then the taxi slowed and stopped. They moved apart. In the most everyday manner possible they got out and Bond paid off the driver.

It was a narrow street on the outskirts of the city towards the port of Piraeus, with a small bar in which a solitary old man dozed, a grocer's shop, a long building that might have been a school, a few houses of variegated shapes but all uniformly whitewashed. One was set a few yards back from the street behind rusty railings. Ariadne opened the gate, which squeaked painfully, and they crossed a tiny paved courtyard overgrown with vine and laurel. An underfed tabby cat rushed past them, squeezed through the railings and vanished. At the front door, Ariadne gave a complicated knock, reached out and gripped Bond's hand.

Bolts were thrown and the door opened. The man Ariadne had called Tzimas stood there. At the sight of them he gave a grunt of consternation, but a gun was in his hand within the time of a heartbeat. He motioned them in and shut the door, bolting it by feel while his eyes and gun remained on Bond. Ariadne led the way across a square tiled hall to an inner door. Bond followed her over the threshold.

There were two men sitting at the cheap barley-sugar-legged table. Both at once jumped up and began shouting questions at Ariadne. During the gesticulating three-cornered word-play that followed, Bond studied the men. One was in his thirties, dark, good-looking, a little overweight for his age: Greek. The other might have been anything between forty and sixty, grey, dried-up, close-cropped, speaking Greek with a heavy accent: Russian. No question about it. Well, that was one point checked off. Bond allowed himself to wonder whether M was in this house. Since the Quarterdeck affair he had, as far as possible, rigorously excluded M from his conscious thoughts, knowing that to speculate in that direction put him at the mercy of useless, senseless rage and hatred. So it did now for a moment: Bond gritted his teeth and concentrated on the present scene.

The Greek, biting his lip, hurried to an open roll-top desk littered with papers and began telephoning furiously. The Russian continued his dialogue with Ariadne for a time. He glanced at Bond more and more often, finally dismissed the girl with a flick of his hand and came over. He looked tired and frightened.

'Precaution, Mr Bond,' he said, his accent no less thick in English than in Greek. 'Take out your gun slowly and give it to me.'

Bond, with Tzimas at his side, did as he was told. The Russian gave the weapon a quick professional glance before reaching across and placing it on the desk.

'Now take a seat, Mr Bond. You like a drink?'

Bond, sitting beside Ariadne on a moth-eaten horsehair sofa, looked up in surprise. 'Very much. Thank you.'

The Russian signed to Tzimas. 'We have only ouzo, I'm sorry. It is known that you prefer whisky, but our budget wouldn't allow this. You call that cheese-paring?'

The thin mouth twitched upwards. You've got guts, thought Bond. You're scared half out of your mind and you're too proud to be seen yielding to it. He nodded and smiled back.

Tzimas handed him a tooth-glass half-full of milky fluid. '*Fíye apo tho, málaka?*' said the man threateningly, glaring into Bond's face. Then he guffawed and slammed him on the back. '*Bravo! Ees iyían!*'

'Now, Mr Bond.' The Russian waved Tzimas away with a frown and leant back against the edge of the table. 'My name is Gordienko and my associate here is named Markos. We may have very little time, so I must request you to be intelligent and answer my questions. As you have gathered, it was arranged for you to be captured tonight and brought here. You are not captured but you come here just the same. Why?'

'What alternative had I? You must see that.'

'I do not. I don't. Now, please. What is the purpose of your visit to Greece?'

Bond stared. 'Good God, you brought me here!'

Gordienko stared back, then shrugged, 'Perhaps it was not intelligent of me to ask this now. Tonight all very confusing. But answer this. In your opinion, who has employed the men who have tried to capture you?'

'I don't know. Some powerful free-lance. Anyhow, it failed. Now let me ask you something. Where's your other prisoner? Is he here?'

'This is ...' Gordienko looked defeated. 'I have no idea what you mean.'

'Now who's being unintelligent? Another one, then. What do you want with me? You've got me here at your mercy. Surely you can let me know that much.'

'I can,' said Gordienko briskly. 'Now, yes, I can. You're

considered to be very important, Mr Bond. So important that the task to plan your capture is taken out of my hands and entrusted to – another official.'

(Ah! thought Bond; I might have guessed that Acropolis caper wasn't your style.)

'On capture you would be kept in custody here in this safe-house for approximately three days and then released. You would also be questioned as to your intentions in coming to Athens. These were my orders. Privately, I had much doubt as to the wisdom of the second item. It is known that you're very resistant to questioning.'

Bond suppressed a surge of excitement. He was nearly certain he saw the truth. Gordienko's obvious air of competence made it most unlikely that he would lie so pointlessly at such a moment. On this reasoning, he, Bond, had somehow strayed out of one conspiracy into another, and the men on the Acropolis had been the agents of the original one, the first, grand, terrifying conspiracy. And that meant that some agreement with this Russian was possible. But caution must be maintained; he was only nearly certain. In this kind of work there are no certainties until the job is over – if then.

He said in a level tone, 'I think I believe you. It rather looks as if we've been at cross-purposes, you and I. We're so used to there being two sides that we never remember there may be a third, hostile to both of us. I propose that, for the moment, we join forces.'

'Agreed.' Some of the tension left Gordienko's lined face. He signed again to Tzimas. 'Let us pool information. Some information, at least. My side is conducting an important, um, event in this region. I must assure you that it's not aimed against your side. It's designed to give strength to my side, naturally, but not so much at the expense of yours. *Efkharistó.*'

Gordienko took the glass of ouzo from Tzimas and looked sidelong at it. 'I too would rather have something else, but at least the use of neutral drink will make sure that our respective national egos aren't offended.' He twitched his mouth as before, with a sort of distant warmth. 'Good luck.'

'We'll need it.' Bond lifted his glass and drank.

'So. My task has been to counter possible outside interference with this event. When your arrival became reported
by our observers, I passed on the news and was instructed to
move against you. Your presence here at such a time could
not possibly be the result of chance. And it is known that you've
had success in the past at interfering with events. . . . *Nai*?'

Markos had finished his telephoning. He came and faced
Gordienko, shaking slightly and sweating a great deal. Now
he burst into a torrent of Greek. Bond made out only scraps,
but they sounded to him disconcerting scraps. To judge by
their faces, Gordienko and Ariadne agreed with him.

When the recital was over and Markos had gone back to
the telephone with fresh instructions, Gordienko turned to
Bond. His face had gone a shade greyer. He carefully adjusted
his wire-framed spectacles before he spoke.

'Our common enemy is proceeding with extreme ruthlessness. The men entrusted with your capture have been mur-
dered.'

Ariadne caught her breath.

'As you know, Mr Bond, assassination of agents is exceed-
ingly rare in peacetime. Not unknown, of course' – the mouth
twitched briefly – 'but rare. I am afraid that nothing less can
be intended than total obliteration of the event I spoke about.
The consequences of this would be serious. Serious as far as
possible war. And the forces at my disposal have suddenly
become almost useless.'

With a convulsive movement, Gordienko drained his glass.
He looked hard at Bond.

'There is a traitor in our organization. Nothing less will
explain what happens. It shames me to admit this to you,
but we are allies. And to say so reminds me. I should like us
to shake hands.'

Bond stood up and complied without much reservation.
The Russian's clasp was firm and dry.

'The official who planned your capture is clearly suspect.'
Gordienko resumed his awkward leaning posture at the table.
'But two persons I can at once eliminate from suspicion. Both
are with us now. Markos is in my company continuously since

your arrival has been reported. Miss Alexandrou was not informed of the details of your capture. Tzimas I can't logically eliminate. But I trust him.

'My procedure therefore is plain. I must move with these three to another safe-house, at a location known only to myself, and operate as best I can from there. Moscow will send me replacements and Markos will recruit fresh local helpers, but these things must take time. And we have almost no time. Will you accompany us, Mr Bond, or do you wish to consult with your own people? If this, I should welcome from you now what information you think you may give.'

Before Bond could reply, the creak of the gate's hinges (purposely left un-oiled, he guessed) sounded clearly from the front of the house. Gordienko's mouth tightened. He nodded to Tzimas, who moved to the doorway. Silence. Then came the code knock on the front door Ariadne had used earlier. Markos relaxed. None of the other three did. Gordienko gave a sharp command. Tzimas moved steadily and silently across the dimly-lit hall, put the chain on the door, and opened it a couple of inches. After a pause of about a second he shut it again. Then he turned and walked back to the inner room, but less steadily than before, and not silently.

When Tzimas reached the waiting group he stared at Gordienko with his left eye. Where his right eye had been there was a red hole edged with black and purple. Finally his body seemed to lose all character, all substance, as if his flesh had turned to sand, and he fell at Gordienko's feet.

Chapter 8

Council of War

THERE WAS no time for doubts now. Bond snatched his Walther automatic when Gordienko threw it. Markos dived for the light-switch and the room went as dark as the bed of the sea. Somebody – Gordienko – began blundering towards the window. 'No,' said Bond urgently – 'they'll be expecting that. It must be the front.'

'Correct. Thank you.'

They moved into the gloom of the hall and Gordienko carefully took the chain out of the door.

'We will allow one minute so that their first vigilance will become dulled. Then we will leave in the following order: Markos, Mr Bond, Miss Alexandrou, and myself. Thirty yards down the street to the left there is an alley with high walls both sides. We will rendezvous there.'

Gordienko switched to Greek and Markos replied briefly. Then more silence. Ariadne caught Bond's hand and held it against her breast. He felt her heart beating, fast but not wildly. He kissed her hand.

'Good luck, my friends.' Gordienko stood with his fingers twisting the door-knob. Bond thought he saw him touch Markos lightly on the shoulder for a moment. Then the door swung wide and they were all running.

The enemy had left the gate ajar – a lucky, a near-vital oversight. All four had gained the shadowy, half-moonlit street by the time the first shots came. Flashes showed from the dark of a shop doorway on the opposite side. Immediately Markos gave a loud grunt of surprise, threw his head back, tottered a couple of paces and dropped. Bond fired three on automatic at the doorway as an aimspoiler, the shots banging out almost as one and filling the little cobbled street with a crackle of echoes. A flying glance to his left showed Ariadne running like an Olympic sprinter, equally spaced from him and Gordienko so as not to offer a double target by bunching. Good girl.

Something fizzed through the air between Bond and Ariadne, knee height, direction ahead. Flashes from what could have been the alley Gordienko had described earlier. Bond veered to the right, halted in a single stride, went down on one knee, saw the next flash, got in a quick but aimed shot that must have passed no more than four feet in front of Gordienko, heard a muffled cry. He bounded up and made diagonally across the street, resisting the natural but slowing and dangerous impulse to crouch. Into the alley and out of danger for the moment. Gordienko and Ariadne there, a body at their feet.

Uncomfortably conscious that he was not in shadow, Bond leaned out and peered to his right, towards the shop-front. A flash came at once; a bullet hit the wall a couple of yards away and buzzed across his front. Instinctively he drew back – but it had been a parting shot. When he looked out again his man was fifty yards away and running hard. Bond did not waste a shot at such a target.

The whole operation had taken less than half a minute, but the street was already coming alive: lights in windows, excited voices, barking dogs. And the party that would have been covering the back of the house must already be starting on its way in their direction. There could be no hanging about, then. But before they moved . . .

Bond ran across to where Markos had fallen. The Greek lay on his face, his arms stretched forward as if he were diving. There was a large thick patch of blood on his cheap cotton jacket below the left shoulder-blade. When Bond turned him over, the limbs moved with the dummy-like lack of all resistance that no living body ever shows. Markos's eyes were open. His face was frozen in a look of mild astonishment, the exact equivalent of the cry he had given when hit. Bond closed the eyes. With a quick look at the house he ran back to the alley. There, methodically, he went straight to the other fallen figure, the gunman he had shot.

This body was perhaps not a dead body yet. The man had collapsed in an awkward half-sitting position, his back against the wall of the alley. Bond spared no attention for the wound the Walther slug had torn in the chest. It was the face that interested him, a pale, hook-nosed face with unusually heavy eyelids, now half-closed so that the eyes were hooded, a face he had seen at Quarterdeck some thirty hours previously: that of the group leader. Here was clinching evidence, if any were needed.

Enough. Bond got up and turned to his two companions. What he saw dismayed him. Gordienko was leaning against the other alley wall, breathing slowly and shallowly. He looked up at Bond and the thin mouth laboured with the effort to speak.

'He was hit in the back, I think,' murmured Ariadne. 'The man in the doorway.'

The Russian went on trying to speak a moment longer. Abandoning the attempt, he brought his right hand up slowly and pointed successively at Bond and Ariadne, Bond and Ariadne in a gesture as plain as any words could have been. Then blood suddenly welled over the lower lip, lots of blood, life-blood, something went out behind the eyes and Major Piotr Gregorievitch Gordienko of the Foreign Intelligence Directorate, Committee of State Security, fell over sideways and lay in the gutter.

Ariadne was crying. 'We must do as Mr Gordienko told us to do.'

'Yes,' said Bond shortly. He had enjoyed his fifteen-minute alliance with the grey man. 'Now we've got more running ahead of us, I'm afraid. Can you find us somewhere safe? Anywhere!'

'That's easy. I've a friend who'll look after us.'

Ariadne's friend, whose name Bond never learnt, turned out to be a plump brunette in a grubby expensive nightdress who showed no surprise whatever at being got out of bed at past 3 a.m. to open the door to two highly suspect-looking people – Ariadne with a ripped seam and earth-stains down one side of her dress, Bond, after his second successive night on very active duty, obviously in the later stages of exhaustion. There was an exchange of Greek between the two girls. The friend smiled and nodded at Bond, said something gracious and incomprehensible, acknowledged his bow, and waddled back to her bedroom. A man's voice sleepily asked a question; there was a shrill reply and a duet of ribald laughter.

'We're lucky,' said Ariadne, smiling at the sound. 'The spare room's vacant. There are drinks in the kitchen cupboard. You go fix yourself one while I put some sheets on the bed.'

Bond kissed her on the forehead and went to do as ordered. The kitchen was small, almost airless and smelt, not unpleasantly, of goat's-milk cheese and overripe figs. In the cupboard, among tins of Italian soup and packets of biscuits showing signs of age, was a huddle of bottles: ouzo, cheap red wine, local brandy, and – blessedly – Bell's Scotch. He poured himself about a gill, cut it with a similar quantity of the excellent Nigrita mineral water, and swallowed the drink in two draughts. Already, as he prepared a weaker follow-up, he felt the familiar spreading, smouldering glow enfold his stomach and seem to blow away the mists of fatigue that had overhung his brain. An illusion, surely that last part: the body must warm alcohol to blood heat before absorption can even begin. Yet, as always, illusion or not, it worked.

It was a pleasant little bedroom with gay hand-painted furniture and brocade curtains, but Bond had eyes only for the girl who sprang up off the bed when he appeared.

'I only put an undersheet,' said Ariadne. 'I thought we wouldn't need something over us.'

'No. It's very hot.'

She hesitated. 'We've many things to do and not much time. But I thought we couldn't do any of them before we'd slept.'

'No. And before we sleep . . .'

The unfinished sentence hung in the warm air. Ariadne smiled, a calm, self-possessed, sensual smile. Then, her sherry-coloured eyes never leaving Bond's face, she stripped naked, unhurriedly but without coquetry or exhibitionism, her movements and expression showing an absolute certainty that he would find her beautiful. She had a truly magnificent body, slender but rounded, longer in the leg than is common with Greek girls, the breasts deep and yet youthfully taut, the belly slightly protuberant with a soft honey-blonde triangle at its base. She narrowed her gaze now and her lips parted.

There was nothing leisurely about Bond's undressing. Within seconds they stood flesh to flesh. She shuddered briefly and moaned; her arms tightened round his neck, her loins thrust against his and he felt the strength of her as well as the softness. As if they had become one creature with a single will, the two bodies sank to the bed. No preliminaries were needed. The man and the woman were joined immediately, with almost savage exultation. She leapt and strained in his grip, her movements as violent as his. The pace was too hot for their strivings to be prolonged. Their voices blended in the cry of joy that sounds so oddly akin to the inarticulate language of despair.

The creature separated, became two bodies once more. Bond tried to think of tomorrow, but his mind, like an over-ridden horse, refused to budge. He fell asleep with his head against Ariadne's bosom.

They left the flat early and made their necessary preliminary moves: coffee and rolls and splendid thin Hymettus honey at the busy little *kafenion* round the corner, a lurching but speedy journey to Constitution Square in one of the big yellow six-wheeled trolley-buses, a whirlwind shopping expedition along Stadíou to equip Ariadne (her apartment in Loukianou would certainly be watched), and straight into the Grande Bretagne, keeping with the crowds all the way. The hotel too was no doubt being watched, but here they would be safe until night-fall at any rate, and long before then they would be gone.

At the same brisk tempo they changed and showered. By the time Bond had finished shaving in the grey-marble bath-room, all traces of fatigue had dropped from him. He even felt guardedly optimistic – no longer the tethered goat at the tiger-shoot, but a hunter on equal terms with the opposition and accompanied by an associate of proven value.

Finally, with Bond sitting on the bed and Ariadne on the

blue-covered couch, the council of war went into session.

'Let's take the most obvious point first,' said Bond, lighting Xanthis for the two of them. 'Your position is horribly dangerous. You're the only survivor of the three people Gordienko felt he could trust. You daren't contact your organization – more than that, after what happened last night this traitor character will be actively interested in having you killed. You can disappear, of course, slide off to Salonika or somewhere and wait for the storm to blow itself out. But you're not going to do that, are you?'

Ariadne smiled. 'No. On at least two counts.'

'Right. Then all you can do is to throw in your lot with my people. I needn't explain you – you'll just be my assistant. Agreed?'

'Agreed.' Very much the earnest young discussion-group member again, she nodded sharply. 'But I must do my utmost to let Moscow know what's happened. You understand that?'

'Yes, quite reasonable. I've been working out how you can set about it. I don't suppose you'll have had any dealings with anybody at the Russian embassy here? That means you'll have to take your chance. Telephone them – on a public line – and just mention Gordienko. That'll get you somewhere near the right quarter. You'll know what to say. Of course, for all you know, you might get hold of the chap who sold out to the common enemy. But there's no way of guarding against that. Agreed?'

'Agreed.'

'Good. Now I must get hold of my man here and arrange a rendezvous.'

Bond picked up the telephone and asked for the number of the small foreign-language bookshop Stuart Thomas managed as his cover. In less than a minute the hotel operator rang back to say that the number was unobtainable: 'No, sir, not engaged, not no reply – unobtainable.' Alarm flickered in Bond. He checked the number, asked the girl to try it again, got the same result, put Ariadne on the job of chasing up Service Inquiries. The engineer on duty was sympathetic but

not helpful. He could find no record of anything that concerned the number in question. He would attend to the matter,
of course, as soon as he had the opportunity. Perhaps the
lady would care to telephone him again later. Meanwhile
had she thought that her friend might have overlooked the
payment of his bill?

Without exchanging a word, Bond and Ariadne hurried
out.

The situation turned out to be quite simple, and quite final.
The firemen had done their work and left; the police were in
possession. In charge of them was a stocky young lieutenant
in smart light-grey uniform, courteous, probably efficient,
and anxious to show off his English to Bond, who represented
himself as an old customer of Thomas's drawn by curiosity
and concern. There was plenty to arouse that: great blackened
fragments of glass on the pavement, jumbled heaps of charred
and saturated paperbacks, atlases, dictionaries, guidebooks,
capsized cases and stands, a strong smell of burnt cardboard
and glue. Some of the stock had escaped damage, and the fire
in the shop itself had not spread to the adjoining furrier's and
travel agency. The inner apartments had suffered worse,
being more or less gutted in parts. One corner was open to the
sky, and the rooms at the back of the travel agency were in
almost as bad a state. It had been a remarkably fierce blaze.

The police lieutenant accepted a cigarette. 'The firemen have
not done badly. They were notified quickly. We're still not
certain what has caused the outbreak, but it's being suspected
that this was no accident. The heat has been greater than we
expect in an ordinary fire. Our expert's working here for the
last hour. Some bomb, perhaps. Do you know by any chance,
sir, if Mr Thomas is having some enemies? Business rivals,
men of that sort?'

This was dangerous ground. Being roped in to help a police
investigation would be a fatal setback. Bond said firmly, 'I'm
afraid I don't know him on that basis, only as a customer.
You'd better ask Mr Thomas himself.'

'Unfortunately this is not possible at the moment. Mr
Thomas is not present. He wasn't present when the firemen

came. I was understanding from the neighbours here that this seems unusual. Normally he's spending the night in his quarters at the back of the shop. A most lucky escape. No doubt the news will reach him soon and bring him. You're wanting to see him particularly, sir?'

'No,' said Bond. 'Not particularly. I'll contact him later. I just thought I'd like to ask him if I could do anything. Thank you.'

'Please, sir. Miss.'

The lieutenant bowed slightly, glanced at Ariadne with admiration, at Bond with cheerful envy, and turned away to meet a middle-aged man in plain clothes who, brushing ash off his jacket, was approaching from the back of the shop – no doubt the fire expert. Bond also turned away. He couldn't get at the information about to be delivered, and in any case it made no difference which particular technique had been used to cripple the British intelligence network in Athens, any more than it mattered – from this point of view – whether Stuart Thomas was alive in enemy hands or lying in the ooze off the Piraeus waterfront. Bond had had his most powerful weapon snatched away before he could grasp it.

As he put it to Ariadne back at the Grande Bretagne, 'It wasn't only him they were after – they wanted to prevent me from getting hold of his records, his lists of contacts, pick-up points and times, locations of letter-boxes and the rest of it, so as to cut me off from our people. All that stuff would have been in the back part of the shop, of course. That was the centre of the fire.'

Ariadne frowned. 'Why not just remove everything? Less to be seen. They could use what they took, certainly.'

'Less safe, too. They couldn't have been sure there wasn't some material in places they couldn't find without pulling the building to pieces and which I might know about. No doubt they took away what they could find easily. There wouldn't have been much of that if I know Thomas.'

'His assistant?'

'I can't see how I dare approach him after this,' said Bond, staring at the wall. 'If he's not dead or kidnapped he'll be watched. And I can't hang on here in the hope that somebody'll come to me. Pretty useless, anyway. The tags Thomas put on me last night have vanished. God knows how many other people have. How did Gordienko put it ? Extreme ruthlessness. You and I seem to be in the same situation.'

'Yes, and so we must deal with it together.' Ariadne came over and sat beside Bond on the couch. She spoke with great determination and force. 'I too have been thinking. We must move immediately. We've a long way to travel and it's only . . . sixty hours exactly until the event Mr Gordienko mentioned. Probably less than that, because—'

'What is this event ?'

'I'll tell you when we're on our way.'

'So that I won't get the chance to tell London beforehand,' said Bond dispassionately. 'Of course.'

'Darling, I know you must tell London if you can, don't I ? Be reasonable. . . Good. Now, we have a sea-trip ahead of us. About two hundred kilometres – a hundred and twenty miles. At least, it's that in a straight line. So we must have a boat and someone to sail it for us. I know who.'

Chapter 9

The *Altair*

'LITSAS WAS in General Papagos's army which fought the Italians when they invaded Greece in 1940. You remember how the Greeks threw them way back into Albania ? Well, Litsas was with the infantry that took Koritsa. His platoon had used up their ammunition and he killed twelve Italians with his bayonet. They made him a sergeant for that. He was eighteen then.'

Ariadne paused in her recital as she and Bond entered the little high-ceilinged café. The proprietor, chunky and grizzled, with the standard tobacco-stained moustache, came bustling forward.

'*Kal' iméra sas,*' said Ariadne courteously. '*Boreíte na mou peite, sas parakaló – pou eínai o Kyrios Litsas ?*'

The man took them to the doorway and pointed diagonally across the road towards the quays. There followed one of the animated discussions that, in Greece, accompany even the most elementary piece of business. Finally, with that ripple of the shoulders that does duty for a shrug hereabouts, the café-owner left them, seeming to imply that he took no responsibility for what use might be made of his information. They moved off in the direction he had pointed.

'When the Germans came,' Ariadne went on, 'they cut Papagos's supply lines and he had to surrender. The soldiers weren't made prisoners, they were just disarmed and sent home. Litsas walked a couple of hundred miles across Greece to Euboea, where his home is. He joined some guerrillas and went on killing Italians. Germans too when they started trying to crush the resistance movement.'

Bond took her arm as they crossed the street. 'You certainly seem to have studied his career.'

'My father was his officer in 1941 and they met again in the resistance. They were very brave, both of them, I have to admit that.'

Ariadne's face had clouded. Bond said, 'Admit it?'

'I know it sounds odd, but. . . . You see, I believe that in our civil war the wrong side won. You'd say the democratic side. It would have been so right for the country if the Communists had been allowed to take over. They were the real Greek patriots. They'd mostly done the fighting during the occupation . . .'

'A large part of which was against rival organizations on the same side,' said Bond dryly. 'But what do you care about the civil war? You can't have been more than six when it ended.'

'Seven. I've studied it.' Ariadne looked sheepish.

'No doubt. Anyway, what about your father and Litsas? They were on the wrong side in it, I gather.'

'Please, James, it was no joke to me. Father became very reactionary. He joined what was known as the National Army. Most of them were Fascists, terrorists, no-good people. Litsas joined it too. He was a liaison officer with the British for a time, but he transferred because he wanted to be in the fighting.'

'And kill Communists. You know, Ariadne—'

'There he is. There.'

They had been moving along the walk that follows the curve of Pasalimani, the larger of Piraeus's two yacht-basins. On the far side, the motionless water held scores of assorted craft, from fishing-boats and twelve-foot sailing dinghies to yachts as opulent as any in the Mediterranean. Immediately below, on the narrow stretch of yard, boats in various stages of repair and conversion were being worked on. Bond immediately picked out a tall white-shirted figure evidently giving vigorous instruction to a couple of cowed-looking employees. As Ariadne and he turned towards the steps leading down to the yard, Bond went on with his train of thought.

'From what you've been saying, this man sounds exactly the opposite of someone who'd help your side.'

'It's also your side for the moment, remember. And he's

very pro-British. And although he's always been mad at me for joining the Communist Party I think he's continued to be fond of me, because he loves my father. And there's something I know about the other side which may help if he becomes obstinate.'

Litsas turned and saw them. He was tanned to a rich brown by years of sun and salt air, a remarkably handsome man in his mid-forties with thick black hair just starting to go grey, neat pointed ears close to the skull, sad and watchful brown eyes, a jutting nose, and a mouth that at the moment looked good-naturedly sensual, though Bond imagined – rightly – that it would harden to a fierce line in times of action. The belly showed no trace of fat and the shoulders and upper arms bulged with muscle. Bond put him down as a loyal friend and a totally implacable and ruthless enemy. He trusted him on sight.

After an instant's pause, strong white teeth showed in an unreservedly warm and welcoming smile. '*Ariadne, khrisi mou.*'

'*Yassou, Niko, ti yínese?*'

The two embraced affectionately. Then the watchful eyes moved to Bond.

'This is James Bond, Niko, an English friend of mine.'

'How do you do, Mr Bond.' The handclasp was strong and warm. 'You've picked a good time for your visit. I'm just finishing here before I go over the road for a drink. I hope you'll join me. Let me manage these two idiots first. They know as much of carpentry as I know of . . . knitting.'

Apart from a few falterings (no doubt from lack of practice) this was said in a manner approaching that of a middle-class Englishman – above all, with less of the difficulty with 'ch', 'sh' and 'j' than most Greeks experience. Litsas now moved back to his workmen. Despite his gay, friendly tone, his brown eyes had not for a moment ceased their discreet but careful appraisal of Bond.

The boat under discussion was a twenty-footer with an unusual pointed stern, broad in the beam, a fishing-boat or perhaps lifeboat part-way converted into a pocket-size cabin-cruiser. Two bunks had been completed, also the skeleton of the superstructure in slender pine beams. Bond guessed that the final result would look grotesque to a yachtsman's eye, but fetchingly 'quaint' to the French or German tourist interested in a not-too-expensive hire.

No doubt feeling that words were inadequate to express his disgust, Litsas put out one large brown hand and, seemingly with a mere flick of the wrist, broke one of the vertical members away from the gunwale as if it had been fixed there with stamp-paper. The two workmen put on exaggerated expressions of guilt and self-reproach. With a final sweeping gesture of contempt, Litsas turned away. He winked at Bond and Ariadne.

'They're children,' he said, making a herding motion towards the steps. 'Nice children, but children. Not just lazy and careless: they cannot see the idea that very much effort is required if you want to make something even a little good. When I tell them that the deck-housing would fall when the first decent wave hits it, they want to say, "Perhaps, but be nice, Mr Litsas. See how beautiful we have made the bunks." That's Greece for you, I'm sorry to say: people that don't try hard enough. But I mustn't bore you with this grumbling. What brings you to Greece, Mr Bond? You're on holiday?'

'No, I'm afraid not.'

Litsas caught the tone at once. 'I hope there's no trouble? If I can—'

'There's trouble all right. We desperately need your help, Mr Litsas.'

'We? Love trouble?'

'I wish it were. Ariadne and I are fighting an international conspiracy which is threatening England and Russia and probably Greece too. I'm sorry to sound melodramatic, but—'

'I don't care what you sound, Mr Bond.' Litsas had stopped dead on the pavement opposite the café. His eyes and voice were full of hostility. 'I've finished with politics altogether, and in any case I would never help the . . . the faction you represent. Now you must excuse me.'

He started to move away. Bond stepped into his path. 'I swear to you I'm not a Communist. I'm on your side.'

'Several Communists have said to me almost those exact words. The last one tried to kill me ten minutes afterwards.'

Ariadne intervened. 'Niko, I promise you that if my father came here and knew what we know he'd ask you to do all you could do to help us.'

This increased Litsas's anger. 'My dear young lady, it's most wrong that you bring the major into this business. And stupid. I don't admire you.'

'Listen to me, Mr Litsas,' said Bond desperately. 'Our cause is just and we're in deadly earnest about it. I give you my word for that as an Englishman.'

'You do, yes?' Some of the fire left Litsas's manner. 'That doesn't mean as much as it has done, to most people. To me . . . well, I'm sentimental, I suppose. Very good, English-man, I agree to hear your story. I promise nothing more.'

With no more said they reached the café and sat down at one of the little oblong marble-topped tables – plastic had yet to find its way here. The speckled wall-mirrors did what they could to give an illusion of roominess. There, amid a buzz of chatter, among games of backgammon and what looked like gin-rummy, over cup after cup of scalding Turkish coffee, Bond gave the full account, all the way from Quarterdeck to the fire at Thomas's shop. Litsas's eyes never left Bond's face. At the end he sat for a full two minutes perfectly relaxed, without a hint of the fidgeting of hands and feet so curiously common in Greek men. When he spoke his tone was cold and measured.

'So it comes to this. You and Ariadne want me to take you to some island of which the name she won't say. There, some-thing she calls an *event*' – the deep voice grew contemptuous – 'will take place, if it isn't prevented by some enemies. A British chief of Security has been kidnapped by the same enemies and may be made use of to damage British interests. When you get there you may think what to do next. At the moment it's clear that you have no plan. And not a very good story either. I'm sorry – I can introduce you to dozen people who will charter to you a yacht and crew to go to the islands. If you're so fussy. There are public steamers which—'

Bond interrupted brusquely. He had settled in his mind on a force of three as an absolute minimum for the task in hand and he felt sure that this man was the best available for making up the number. 'Look,' he said, 'that line of talk won't get any of us anywhere. What do you imagine is at stake for you is this? Do you think Ariadne and I have told you all this because we're out to steal one of your boats? What are you afraid of?'

'That's enough from you, Mr Bond, I won't stand—'

It was Ariadne's turn to cut in. 'Niko. Listen to me. One fact, or almost certain fact Von Richter is involved.'

She got her effect. Litsas snarled like a wild animal. *'To poústi! To thráko, to* ... That ... savage! The butcher of Kapoudzona! Come on, Ariadne, I must know more. How was this found out?'

'He was seen quite accidentally by a guy who was a resistance fighter. The man told the local Party chief, and so on. We got the news yesterday.'

'So? He's in Greece. Nothing strange in that. Those German bastards are coming back here always, to enjoy in peace the beautiful country they began to love while they were burning our villages and shooting our men and sometimes also our women and children. He was on his way to Kapoudzona to enjoy his pleasant memories.'

'No. He was making inquiries about boats to ... the place of the event. Yesterday we hadn't thrown away the idea that it might be coincidence. Lots of people go to this place in the summer. But I don't think now it can be coincidence. Do you?'

'No,' said Litsas grimly. 'No, I don't.' He took a deep breath and looked from one to the other with the beginnings of a grin. 'All right. You've caught your fish. I'll do anything you say. It's time for a change for me. Don't think I believe completely, though. This sweet girl here might still be lying when she tells me about von Richter. But perhaps she tells the truth and that's enough for me. I'd go halfway round the world for a chance in ten of seeing that squarehead in my sights.'

Bond's heart had lifted in relief, in exultation. He said, 'How soon can we leave?'

'Soon. We'll take the *Altair*. She's a fifty-footer with a Diesel. Strong. Not easy to be noticed. Do you know anything of boats, James ?'

'A bit. I spent a lot of summer holidays years ago in a converted Brixham trawler.'

'You'll be useful, then.' Litsas turned authoritative. 'Right. If things were different you could cross the road and eat clams at Diasemos, but you must put up with what I bring you. The *Altair* is moored along by the clock-tower. Panamanian flag. Next to a big Yankee thing for millionaires. The two of you go on board now and remain out of sight until we sail. Do you think you were followed from the hotel ?'

'Doubtful. In what we stood up in and just carrying a shopping-bag we stood a fair chance of not being assumed to be leaving. Our most vulnerable moment was when we stopped for me to wire London and Ariadne to warn her people. But we had to take that risk.'

'You must take the next risk too. It's not far and nobody's on board. You have just one gun, James ? Yes. Leave everything to me. Be off with you.'

Within ten minutes Bond and Ariadne crossed the after-deck of the *Altair* and made their way into the tiny saloon. Here everything was squared away, the floor scrubbed, the windows polished, the miniature royal-blue curtains freshly laundered. Bond guessed that the boat had been about to go out on charter, and grinned to himself as he visualized Litsas airily riding over the protests of the party who had rented her.

They explored briefly. The narrow companion-way led below to a cupboard-sized galley on the starboard side, a head and shower to port. Bond lowered himself from the galley into the engine-room, gasping at the heat and the reek of oil, and looked over the single-drive 165 hp Mercedes engine. New condition; clever use of available space; maintenance up to Royal Navy standard. Bond's respect for Litsas rose a further notch.

For'ard of galley and head were a pair of cabins with double bunks and, for'ard again, another pair with tiered single bunks. They took the port midships cabin. Ariadne unpacked and stowed away their minimal luggage: changes of under-clothing, handkerchiefs, a couple of shirts, toilet gear and, incongruous among these humdrum necessities, eighty rounds of ammunition for the Walther. She smoothed back a tendril of brown-blonde hair and turned straight into his arms.

With her face against his neck, she murmured, 'So I have you for a little longer. It seems like it was days and days before I thought I'd have you at all. I don't care what happens tomorrow. Now. I know I'll care if you're taken away from me. So let's use every moment we have.'

She drew her head back and desire made her eyes look unfocused, opaque. 'Don't shut the door. We're alone here.' Her breasts seemed to swell against his chest.

There on the hard unluxurious bunk Bond made long love to her, both of them taking their pleasure easily, slowly, searchingly, with none of the near-hysterical frenzy of the early hours of that day. The buzz of activity all around them, the shouted orders, the rattle of anchor-chains, the fluctuating hum and roar of engines, lost all meaning and vanished. At last, exhausted, they drew apart and slept.

Bond was woken by voices and footfalls overhead. He dressed swiftly, his eyes on the uncovered form of Ariadne, fast asleep on her back, one knee raised in an attitude of total abandonment. He stooped and kissed her warm cheek.

By the time he had moved the few yards back to the saloon Litsas was standing alone, hands on hips, among heaps of various stores, and the voices were retreating in the direction of the dockside.

'Ariadne is asleep?'

'Yes.'

The big man looked directly at Bond with eyes that were sad and pleading now, not watchful. 'You'll be good to her, won't you, James? The way you think, it isn't my business, but her father's my best friend and that means very much in Greece. If you treat her bad, drop her suddenly, make untrue promises to her and so on, then I shall come for you and neither of us would like that. Especially you. You understand me?'

'Yes. You won't need to come for me.'

'Then we shall all be happy.' Litsas slapped himself on the chest a couple of times and his manner lightened. 'I envy you, taking a girl on this trip. I couldn't have found one in the time. Five years ago things were very different. Litsas is not like he was. Anyway, if I bring one, that's not serious enough. I don't know any female spies. Honestly, James' – he shook his head defeatedly – 'to think little Ariadne is working for the Russian bloody Secret Service is fantastic. I thought she's just making cups of coffee for the workers and reading Karl Marx in the evening. Instead of this. . . . Oh well, it's good that the world can still surprise us.

'Now. Fuel and water. Full up. Food. That can wait. Drink. That can wait too, but not so long. Weapons. You'd better look at them now. Here.'

Bond moved to the table. On it were neat oilskin bundles which Litsas untied to reveal one of the excellent Beretta M.34 9-mm automatics and a couple of boxes of ammunition, four Mills HE grenades, and – almost unbelievably – an example of that greatest rifle in the history of warfare, the British short magazine Lee Enfield, with perhaps sixty rounds in clips of five. All the items were in beautiful condition, the metal surfaces of the guns shining dully with a thin film of oil. Bond picked up the rifle and squinted along the V-and-blade sight. 'You got this little lot together in pretty good time.'

'Oh, it was easy. This is my private store. I've had all this stuff for over twenty years. The British gave me the Lee Enfield in 1944. It seemed perhaps not such an expensive gift, since it was made in 1916. Anyway, I made very good results with it, and kept it when they made me an officer. I picked up the other stuff in the same sort of way.'

Bond nodded. 'What made you keep it all?'

'Yes, it must seem rather silly. It isn't really. Not in Greece. You see, here you can't be sure. Oh yes, the Communists were completely beaten in 1949, but you'll agree that Communists don't give up easily. I must admit that they're not being violent now. But recently they've begun to be active again. Anyway, if they do try again, they won't get rid of me without some trouble. And it isn't only the Communists by a long chalk. Only last year I had some trouble down in Crete. Some of them are a bit primitive there, poor chaps. I'll tell you the story some time. Anyway, I was facing a bunch I had to pacify with this. Just waving it at them was enough, thank God.'

While he talked Litsas had taken the wooden lid off the starboard-side bench and brought out another oilskin package. This one proved to contain a Thompson MI sub-machine gun of World War II vintage. It had been as lovingly cared for as the other pieces.

'A present from the USA. It lives on board. Stacks of ammunition. I hope you think now our fire-power is enough?'

Bond grinned delightedly and slapped Litsas on the shoulder. 'With what we've got here we can take on anything short of a tank.'

'A cruiser tank at least. We shan't be shooting until the morning, I suppose, so let's stow the stuff, eh?'

They had about done so when a light step sounded on the deck outside and a youth of about sixteen, not tall but powerfully built for his age, stepped over the coaming into the saloon. He nodded gravely to Bond.

'This is Yanni,' said Litsas. '*Yanni, o Kyrios Tzems....* You and I could manage the boat together, but we need a relief for the wheel. Yanni knows boats and he knows these seas. This is all we need. I shall slip him a couple of hundred drachmas and put him ashore somewhere before we begin the shooting. Well, since you like the weapons we can get the gangway up.'

He spoke to Yanni, who nodded again and slipped away with the same almost noiseless tread. Just afterwards Ariadne joined them.

She looked coolly desirable and at the same time impressively businesslike in blue jeans and a man's fine cotton shirt several shades darker, her hair pinned back close to her head. She looked quickly from Bond to Litsas.

'Well, why aren't we moving?'

'We're ready, my dear. But only you know where we must move. Isn't it time you trusted us?'

'Not until I have to.' Ariadne, at her most strict, avoided Bond's eye. Her tenacity in holding on to this information struck him as about equally absurd and admirable. She blinked, came to a decision. 'Go toward the Cyclades group. I'll tell you which island when we're sailing.'

'Very good. Right, James. Let's go.'

Five minutes later, a man in a grubby linen suit arrived panting at the quayside, peered after the receding shape of the *Altair*, turned and ran for the café and its telephone.

Chapter 10

Dragon Island

'THAT'S WHERE we're going.' Ariadne's finger came down on the map. 'Vrakonisi.'

Looking over her shoulder, Litsas nodded. 'Fourteen hours at least – I don't want to make her go more than about eight knots. Longer if the weather's bad. And it might be.'

'It's calm enough at the moment,' said Bond.

The dark indigo-blue sea slid past almost unwrinkled. Two miles away, the larger detail on shore was still perfectly clear, but its colours were just beginning to change in the approaching September dusk, the white of the scattered buildings losing its glare, the green of the trees fading and turning bluish, the tan and ochre and gamboge of the hillsides seeming oddly to have become more intense. A fishing-boat with a chain of dinghies passed towards Piraeus between the *Altair* and the coast, all the craft moving as smoothly as if they were running across ice.

'It's usually calm here,' said Litsas, 'but wait till we get past Cape Sounion and leave the shelter of Attica before you be sure. Out there you can meet a norther and it's often quite bloody. Right. We make over here towards Kea, run south past Kithnos and Seriphos, round Siphnos and sail due east. That part may not be good either, but if it's rough we'll get some shelter from Antiparos and Paros for the last miles. Right. I'll just go and speak with Yanni.'

Litsas left them. Bond sat back and gazed out at the coast with eyes that hardly saw. He felt wonderfully relaxed and confident. The broad caique hull thrust its way sturdily through the still water, the muffled roar of the engine was even and regular, accompanied by no vibration. There were big questions yet to be settled and battles to be fought, but until first light at least everything was secure. He had had to learn to get everything possible out of such interludes before action, to savour each moment of calm that lay between him and the shooting, the running in and out of cover, the final assault and the blood.

He glanced sidelong at Ariadne's profile. Along with its abundant sensual beauty, its strength and intelligence impressed him anew. In America, in England, anywhere in the developed countries a girl of this calibre would be carving out a brilliant career for herself in journalism or entertainment. In Greece these opportunities barely existed. He felt he understood a little more than nothing of what had driven her into the arms of Communism.

Bond picked up the map and found the sickle-shaped island. A memory clicked in his mind. 'Vrakonisi. So that was where Theseus went after he'd dumped your namesake on Naxos.'

'I thought you didn't notice,' said Ariadne, smiling and biting her lower lip like an embarrassed schoolgirl. 'That was a silly mistake of mine.'

'I'd only to look up the books and I could have identified the place straight way.'

'You won't find this story in the books; it's just a local legend the old people tell.' Ariadne settled down to impart information, but with a warmth of manner she never showed when the subject was politics.

'None of the scholars know why Theseus took off from Naxos in so much hurry. The Vrakonisiots do. Their king had heard about Theseus slaying the Minotaur and so he sent some men to him and they begged him to come over and fight a dragon who was burning up their island with the flames of its breath. So Theseus left Ariadne sleeping and went over to Vrakonisi with the messengers. He thought he'd be back very soon.

'But the dragon was dangerous because he could hurt you when you couldn't see him. He'd hide himself behind the mountain and breathe fire at you over it. Theseus waited for him to get started and then swam around the island and took the dragon from the rear and pulled him into the sea. And the water boiled and the steam rose so high in the air that the gods on Mount Olympus saw it and wondered what it was. At last the dragon was drowned and sank to the bottom of the sea. When Theseus got to shore he found that the boiling waves had melted so much that only a tenth part of the island was left, but the king and his family and his palace had survived and his daughters took care of Theseus while he recovered from his burns. That was a big job, and when he got back to Naxos and looked for Ariadne she'd gone. He'd been too brave for his own good.

'They'll tell you that that's just a mythical story of what happened when the island was formed as it is today. A volcano was erupting and pouring down burning lava and at last it exploded and the sea rushed in. But I'd as soon believe in the dragon. Vrakonisi — they'll tell you it means just "rocky island", not exciting. But that ought to be Vra*kh*onisi, with the letter *khi*. What it must really be is Thrakonisi. Dragon Island.'

'And now there's a dragon round the place again,' said Bond flatly. 'Only this time it's a Chinese dragon.'

Litsas reappeared at that moment and the words caught his ear. He checked in his stride.

'There's Chinese handwriting over every part of this business.' Bond offered cigarettes. 'The scale, the disregard for the unwritten rules of peacetime intelligence work, above all the recklessness. None of the smaller Powers who might want to resist Russian influence in this part of the Mediterranean or the Near East — Turkey, for instance — would or could risk a fraction of what these people have done. But before we go on theorizing, let's have a dose of fact. Ariadne's told us the location of this event. What we need to know now is what it is.'

'All right. This is it.' Ariadne drew her legs up on to the bench and clasped her knees.

'A secret meeting has been arranged between a top Russian official — you're sure to know his name — and representatives of some countries around here and in North Africa. High-up representatives; I heard that Nasser intended to come himself, but in the end he had to appoint a substitute. All the invitees accepted the Russian invitation at last, but a snag happened when they tried to fix on a place to hold the meeting. Russia would have been the obvious one, but two of the delegates got very reactionary and said they wouldn't go there. And then they all started fighting about prestige. So they finally settled on some halfway spot on neutral ground – for some reason Greece wasn't invited. The Turks must have been behind that. Russia should have stopped them.'

Ariadne's momentary but real indignation spoke of the undying nationalism that sits in the heart of every Greek, even the most sophisticated. Litsas responded at once, nodded in sympathy, but Bond failed to notice. His thoughts were racing ahead, outlining the consequences of what Ariadne was saying and fitting this picture into the information he already had. What looked up at him was frightening.

'So,' the girl went on, 'an island seemed just ideal – out of the way, but enough tourists and people around so that a lot of visitors suddenly coming wouldn't be noticeable. Vrakonisi was chosen because at one end of it there's a big house on a kind of rock that you can only get to by water.'

'I know the place you mean,' Litsas put in. 'That was clever of them. It'd be damned difficult to take them by surprise there. And that's what the enemy must want to do.'

Bond's eyes narrowed thoughtfully. 'Let's consider his strategy,' he said.

'Over a glass of ouzo, please, James.' Litsas got up from the table and went over to the ice-box on the port side of the companion-way. 'In Greece you consider nothing unless with some stimulating drink, and it's the wrong time for coffee. We modern Hellenes must help our poor brains with something.'

From a tall wicker-covered flagon he poured three stiff drinks on to chunks of ice and handed them out.

'This stuff is from the barrel – much better than the bottled. Stronger and not so sweet.'

Bond sipped and agreed. It had the bland fieriness he looked for in all short drinks: cool and dry in the mouth, warmly powerful in the belly. He pondered for another few moments.

'The intention,' he said slowly, 'is to break up the conference by violence, killing as many people as possible in the process, and making the whole thing as public as possible. After that, the plan would have been to make it look as if my chief and I had done the job, and put us in no position to say we hadn't. Our bodies would be found with the deadly weapons in our hands. No doubt we'd have papers on us "proving" we were acting under orders. The whole affair would stink to high heaven of being fixed, of course, and nobody who understands the British would be taken in, but that's a long way from being everybody. Enough people would believe it, or go on as if they believed it, for British influence hereabouts – which is still not negligible – to vanish overnight, British prestige to be ruined everywhere, rioting to break out, burnings, shootings, and worse . . . Gordienko wasn't fooling when he talked about a risk of war. I think he was making even more sense than he probably knew.'

'One moment, James.' Ariadne leaned forward earnestly. 'I agree with all this, but I still don't see why you're so sure that the Chinese must be responsible. The Americans are quite capable of this sort of thing. Consider their behaviour about Cuba, the Dominican Republic, Vietnam; they don't hesitate to—'

Bond started to speak, but Litsas held up a hand. 'Let me reply, James. Listen, young lady. At Pierce College in Athens the Americans educated you, taught you English, explained to you their way of life. Were you such a bad and lazy student that you're forgetting all that? Can you see no difference between fighting aggressive Communists and this caper, killing chaps in the public streets of a friendly and peaceful nation, taking a Security chief from England completely openly? Even the worst men in Washington would not advise that. I beg you, Ariadne, forget your Leninist Institute and start to think!'

'And,' said Bond, 'if they're still telling you there that the United States is world enemy number one they need to catch up on their studies. The Kremlin knows perfectly well that the main threat isn't the West any more, but the East. Surely that's not news to you?'

Ariadne had flushed. She gazed at Bond and said, still with a touch of defiance, 'Maybe. You could be right. I don't know.' Then she turned to Litsas and went on as before: 'But don't tell me about aggressive Communists. That's straight out of the . . . the Lyndon Johnson Institute!'

Bond chuckled. Litsas roared with laughter and slapped Ariadne on the thigh. The three shared a moment of total understanding and pure uplifting gaiety. It was gone in a flash. Bond sipped ouzo and took up his exposition.

'What really frightens me,' he said quietly, 'is the thought that this thing is so violent, so ruthless, so . . . so *crazy*, that it might easily not be a one-shot deal, but the first step in something on an even more ambitious scale. Let's consider what might conceivably happen, how bad it could be. Stage one: Britain fatally damaged, Russia's prestige weakened, in this part of the world very seriously weakened – so she couldn't even protect the delegates to a conference she'd convened, couldn't she, and what about the gross infringement of Greek territoriality? The eastern Mediterranean laid open for Chinese penetration. Stage two: the whole Arab world and/or Africa. I'll leave it to you to wonder what Stage three might be.'

Nobody spoke. The *Altair* moved peacefully and purposefully on its way. Litsas fetched fresh drinks.

'That could be the big plan,' he said, sitting down again. 'But now the details. What might be the Chink plan of attack? Sea or land? Or air, perhaps? A few bombs would make plenty of casualties.'

'Air I rather . . .' Bond shook his head. 'They'd have to crash the aircraft somewhere near by, and crashes are tricky things to rig. There's the question of getting the pilot away – oh, they wouldn't think twice about his being killed, but he would. If they put the machine down on land they risk burning everything beyond recognition. In the water you're in even greater danger of losing the lot. I suppose you could try a duplication, one aeroplane for the assault and a twin for the crash, but that way you'd more than double your risks. No, for the time being I think we can rule out the air. Now, land. How well do you know the place, Niko?'

Litsas screwed up his face and sighed. 'I'm trying to remember. . . . That end of the island's pretty wild. Parts of it were never cleared for cultivating. Big blocks of stone and some dense bush. Difficult to move about, but first-class cover. If you knew your business you could hide a platoon in there.'

'In a different way that isn't very promising either,' said Bond. 'You'd need something a good deal heavier than small arms to make any impression on a house. And any sort of artillery would take some installing, if the going's as rough as you say.'

'One of those anti-tank things – what are they called, bazookas?'

Bond shook his head again. 'I doubt it. They couldn't do much more to a tank than blow its track off. I suppose – if you could get at a window. . . . But you'd have to get up bloody close. Of course, atomics would solve everything and to spare, though you still have a delivery problem. On the whole I think the sea's the most likely. Well, that's as far as we can go now. All we can do is get there.'

Bond's voice and manner had turned suddenly cold, so much so that Ariadne glanced at him in concern. In fact he had gone cold inside at the mental picture, hideously clear, of a thirty-knot cabin cruiser with a stolen tactical atomic device on board slipping round the corner of the island, throwing its insanely destructive punch, and making at full speed for the horizon and a rendezvous. God, that would rock the world all right!

To conceal his agitation from the others he got to his feet and went to the saloon doorway, unconsciously allowing for the motion of the ship as he did so. By imperceptible degrees the weather had been freshening. Whitecaps were beginning to break up the surface of the dark water. The lights of a village clustered at the shore and wound away upwards and to one side. The day had not yet quite gone. Against the faint luminosity of the sky the columns of a ruined temple could be made out, an image of defiant integrity and loneliness that quietened Bond's fears. Its makers could have had no notion of how long even these remnants would outlast them and their god, but had they known they would have gone on building just the same. That was the only way to behave: to see to the doing of what had to be done.

Litsas joined him. 'We should get busy. I suggest an early supper, because the wind and sea are getting up.'

He glanced at the sky, moved a couple of yards for'ard and looked over the cabin-top out to the fading horizon. 'It'll be Force 5 or 6 in a couple of hours and the old *Altair* does roll a bit. She only draws just over five feet – that's the bad thing with *karavóskaro* hulls. Anyway, eating's better if your plate stays still. Afterwards an early bedtime; for you two, that is. Yanni and I will split the watches. We'll be off Vrakonisi about six. I'll check the course and the weather reports and then we'll see what's in the larder.'

When they were alone on the narrow strip of deck, Ariadne turned and clung to Bond. Her lips tasted faintly of salt. As he closed his eyes and kissed her more deeply, he recognized the old feeling of surrender to another person, as always with the illusion of permanence, the seeming certainty that this, here, now, was the end of the torturing quest for fulfilment. But knowing that the illusion was an illusion, the surrender destined to be revoked, curiously made the moment sweeter. Bond yielded himself to it utterly. On all that enormous plain of black water it was as if only two human beings existed.

That was an illusion too, and a dangerous one. He heard the mental alarm-bell that warns the experienced campaigner of duty left undone, the unlikely but possible approach-route unguarded, the vital item of equipment checked but not double-checked. It was not even so very unlikely that, somewhere on that watery plain that just now had seemed a guarantee of solitude and safety, a group of enemies, cruel, intelligent and well armed, was looking for him, bent on capture or murder.

The three of them accordingly made what defensive plans

appeared most flexible, and the necessary preparations. Then they ate a meal of black olives, fresh bread, delicious plum-shaped tomatoes, sliced raw onion and manouri cheese, followed by peaches and tiny sweet seedless grapes. They drank the light Mamos retsina and rounded off with Votris, which Litsas declared was the only drinkable Greek brandy. Two small glasses of it were enough for Bond. It carried the hint of treacliness which he could never stand in a drink. But he made the necessary polite noises.

At ten o'clock Litsas got up and stretched. 'Good night, you two. I'm going to bed down here for a few hours. I hope I won't be seeing you before the morning. But if I do, remember: keep quiet and keep low.'

The weather was coming from behind them now and the *Altair* was pitching in a steep, short rhythm. Making love in a small ship with a sea running is not unlike flying through some strange element that at one moment seems thinner than air, at the next thicker than water. For an instant, at the climax, Bond and Ariadne hung weightless, then plunged as if into the still black depths above the ocean floor.

Bond lay on his face with his arm across Ariadne's belly and sleep came quick and heavy. But he was awake in a flash when a hand pressed his shoulder and a young Greek voice whispered: '*Kyrie Tzems. Despinís Ariadne.* Boat.'

Chapter 11

Death by Water

THE DECK was in darkness, apart from the glow aft, where Litsas would be at the wheel. Elsewhere there seemed to be no light at all. Cloud covered the moon and stars. The wind had abated a good deal, to Beaufort 2 or 3. Keeping below the gunwale, Bond crawled aft and round the corner of the deck-housing.

'Dead ahead,' said Litsas quietly. 'Stay close to the mast and have a look.'

Bond raised himself with caution. He narrowed his eyes. A shadowy bulk, showing its starboard green and a light in a pilot-house amidships, lay almost broadside across their bow perhaps six hundred yards distant. It appeared not to have way on. Bond caught a glimpse of a swept-back stub mast above the cabin top, a movement in the pilot-house. Not much else.

'They came at about twenty knots from where Paros is,' Litsas went on. 'Then, when they were on our port bow, they lost way and hove to. Engine trouble, or they're imitating it.'

'Is real engine trouble likely?' Bond still kept his eyes on the other ship.

'It's possible. Some boat-owners forget their maintenance. They're Greeks. Don't try enough. Anyway, if these people are true they'll have trouble if the weather gets worse again. You could hang no more than a sail like a handkerchief from that little penis which is all their mast. I'm at half-ahead now. We'll go in slowly.'

Neither spoke while the distance between the two craft lessened. Bond found that he could make out an intenser patch of darkness to his left that must be Paros. On the starboard bow was an even vaguer shape; he guessed it to be the smaller island of Ios. Ahead, beyond the gradually expanding profile of the other boat, there lay something above and around which an almost indefinable change was taking place, as if an infinitely thin sheet of water were being lowered on to a pool of black ink: Vrakonisi, and the first hint of dawn.

When the gap had narrowed to something under two hundred yards a faint hail came from the cabin-cruiser.

'*Kapetánie!*'

'*Akoúo – ti thélete?*' shouted Litsas, and throttled his motor right back.

The exchange continued. Litsas relayed excerpts and comments to Bond.

'Both their engines are overheating. They say. They say they've nobody on board who can make repairs. A *meltémi* – a northern gale – was blowing for four days and they're afraid it'll freshen again when the sun comes up. That's reasonable. If they're true they must call for assistance. Left alone they could pile up on a reef in a couple of hours. They want us to give them a tow into Vrakonisi. Somebody else might come by, of course. But nobody might. Probably nobody will. What do we do, James?'

Bond considered. 'This is one line that we more or less predicted. I don't suppose for a moment that this lot is anything but a boat-load of the opposition. But we're not entitled to ignore the faint chance that they're what they say they are and in serious difficulty. Whatever we're up to we're still sailors. Tell them we'll take them in tow.'

'I agree.' Litsas shouted acceptance, then lowered his voice. 'Right, James, here are your parcels. I hope to God we've fastened them well.'

Within twenty seconds Bond had tied the string of small plastic-wrapped packages round his waist and donned the only two useful items of equipment that chance had stowed in the *Altair*'s odds-and-ends locker: a pair of flippers and a hunting-knife for underwater fishing. In similar adventures in the past Bond had had a luxurious armoury of devices to choose from. This time, he realized without dismay, it had been and was going to go on being a matter of improvisation, guts and what physical skills he could command.

He was ready. Litsas turned from the wheel and spoke low and urgently.

'The only thing we at this end must fear is ramming. With their speed and ours I couldn't avoid that. Now over the side with you. Good luck, James.'

They gripped hands for a second. Bond threw a leg over the rail and slipped silently down into the invisible water. It struck chill, but he knew that in this sea at this time of the year it would be no worse than cool once he started to move. For the next few minutes he would be confronted with nothing more severe than a simple test of his sense of position and timing – the need to ensure that the bulk of the *Altair* lay continuously between him and the presumed opposition. He found time to smile at the thought of the presumption turning out to be comically mistaken, elaborate and highly lethal preparations being made against a party of Dutch businessmen or Swedish teachers on vacation. Then the *Altair*'s engine revved up, her bow began to come round to starboard, and Bond was breast-stroking gently to keep his position.

To take and secure a line from a craft without steerage-way in anything but a flat calm is not straightforward. To do it single-handed is hazardous, but all three had agreed that Yanni was not to be involved in what was not his quarrel and must stay below in the fo'c'sle as long as danger threatened. And Ariadne could not leave her post.

Every minute counted – or might count. While the two vessels approached closer and shouted directions were being swapped, Bond pushed off from the *Altair*'s hull and began to swim on a slowly turning path that would keep him well away from the strongest light now burning, a fairly hefty installation mounted at the point where the cruiser's stub-mast joined the deck-housing. Even so there was no guarantee of not being spotted, but Bond intended as far as possible to make the trip below the surface, and a really safe circuit would have taken too long.

It was not a particularly tough swim. His burden served as a

makeshift diving-weight and the flippers added bite to every
stroke. Even a yard or so down most of the turbulence sub-
sided. The deeper swell, a long swaying motion, remained,
but this was no hindrance, nothing more than the familiar
feel of the element. He surfaced a dozen or more times to
breathe and check his position. At last he was within twenty
feet of the cruiser and dead astern of it. He made his way
cautiously forward into the shadow cast by its hull, found
and noted a fender hanging overside amidships, then moved
for'ard again until he could watch and listen.

Litsas was securing the tow-rope. Four men incongruously
dressed in city suits were at the cruiser's bow. A conversation
was in progress. Bond waited for the expected next step. It
soon came. The four reached some agreement with Litsas,
took up positions at the tow-rope and began clumsily hauling
at it. In a minute or two they would have brought themselves
up to the *Altair* and be in a position to jump on to the counter.
It was time for Bond to get going.

He stripped off the flippers and let them sink, moved back
amidships, grasped the rope of the fender, heaved himself up,
grabbed the rail and rolled inboard without making a sound.
Crouching in the shadow of the deck-house he unfastened the
packages at his waist but left them in position. He drew the
knife from its scabbard below his knee and glanced for'ard.

One of the cruiser's men had reached the *Altair*; the next,
in obvious apprehension, was studying the fluctuating gap
between the two boats while his two companions struggled
with the tow-rope. No immediate hurry, then. After a swift
prowl on hands and knees Bond had satisfied himself that the
party numbered five: four men for'ard, one, in the faded shirt
and slacks of a sailor, leaning on the instrument-panel in the
pilot-house, closely watching the movements of his companions. On the assumption that this was an opposition force,
there would be nobody below at such a time.

Bond moved to a point just aft of the open door of the pilot-
house. There was one more detail which with luck could be
settled now. He edged forward for a risky look. Yes. In the
flooring by the pilot's seat was a brass-edged trapdoor with a

countersunk ring at its centre. Bond settled back and waited, a mere couple of strides from the fifth man's back, knife in hand.

Three of the party were now on the after-deck of the *Altair*; the remaining one was evidently to stay where he was. An altercation broke out. Litsas was spreading his hands, protesting, the picture of outraged innocence. Bond caught a mention of his own name, then Ariadne's, then the word *astinomía* – police.

This was no shaker; quite the contrary. It was as if the group were interpreting, without much imagination, a rough shooting-script drawn up for them by Bond and the others the previous evening. Real police would have approached openly, with all the paraphernalia of searchlight, loud-hailer, uniforms and levelled guns. The thing was virtually certain now – but that was not certain enough. The other side must somehow be provoked into declaring itself unmistakably.

Litsas continued to protest, gesturing back the way they had come, no doubt explaining, as planned, that he had put the Englishman ashore at Sounion. One man stepped forward and tapped Litsas's trouser pockets, then gave an order. The other two filed forward and turned in at the saloon door. The search had no need to be prolonged. Within a minute the two reappeared. The leading one gave the slow upward nod that means 'no' in these parts. Another order, and the pair went further for'ard and out of Bond's sight.

Complete silence, except for the faint creakings in the cruiser's superstructure. Then a man's laugh, shockingly out of key with the atmosphere of strain. Then the lunatic metallic chattering of the Thompson, sounding flat and echoless across the water. A loud moan. Bond had a glimpse of Litsas grabbing for the place on the roof of the deck-house where the Beretta lay hidden under a folded tarpaulin. The man near Bond moved at the same moment, flung himself into the pilot's seat and pressed a stud on the panel. Two powerful engines came instantly to life below decks.

Now Bond acted. He leapt forward, flung his left arm round the man's face, covering the mouth. The knife thudded into the chest once, twice, three times, the torso jerking at each blow while the hands fought unavailingly for a grip. Bond heard a thin wailing that would be inaudible a couple of yards off. Poor bastard, he thought – they told you it might just involve a bit of tricky sailing with a couple of thousand drachmas at the end of it. A fourth thump of the knife. Then trunk and limbs relaxed, warm blood flooded out on to Bond's left sleeve, he stepped aside and helped the body out of the seat.

There were yells and shots from the *Altair,* but Bond had no time to spare for them. He darted one glance for'ard. The enemy there was crouched behind the gunwale, pistol in hand, evidently trying for a shot at Litsas. Bond dropped to his knees, shoved out of the way the legs of the man he had stabbed, got his finger through the brass ring of the trapdoor and heaved it aside. The roar of well-tuned machinery and an engine-room smell came up at him. He moved to the deck immediately outside the doorway and there, swiftly and methodically, drew from the pouches at his waist the four Mills grenades. Each was surrounded by a half-inch-thick protective coating of heavy-duty grease from the *Altair*'s stores. Again he made no delay, but with quick deft movements grasped one grenade after another in his right hand, drew out the safety-pin with his left index finger, and had tossed all four down the hatchway before the seven-second fuse of the first had had time to release the firing-pin.

Then it came, a monstrous pounding, shivering bang underfoot that made the deckboards leap as if struck with a massive hammer, the buzz of flying metal, a wash of flame above the hatchway. Immediately afterwards a revolver bullet fizzed through the air four or five feet above Bond's head: a poor shot, but the next might be closer. Knowing better than to poise himself for a dive, he vaulted the rail and fell anyhow into the sea. Just as his ears went under he thought he heard a second explosion. Then he arched his back and kicked out and swam at top speed a couple of feet below the surface for a hundred counted seconds. Finally he turned and let his head come up.

One glance told him that anybody who might be still alive in the cruiser would not be standing at the rail in the hope of getting a shot at a swimmer. Nor was there now any question of the vessel ever ramming anything. Amidships she was burning heavily, with the rich fat glow of oil. The breeze was whipping the blaze for'ard and Bond caught the glow of flames sweeping the deck-house. He could hear the roar of fuel-fired combustion. Something aft went up with a kind of puffing bellow and a bunch of flame, intensely orange in colour, jerked and eddied outwards. Not for the first time in his career, Bond felt a surge of sickening remorse at the gross, outrageous destruction he had caused, the stabbing of the man in the pilot's seat and the unknown, but probably dreadful, fate of the other. He tried to push the thought out of his mind. It was necessary, he told himself. It was duty.

The sky beyond Vrakonisi had become a couple of degrees more transparent. No colour could yet be pointed to, but the dawn was gathering. Three short blasts – the success signal – came from the *Altair*'s horn as she made slowly away from the burning wreck. Bond leant forward in the water and swam with leisured strokes towards her.

*   *   *

'I think two of them went off,' said Litsas, 'but it was hard to tell. The fuel was exploding too. Anyway, it was enough.'

From his place at the wheel he nodded towards what was left of the cruiser. It was a mile astern now, burning less fiercely, partly obscured by the ragged smoke-cloud that was being blown almost directly towards them. If not earlier, she would begin to settle when the fire reached her waterline and the first waves came inboard.

As soon as Bond was safely picked up it had been a matter of first things first. The *Altair* had to get out of the area before boats from Paros or Vrakonisi could reach the scene. Bond had taken the wheel while Litsas and Yanni hoisted the main-sail, foresail and jib. Now, before a stiff following breeze, the little caique was making close to ten knots. They had decided to run south and circumnavigate Ios before coming up to Vrakonisi – another couple of hours' sailing time, but worth it to provide the makeshift alibi that would protect them against involvement in official, and unofficial, inquiries. It was not until now that they had had the leisure to compare notes.

Bond told his story squatting on the after-deck, sipping the glass of Votris and drawing deeply at the Xanthi that Ariadne had handed him. The cigarette tasted wonderful and at this moment he did not mind the sweetish tang of the brandy. He ended by asking, 'Did anybody see what happened to the man who stayed on the cruiser's foredeck?'

'I certainly didn't,' said Litsas. 'He made one shot at me, a bad one, I made a much better one and he ducked down. Then the explosions started and I never saw the chap again. Their dinghy was lashed down for'ard and he didn't go to it.'

'He's had it anyway.' Bond forced callousness into his voice. 'Fire or sea. But tell it from the beginning.'

'Oh, they asked very many questions and I was the stupid peasant – perhaps you saw some of that. Then one bloke stayed with me and the other two went for'ard to look at my daughter sleeping on the cabin-top and to make sure the dangerous criminal James Bond wasn't hiding in the fo'c'sle. Then . . . but I must let Ariadne tell the next part.'

'Like Niko says, it was all luck really.' Ariadne, sitting beside Bond with her knees drawn up and her shoulder touching his, was at her most direct and matter-of-fact. 'I recognized one of the men. His voice was familiar right away and just then the ship turned or something and I saw it was a guy called Theodorou, who was in the same Party branch I was for a while before they expelled him for being a criminal and a leftist – you know, attacking the USSR for leading the world to peace at the time of Cuba. Well, the Greek police are very corrupt and Fascist and everything, but even they wouldn't sign up a skunk like Theodorou. When he saw I recognized him, he made a horrible laugh and said I must come to his boat for questioning and . . . something more besides. Greek police don't behave that way either.

'So then,' Ariadne went on, taking another cigarette and lighting it from Bond's without ceasing to talk, so that her words came in jerks – 'so then . . . I said . . . that would be just fine with me . . . and he must wait a minute while I . . .

found my sweater. But what I found was the Thompson under the blanket and I shot him with it.

'It was just like you said, Niko: vibration and a pull to the right, but mostly I hit him and he yelled and went down. But the other man got down too and that worried me, because I hadn't had time to shoot him and he obviously had a gun, and I was kneeling on the cabin-top while he could move around on the deck without me seeing him and might pop up anywhere and shoot me before I could turn. – Darling, could I have some of that, please ?'

She took Bond's glass with both hands. They were shaking. He put his arm round her shoulders as she drank.

'That was where young Yanni turned up,' Litsas put in. 'He said he didn't want to be sent to bed like a child before the trouble had even started. He wanted to help. So he went to his bunk and got out his knife and stood on the little ladder that comes up from the fo'c'sle. When the first bad man was knocked over, the second bad man was getting ready to shoot at Despinís Ariadne. But unluckily for him his back was to Yanni. The distance isn't more than about a yard and Yanni can walk like a cat. He came up from the fo'c'sle and shoved four inches of the best Sheffield steel under our friend's left shoulder. He gave no trouble after that.

'I asked Yanni if he wanted some brandy and he said no, thank you, he thought he mustn't start drinking at his age. After knifing a man with a gun!' Litsas laughed heartily. 'He's back on the job now, washing down the deck. It did get rather messy.'

Bond shuddered. He had had to get used to the idea of involving innocent outsiders in the kind of savage, unpredictable violence he traded in, but to have brought about the initiation of an adolescent into the ways of killing was something new to him. He hoped desperately that the relative unsophistication of Greek youth would protect Yanni from the progressive intoxication with lethal weapons that, in an urban British lad of this age, could so easily result from such an episode. The alternative was not to be thought of. He asked with assumed eagerness, 'What happened at your end, Niko ?'

'Oh, that was nothing at all. My chap had had the common sense to get his revolver out, but when the Thompson started up the poor devil couldn't help moving his eyes off me for a second. I kicked his gun half out of his hand and then shot him in the face. Child's play.'

There was a call from Yanni amidships. They turned and followed his pointing finger. But there was nothing to see. Steel-coloured water, lightly touched with the lilac of the opening dawn, stretched unbroken over the place where the cruiser had been.

Chapter 12

General Incompetence

I T WAS a beautiful morning. Out at sea the rising *meltémi* was blowing the tops off the waves, but off the southern shore of Vrakonisi it did no more than impart a pleasing sense of motion to the slightly flawed surface of the water, as if a giant mirror of liquid blue stone were perpetually moving south and perpetually renewing itself from the edge of the land. And on the land, in the house on the islet, all that could be felt was a mild breeze, gusting a little at times and fluttering the natural-coloured linen curtains, raising the corners of the papers on the long pale Swedish desk by the window, but cool and delicious.

Sitting at the desk with a glass of tea before him, Colonel-General Igor Arenski felt comfortably relaxed. This was his first undercover assignment outside the Soviet Union, though as a high official of the K G B (Committee of State Security) he had naturally made frequent trips to foreign countries in the guise of trade delegate, manager of cultural mission and the like, and had worked for over five years as a counsellor at the Russian Embassy in Washington.

Arenski folded his hands behind his bald head and gazed out over the placid stretch of the Aegean. Supervising the security arrangements for this conference had been a simple matter to a man of his experience. All the real work had been done weeks before in his Moscow office. Coming all this way merely to witness the operation of the foolproof machinery he had devised was, between himself and his professional conscience, quite unnecessary. Half a dozen of his subordinates —that charming dark-eyed lad Gevrek from Soviet Armenia, for instance – could have done this part of the job equally well.

That was the sort of thing these *yobannye* politicians never understood. They thought in terms of rank, of roubles, of protocol, of producing senior Security officers when senior diplomats were being taken under protection. As if these Arabs and Levantines would know the difference between a distinguished higher member of the *apparat* and a provincial area-controller!

Still, he must not complain. It was a good thing to have got away from Moscow for a time; even a short trip like this helped one to maintain an international outlook. And, although not up to the climate and standard of comfort to be enjoyed at his villa outside Sevastopol, this was an agreeable enough location. The inhabitants were a barbaric lot in general, uncouth and suspicious, but his contact with them for intelligence purposes had had to be no more than minimal, and it was true that his contact with one inhabitant – a fisher-boy or something of the kind from the port – was turning out to be unexpectedly interesting. Life was treating Igor Alexeivitch well.

Though he would have denied it strenuously, Arenski was himself a politician of the most durable sort. Under Beria in the MGB, the old Security Ministry, he had conducted himself with a sort of inspired circumspection, making neither friends nor enemies and yet avoiding the dangerous status of the individualist. His sexual tastes had paradoxically stood in his favour – the consensus in the corridors of the Kremlin had been that someone as obviously vulnerable as that was no danger in any quarter. When Beria fell, when the fat baron and all his vassals went down in the bloody aftermath of Stalin's death, Arenski had moved a major rung up the ladder. He was nobody's man, anybody's man, safe, silent and slow, the perfect politicians' choice, and therefore unqualified to rise to the occasion in any real emergency.

At last, bored with the play of sunlight on the most beautiful water to be found off any European coast, Arenski sighed and glanced at the file that lay open in front of him. It was necessary to go through the motions of work in order to preserve good habits. His small blue eyes moved idly over the topmost sheet, although he knew its contents by heart. The closing lines ran:

DAY 4

Time	Event	Remarks
1200	Degree of readiness yellow	Cordon round house
1600	Arrival of Ministerial group	Sea patrol begins
1700	Degree of readiness red	
1800	Arrival of delegates	Identity checks
–1930		
2000	Speech of welcome, toasts	Check on cordon
2030	Conference in session	Land staff fed in shifts
2330	Dinner	

DAY 5

0030	Conference in session	
0300	Refreshments, rest period	Check on cordon
0400	Conference in session	
0530	Speech of thanks, departure	
–0600	of delegates	
0630	Degree of readiness yellow	Sea patrol returns
1200	Departure of Ministerial group, degree of readiness blue	Cordon withdrawn, close down radio links
1700	Departure of staff	

Arenski himself would not be departing with his staff. He had ten days' leave coming to him and proposed to spend as many of them here as he felt like. At the moment he felt like spending them all here. There was something about that boy's way of laughing . . .

A knock at the door brought him out of his reverie. '*Da?*' he called irritably.

One of the two men who had first occupied the house entered and spoke in an appalling Ukrainian accent.

—Good morning, Comrade General.

—Good morning, Mily. Please sit down.

The general had quickly mastered his irritation and spoke amiably. It was a rule of his never to antagonize anybody, not even a worthless peasant like Mily who ought to be doling out bowls of soup at a labour camp.

The man perched himself awkwardly on a bad copy of a Venetian stool by the empty marble fireplace.—Only one thing to report, sir. There was a fire at sea about five o'clock this morning, I was informed by a man at the harbour. Two boats went out to investigate. They made a search of the area but the ship had sunk without trace. They picked up one survivor, rather badly burnt. There's a hospital of sorts in the town above the port and he was taken to it. He had some story about a fire in the engine-room.

—A sad story, Mily. But I don't see that it concerns us, do you? Some fool of a Greek throws a cigarette-end into a tin of petrol and blows his ship up. It would be surprising if something like that didn't happen every week in a country as backward as this. You really mustn't go about flapping your ears at every piece of local gossip. A good Leninist like you should be able to distinguish at once between the essential and the inessential.

Mily flushed and said humbly, —I'm sorry, Comrade General, I didn't think.

—It's of no consequence, my dear Mily. Anything else?

—Boris kept listening watch on the Athens frequency at the usual time, sir. No transmission.

—Very good. See what that is, will you?

There was movement on the terrace outside and an excited murmur. A man's voice shouted in Greek. Mily went to the door, opened it, letting a bar of intense sunlight and a surge of heat into the shadowed room, and went out of sight for a moment. When he reappeared he seemed agitated.

—A rowing-boat is approaching, sir. A girl and a boy of about sixteen. They're making for the anchorage.

This sort of situation had arisen a dozen times since Aren-ski's arrival on the islet – tourists coming to ask if and when the house would be available for rental, tradesmen from the island touting for custom – and had been easily dealt with, as he had known it would be, by one of the Greek members of the team following laid-down procedure. Normally the general would have allowed this procedure to run its course without rising from his chair, but this time he decided to oversee the matter in person. He got up, pulled his green-and-turquoise check shirt into position and sauntered outside.

The sun beat down at him and its reflection on the water was dazzling. He shaded his eyes. A hundred yards away a white-painted dinghy was being rowed straight towards him. The senior Greek employee, binoculars in hand, asked him for instructions, but Arenski went on studying for a moment the play of strong bare brown shoulders at the oars. Finally he said in English, regrettably the only language common to himself and the man at his side, 'Have you asked them what they want?'

'Oh yes, General. But they are not answering me.'

'Try them again. Ask them who they are, tell them that this is a private house and so on.'

The Greek did as he was told. This time there was a response, from the girl. It was gibberish to Arenski except for one name, a name he recognized and reacted sharply to.

'General, she is saying she is a friend of Comrade Gordienko and she is wishing to speak with the gentleman of the house, please.'

Arenski fingered his pendulous lower lip. What was happening was inexcusably irregular, but he recognized with some weariness that he could not afford to send this person away. And there was another consideration. He said with fair cheerfulness, 'Tell them we don't know any Mr Gordienko, but the girl and her . . . her escort are very welcome to come ashore for a chat.'

Two minutes later the general, hands on hips, was on the mole surveying the two arrivals. The girl, a Greek or Bulgar, was cheaply pretty, over-developed about the bust. The boy, he assured himself out of the corner of his eye, was satisfactory, muscular, and tanned. Arenski waited: always let the other speak first.

The girl faced him. 'Do you speak English?'

'Yes.'

'My name is Ariadne Alexandrou. I am an employee of Mr Gordienko in Athens. I have an urgent message for the man in charge here.'

'I'm the tenant of this house, if that's what you mean. But excuse me one moment.'

Leaving the pair in the sun, Arenski strode briskly on his short legs back into the room he had just left. He took out a spring-back file bound in the yellow of Personnel and containing photostats of identity documents and dossiers. Alexandrou. Here it was. The hair in the photograph was longer but the rest was the same. He shut the file and returned to the doorway.

'Come over here, will you? Both of you.' When they had reached him he went on pleasantly, 'Your credentials are in order, Miss Alexandrou. You may come inside.' Then, his little eyes running over the boy's body, he added, 'And please ask your young friend if he would care for a glass of something cold in the kitchen.'

The boy looked back at Arenski while the girl put the question. His look said, as plainly as any words, that he knew what was in the general's mind and found it total filth. With a word to the girl he turned his back and strolled away.

Arenski swallowed and drew himself up. By a tremendous effort he managed to smile at the girl, introduce himself, and say, 'Let's sit down in the cool, shall we?'

The contentment he had felt half an hour earlier had totally departed. All things considered, he was probably the least suitable man in the whole of Soviet Security to react appropriately to Ariadne's story. Nevertheless he heard her out to the end without once interrupting.

When she had finished he sat silent and motionless for a time in his revolving chair, hands behind head. Then he turned round to his desk and reopened the Personnel file. Finally he said, looking out of the window, 'You were recruited by the Chief Intelligence Directorate, the GRU.'

'That's correct.'

'Why was that? What's a girl of your sort doing as an agent

of the Red Army? Surely it would have been more natural for you to come directly under the orders of the KGB.

'Maybe it would, sir. It was just that ... well, the man who originally signed me up to work for Russia was the Number Two of the GRU in Athens.'

'Yes.' Arenski still stared out of the window. 'He was your lover, this man?'

'Please, General, is this important?'

'He was your lover, this man?' It might have been a tape-recording of the previous query.

'Yes. He was.'

'And it was he who ... converted you, I think would be the right word here – converted you to Marxist Socialism?'

'Yes.'

'Have you done much counter-espionage work?'

'Not a great deal. Chiefly on jobs that called for a girl like me.'

'A seductive temptress,' sneered Arenski. 'Really, some of us behave as if we're still in the pre-Revolutionary era. Now, your father' – he glanced at the file – 'your father is an official of Pallas Airlines. A comfortable bourgeois.'

When this drew no reply, the general swivelled his chair round again and studied her impersonally. Eventually he drew in his breath and said in what he meant to be a kindly tone, 'You know, Miss Alexandrou, you're not the sort of person one expects to find working for peace in a primitive country like this one. What can be your experience of the class struggle? Where are your roots in the workers' movement? You know what you are? You're a romantic. Drawn to Communism by sentimental pity for the oppressed and to Intelligence work by false notions of glamour. And this means—'

The girl cut in sharply. 'General Arenski, I came here to discuss something much more important than why I became a Communist. There's a terrible threat against your country and against what we both believe in. I'm awaiting your instructions.'

Arenski wrinkled his nose and sniffed. 'Romantics like you are peculiarly apt to lose their sense of proportion. Let us look calmly at what you've told me. This episode in which Major Gordienko and two of his assistants are killed. Were any of the assailants identified?'

'I forgot to tell you that. Mr Bond recognized the man he shot as one of the group who kidnapped his chief in England.'

'Just so. I must say that kidnapping appeals to me. It has such an air of fantasy about it. But of course we know that fantastic things do happen. It's a pity that we have no way of obtaining confirmation of this one. And then the episode of the fight in the boats. You yourself recognized the man called Theodorou. A traitor to the working class, clearly. A criminal, you said. There you are likely to be right. That episode carries conviction of a sort. It would be interesting to interview the man who survived it.'

'There was a survivor?' asked the girl, sitting up sharply.

'Oh yes. He's in the hospital here. I will institute inquiries.' Arenski's tone carried no sense of purpose. One of the minor irritations of this intrusion was the way it had compelled him to change his mind about the significance of the fire at sea. He forced himself to continue his analysis.

'There are other elements of fantasy in your story. Consider this idea – put forward by Bond, naturally – that the Chinese People's Government is conspiring against us. Now I know it's fashionable to take the view that China has replaced the capitalist West as the chief threat to world peace. And it's true that our leaders have been properly severe on the ideological mistakes of the Chinese. But it would be disastrously un-Marxist to jump to the conclusion that their pride, their ambition and their envy of the USSR could ever drive them to the attempted use of violence against our conference tomorrow night. That would be gangsterism; gangsterism of the same kind as you have twice been involved in, though of an infinitely greater degree. And gangsterism is the typical resort of Western warmongers.

'My dear young lady,' – Arenski tried another smile – 'the key to this whole affair is the character of the man Bond. I know him well by repute. He has conducted terrorist activities in Turkey, France, and the Caribbean. Quite recently he committed two assassinations in Japan for motives of pure personal revenge. He is a dangerous international criminal. He has very cleverly involved you in his schemes with tales of kidnapping and wicked Chinamen – the very thing to appeal to your romantic nature. Who his opponents really are is scarcely worth conjecturing about. Some rival gangster group, probably American. Our concern lies elsewhere.'

'May I ask a question, Comrade General?' For the first time, the girl spoke with proper respect.

'Certainly, Comrade.'

'How does this theory square with the murder of Mr Gordienko and his two assistants, and with Mr Gordienko thinking for sure that there is a traitor in our organization in Athens?'

'That is two questions, but we will examine them. Gordienko and his men were killed because the rival gang wanted Bond and they were in the way. Very regrettable, but not mysterious. Gordienko's notion of a traitor . . . well . . .' The general turned over a small, well-manicured hand. 'I respected old Piotr in a way, but he was never the most efficient of men. And he's been out here too long. By your own account a breach of security had clearly taken place. There'd been a leak. Gordienko had slipped up, but he didn't know just how or where. What more natural than to create an unknown traitor who takes the blame for all your mistakes?'

'I quite understand that, sir. You make it very clear. But I would like you to explain why, if there is no traitor, my message to you via the Embassy in Athens has never arrived.'

Arenski sighed. 'You said you don't know who you spoke to there. Some junior clerk, no doubt, probably a Greek, who was too stupid to understand your no doubt guarded phrases, went out to lunch and forgot the whole thing. And your zeal was commendable, but before very long I shall be reading all about the affair in the newspapers when they're fetched from the port. It'll be interesting to see how they treat it.

'There, then, is your explanation. There are half a dozen other such explanations. Whereas your explanation, of course, involves the mysterious traitor.'

'Well . . . yes, sir.'

'Kidnapping, Chinese terrorists, traitors: is there no end to it?' Arenski turned businesslike; he had spent too long being reasonable. 'Now, I will outline our course of action. I want Bond here. He clearly has designs of some sort against our conference. Aided by this Greek ruffian and an unwashed small boy he has little chance of achieving anything spectacular. There are weapons here that would drive off a small warship. I think I can say that I've neglected nothing.' The general gave a narrow smile. 'But Bond may be a nuisance. He must be kept out of harm's way until our delegates have departed.'

'Anything I can do, Comrade General . . .'

'Yes, Comrade Alexandrou, there is a great deal. I take it you have been sleeping with our Mr Bond?' Arenski managed to keep out of his voice very nearly all the distaste he felt at the idea.

'Yes, sir. He won't let me alone.'

'Is he infatuated with you?'

'Oh yes. I've very much influence over him.'

'Better and better.' Arenski almost beamed. 'Persuade him to come here for an interview. Say I am gravely concerned about what has happened and need his help. Give him my word that he'll be able to depart unmolested at any time he may wish. You'll know what arguments to use. Is that clear?'

'Perfectly clear, Comrade General,' said the girl, getting up. 'I'll bring him here as soon as I can, but you must give me a little time.'

'By all means.' The general also rose. 'Tell me, how did you persuade him to let you come here this morning?'

'By the same sort of methods as I shall use to persuade him to come himself.'

'Just so, just so,' said Arenski hurriedly, then, remembering his manners, added, 'A glass of something before you go, my dear?'

'No thank you, sir. The sooner I return the better.'

'We shall make a Marxist of you yet. Let me say how much I appreciate your services.'

The girl smiled gratefully and said with obvious conviction,

'And let me say, Comrade General, how grateful I am to you for interpreting the situation scientifically to me and for being merciful with me about my bad attitude to this spy's deceptions. I hope I have learnt from the experience.'

Arenski bowed. He had thought her a typical Balkan whore, foolish, sentimental and pleasure-loving with a streak of gangsterism, but she had determination and her readiness to correct her mistakes was promising. He would mention her favourably in his report. 'Au revoir, Comrade Alexandrou, I look forward to seeing you very soon.'

Left alone, he paced the floor for a time, frowning. It crossed his mind that the notion of a Chinese attempt to sabotage the conference was not entirely fanciful. According to report, Mao Tse-tung had been in some odd moods recently, as his retirement approached. And the behaviour of the Red Guards, the new hostility to foreigners. . . . Then the general's brow cleared. Fantasy must be catching. Overt violence on the scale required was unthinkable in peacetime, even granted the uttermost in neo-Stalinist irresponsibility among the Chinese leaders. Nevertheless, one or two points must be cleared up at once.

He went to the desk and rang a small brass hand-bell. Mily came in.

—Go to the wireless room and tell the operator to contact Athens immediately. I'll come along and speak in a couple of minutes.

—And break wireless silence, sir?

Arenski clenched his small fists. This ploughboy gaping would drive him mad. He answered in a tone of caricatured patience—Yes, Mily, and break wireless silence. Exactly that. Now go and do as I say. And get one of the Greeks, the fat one, to go up to the hospital in the town and inquire about a – no, tell him to come and see me.

The fat Greek arrived, was briefed and sent on his way with Arenski's usual politeness. (Once outside the door, the man made the traditional five-finger gesture, meaning roughly, 'May all your senses leave you.') Then the general went up to the tiny oven-hot cubicle on the top floor that housed the

T–E

wireless station with its R/T links to Athens and to Plovdiv in Bulgaria, which would act if required as a relay to Moscow. The latter circuit was not to be used except in conditions of threat-to-peace emergency. The room reeked of sweat and cheap Russian cigarettes. An unmade bed filled most of the space not occupied by the grey-enamelled set. Arenski pulled out a scented silk handkerchief and inhaled.

The operator, a bull-necked Muscovite with a heavy shaving-rash, handed up the microphone and Arenski got down to it.

It was frustrating, it was unbelievably prolonged and the howl of static surrounding and blurring the incoming voice set his teeth on edge, but at the end of twenty agonizing minutes he had the situation clear. He thanked the operator and left the room, sweating freely.

Descending the broad whitewashed stone stairs to the terrace, where he would sit out of the sun and enjoy his mid-morning glass of fresh lemonade, Arenski almost smiled at the predictability of the answers to his questions. Why had the shootings – 'the forcible retirements of the sales manager and two representatives' – not been reported? Because on attempting to make this report the transmitter had been found to be defective. And repairing it had taken a long time. It had only been functional for the last two hours or so. Why had not the report been made then, at once? Because it had been thought better to wait until the allocated transmission period at 1200 hours. Why had the arrival of Bond – 'a dangerous English competitor' – not been reported? Because by the time the plans to detain him in Athens had broken down the transmitter had become defective. Apologies were offered, plus an assurance that the assistant sales-manager was now in complete control of the situation.

Arenski relaxed in his basket chair and sipped his lemonade. On further reflection he actually did smile. How like poor old Piotr Gregorievitch to have imagined he could deal with Bond by himself. How like him to have failed to institute an efficient maintenance-and-repair system at his wireless station. And how totally, hopelessly like him to have got himself killed in a quarrel between two bands of Western thugs. It was painful to think ill of an old comrade, but it was as well that Piotr had gone before doing any real damage.

Bond ... Arenski was looking forward to the encounter. And not only that. It would be satisfying as well as advantageous to him to be able to tell the minister, 'I have a prisoner who may interest you. A Western gangster called Bond. No, oddly enough I found him quite easy to capture.' Then, when the conference was over, Bond would snatch a gun and the general would have to shoot him in self-defence. Perfect.

After a moment Arenski muttered to himself in English, 'The man who killed James Bond,' and chuckled wetly.

Chapter 13

The Small Window

'HERE THEY come.'
Litsas lowered the Negretti & Zambra binoculars and put them down on the cabin-top. Through the sun-dazzle Bond saw the smudge that was the dinghy, seemingly stationary at this distance, just off the point of the island beyond which the islet lay. The *Altair* had dropped anchor in a tiny cove whose granite sides dropped steeply into the water. Here they were secure enough from observation, but the north coast of Vrakonisi is never really comfortable in anything but a flat calm, and the caique, moored to a pinnacle on an odd tongue of rock and anchored on its narrow underwater continuation, was swinging and lurching unhealthily.

'Go on, Niko,' said Bond from his canvas chair on the tiny foredeck. 'By the way, where is Kapoudzona?'

'Macedonia. Mountain village. They're quite tough people there. I don't like them much, they have too many Bulgars and Turks, but they're tough. Well, just after the village the staff car comes to a road-block, some chaps rise up behind the rocks and blaze away, and all the German colonels are killed.

'Von Richter is commanding the support company of an SS infantry battalion who are training close by. There's a new German order saying that attacks of the guerrillas must be punished in a quick and – and severe way. That's enough for him.

'In two hours he's put a cordon round the village and he's lined up everybody in the square. He makes the women and the children under fourteen go into the village school. It's big and it's made of wood. Von Richter makes his men lock the doors, throw petrol down the walls and set fire to them.

Some of the mothers try to push their kids out of the windows, but for them he has tommy-gunners. Then he shoots the other people. Two hundred and eight killed altogether. Two old men somehow survive to tell the story.'

After a short pause, Litsas went on: 'I'll always remember one thing. Von Richter was standing at the school door while the women and kids were going in. When he saw a child who looked nice he patted its head or pinched its cheeks like an uncle, and spoke kindly to the mother. Oh, all the Germans love the family values.'

The last words were spoken in a thick, choked voice. Litsas had turned his back. Bond went up and put his arm round the heavy shoulders, saying nothing.

'Promise me you'll let me have him, James. I must kill him myself. You understand that.'

'Yes, Niko, I promise.'

Bond moved away and looked towards the approaching dinghy. It was near enough now for him to be able to see Ariadne's blue shirt and her fair hair shining in the sun. He waved to her and got an answering wave. Thank God she was near. He realized he wanted to see her – not make love to her, just look into her face and touch her hand – with more longing than he could remember feeling towards any other woman.

A movement on the hillside above the dinghy caught his eye. Somebody, a man, was making a painful diagonal descent through the piles of rock and clumped bushes, moving across the steep shoulder of the cove. His movements were peculiar, as if he were handicapped in some way. Bond, idly curious, picked up the binoculars, but by the time he brought them to bear the figure had gone out of view.

*　　*　　*

The roughly-flagged terrace where Colonel Sun was sitting, like his whole establishment on the island, was on a more modest scale than that of his Russian opposite number on the islet. It was also far more secluded, facing inland at the back of the house. A lot of persistence would have been needed to make an inquisitive stranger climb either of the precipitous spurs that cut the colonel's headquarters off from the neighbouring coves, and a good deal of physical toughness to approach directly by scrambling down the barren hillside, overgrown with thorn bushes, littered with great chunks of granite and marble, most of them shapeless, a few of weird geometrical regularity, like building blocks for some colossal unconstructed temple.

The man who had made this uncomfortable journey, and who now sat facing the colonel on the terrace, was physically tough all right. He would have had to be, after sustaining fairly extensive second-degree burns on board the cabin-cruiser, spending an hour in the water and walking five miles in the sun in order to gain the ridge above the house. His left arm was bandaged and in a sling and he had fallen badly twice during his descent as a result of this handicap. Because, as well as being exhausted, he was still suffering from shock, he told his tale ramblingly and with repetitions.

Sun was tolerant about this. Hands on knees, he sat on an olive-wood stool in an upright posture that would have put a crick in any Western back in five minutes, and gazed almost benignly at the unimpressive-looking small-time crook from the Piraeus waterfront who had endured all this for two hundred American dollars. Between them Doni Madan lounged on foam-rubber cushions wearing a black-and-green check bikini, an incongruous get-up for an interpreter. Now and then she sucked noisily at the straws of a tall pale drink.

'Tell Mr Aris I think I have it all clear now,' Sun said to her, 'thank him for his services, and offer him another drink or whatever refreshment he may desire. Then I have some questions. First: how was he able to find me?'

While this was being translated, Sun kept his pewter-coloured eyes fixed on Aris's sallow, pitted face, then watched the mouth show its plentiful gold fillings as it answered. This man had behaved well, no better than any politically-conscious Chinese would, but surprisingly well for a Westerner and a non-Britisher.

Doni had leaned forward to pour more brandy into the

glass that was being shakily held out to her. Now she heaved her body back on to the cushions, adjusting a shoulder-strap and revealing light wisps of uncut fine hair in the armpit. She enunciated carefully in her dry voice, 'He said he thinks it's necessary to warn you, and he had received half only of his money before.'

'That's why he made his way here, not how he knew where to come. Again.'

The colonel, sitting just as before, waited with his invariable and unnerving patience.

'He said they all were showed a map, in case that a man was killed.'

'Remarkable forethought and pessimism. Fully justified, as it's turned out. Well, I think I have enough for the moment.'

Aris gulped brandy and said something on his own account. He appeared uneasy. Perhaps he was discomforted by the bland politeness with which his story of abject and spectacular failure had been received. Fear, much more than conscientiousness or the thought of his money, was what had made him walk out of that hospital when his whole being had whimpered for rest. There were tales going round Piraeus. . . . But he did not dare mention such matters. He talked on, gesturing painfully.

After listening in grave silence to Doni's rendering, Sun turned thoughtful. 'How these people worship words. They have no concept of the relation of words to action. If I had to take a serious view of this fellow's actions, he could not be saved by words in any language. How can he not know such a simple thing? He is divorced from reality.'

Doni waited for this part to be over. A sleepy languor possessed her, compounded of sun, sea air, the hot scents of thyme and fennel from the hillside, the effects of bed and the anticipation of lunch and more bed. She felt dimly, complacently, that nobody was ever going to take a serious view of *her* actions. Pretending to be rubbing oil into her skin to aid her tan, she stroked her thighs slowly.

The colonel went on in a brisker tone, 'Tell Mr Aris I quite understand the difficulties that had to be faced. Assure him that the escape of the man Bond is not serious. It will be turned to account in the interests of peace. And tell Mr Aris too that his money will be paid in full, plus a bonus of fifty American dollars for devotion to duty. He may receive medical attention now. Take him to Dr Lohmann. And get Evgeny to cook him something. Then you or your colleague may comfort him if he so wishes. But remember that he's in a weak physical state, so be sure not to comfort him too energetically.'

With a smile that cut off abruptly when she woke up to who she was smiling at, Doni pushed herself on to her knees, turned away and began talking earnestly to Aris. Sun got up from his stool, unfolding himself vertically like a puppet on a string.

Still keeping in the shadow, he moved to the corner of the stone balustrade at the outer edge of the terrace. There, perfectly impassive, he waited, his half-shut eyes flickering over the wild and glaring but motionless scene before him. They took in nothing. The rattling chirrup of the cicadas beat at his ears without penetrating them. Even if his mind had been unpreoccupied, he would still have had no attention to spare for this irrelevant alien landscape. What was important was action, not its setting. History was a matter of deeds and their doers. If people had to ask *where* a thing happened, it was a scientific certainty that the thing itself was not unique. And within a short time, a good deal less than forty-eight hours, he, Sun Liang-tan, was going to have accomplished something unique.

When the conversation behind him had ended and the two had gone back into the house, the colonel's face changed, though his body remained immobile. A dim slow fire seemed to be kindled behind the grey layers of the pupils and the liver-coloured lips stretched and parted. There was a rhythmical hissing like the sound of a distant air-pump. Sun was laughing.

He recollected himself, hurried indoors and bounded actively up the stairs. In excellent spirits he shot the bolts on the door at the end of the corridor and entered.

'Good morning, my dear Admiral. Or rather,' – Sun consulted the black dial of the Longines at his wrist – 'since I know you sailors are meticulous about times of day, good afternoon. How are you? I hope you have everything you want?'

M had been looking out of the tiny window. It gave him a view of a thin sliver of sea and, once or twice a day, the blessed, almost unbelievable sight of a yacht or fishing-boat, a reminder and a reassurance, for the dozen seconds it was visible, that the world still went on and was still sane. He could not manage more than a few minutes on end at the window, because standing tired him and the one chair the tiny airless room contained (its other furniture consisted of a single bed) was too low to let him see over the sill. Two things in particular tormented him: the fear that a vessel might be going by unseen while he was resting in the chair, and the knowledge that he was beginning to look forward to Sun's visits as some sort of relief from total vacancy. He was in a position to understand the first stages of that sickening and mysterious intimacy that gradually comes to unite prisoner and interrogator. He turned and faced Sun now, pale and hollow-eyed, the skin drawn tight over his cheek- and jaw-bones, but the look he gave the Chinese was steady and his voice, though strained, was firm.

'What does it matter to you, you yellow slug,' said M with great distinctness, 'whether or not I have what I want? Talk as you think, for God's sake.'

'No abuse, please, sir. It causes hot blood and obstacles to thinking on both sides. In answer to your question, of course it matters to me whether you have what you want, or at least your fair share of what's available here. Your strength must be kept up for your part in the experiences which lie ahead of us – which, I venture to assure you, will be far in advance of anything we've so far undertaken together. And to keep you short of food, deny you access to the lavatory and so on, is no part of my plan. I will not have you subjected to any petty privations during your last days.'

M's gaze did not alter. 'That's decent of you.'

'But I didn't come up here only to inquire after your health, important as that is to me. I also bring you news. News of your subordinate and fellow-terrorist, James Bond.'

The effort of self-control needed to avoid betraying any sign of hope, of anything more than mild interest, almost made M stagger. He put out a hand, not too fast, and gripped the edge of the window-sill. 'Oh yes?' he said politely.

'Between ourselves. I don't mind admitting that Bond has been conducting himself with some skill and energy. He has done considerable damage in the Athens sector of this operation. However, that phase was not my responsibility and is now concluded. Bond is here in the vicinity.'

No reaction from M.

'Our habit of working in separate units, each answerable to the top, has had the curious result that while Athens was seeking to neutralize Bond at any cost I have been preparing to receive him undamaged. It will turn out my way. I'm sure we can both trust the resourceful 007 to find his way to this house. When he does so, some time tomorrow, perhaps, if not today, he'll be taken prisoner. In himself he's formidable enough, I grant, but he has no allies of any substance – merely a local whore who has done some messenger work for the Russians and a Greek Fascist cut-throat from the dockside taverns. Whereas very shortly I shall have five experienced men here to deal with him. The outcome is not in doubt.'

'To adopt your own hideous jargon, it would be unwise of you to set too much store by your superiority in numbers.' M managed a grin. 'Bond has successfully taken on far worse odds in the past. Organized by much more dangerous intelligences than a sadistic Chinese infant living in a world of fantasy. Say your prayers, Sun, or burn a joss-stick or whatever you do.'

The colonel showed his inward-pointing teeth. 'Burning is a topic you should have the tact to avoid, Admiral. How is the skin on your chest?'

M went on looking at him.

'Later we might see what we can do with your back. There we have the added factor that the recipient is unaware of where and when each successive stimulus will be applied.

The uncertainty can have interesting consequences. But it's vulgar to exchange threats. I'll leave you to your lunch. Evgeny has promised something special in the way of an omelette. And today I think we might allow you a glass of wine. You'll want to drink to the safe arrival of your friend and colleague.'

Turning away, M gazed out once more at the empty sector of sea.

Chapter 14

The Butcher of Kapoudzona

'THE GENERAL was very worried by what I had to tell him,' said Ariadne. 'He wants you to go see him and have a talk. I think he proposes to join forces with you. He said he needs your help. After the interview, of course, you're free to go if you want to.'

Bond examined the tip of his cigarette. 'What guarantee have I that he'll let me go once he's got me there?'

'Oh, you have his word for that. The word of a colonel-general in the KGB.'

There was silence for a moment in the saloon of the *Altair*. Then Bond and Litsas exploded into laughter.

'Did I do it well?' asked Ariadne eagerly. 'Did I have you fooled any of the time?'

Bond put his arms round her and kissed her cheek. 'No,' he said, 'I'm afraid not. You'll never make a proper spy; you're too honest. We could tell you were hating every word you said and despising the whole thing for being so unbeliev-able. A very poor performance all round.'

'That chap seems to be raving mad.' Litsas was pouring ouzo for the three of them. 'What was he thinking? You told him the whole story, I suppose?'

'Everything. He didn't believe me. Oh, he believed the part about Mr Gordienko because even a moron like myself wouldn't tell a lie he could check out. But the rest was that James was smooth-talking me to help him fight some gangsters so that he could try to blow up this conference. He wouldn't succeed, of course, because the general's precautions are so marvellous, but the man Bond is a dangerous criminal,' – she mimicked Arenski's accent scornfully – 'and might be a nuisance. I had to pretend to go along with him or I would not have gotten away myself.'

'In other words,' said Bond, 'he went on as if he'd decided not to believe you as soon as he set eyes on you.'

Ariadne nodded vigorously. 'Right. I was exactly the person he couldn't believe. I'm Greek, so I'm backward and stupid and a peasant. Then I'm a woman.'

'Oh, he's . . .' – Litsas gestured – 'one of the boys, is he?'

'Yes: you should have seen the look he gave Yanni. You ask him. Well, also I'm middle-class, so I'm a sentimental idiot who can't understand politics. And finally I'm GRU and Arenski's KGB.'

'Yes, that would certainly make you enemies,' said Litsas dryly. 'It must.'

Bond grinned. 'The GRU is the Intelligence agency of the Red Army, Niko. They go in for ordinary regular spying too. That brings them up against the other lot, the KGB. They're the secret police and much larger and more powerful. There's quite a bit of rivalry there.'

'Rivalry!' said Ariadne with a snort. 'Jealousy and hate. A private cold war. You remember Oleg Penkovski, the GRU colonel who spied for the West with that English businessman, Greville Wynne, and committed suicide in prison in 1965. 'Yes,' she went on as Bond looked up quickly, 'the official story is that he was shot in '63, but really they were keeping him in the hope of using him in a conspiracy against the Americans. Then by poisoning himself he escaped them after all. Anyway, everybody in the capitalist countries wondered why he became a spy – it wasn't money, you see. All of us in the GRU know that Penkovski was having revenge on the KGB, getting back at them the only way he could for what they'd done to him and his friends and . . .'

Ariadne checked herself. Bond gave her a sardonic glance and chain-lit another cigarette.

'Well, no help from the general,' he said. 'In fact we must keep out of his way. We've learnt that much.'

'More. A survivor from the cruiser is in the hospital here. Arenski's going to check on him.'

Bond and Litsas exchanged a glance. 'So he was picked up after all, James. Interesting.'

'That's about as much as you can say. We haven't the resources to watch him and find out who goes to see him and I can't believe he's any threat to us. Von Richter is our lead. Where do we start looking?'

'The harbour. Always the harbour. We can be safe there for a short time and we must get some food, real food, hot food, meat, not these meals of a shepherd. And I'd like to refuel; the range of this tub is only a couple of hundred miles. Off we go, then.'

Litsas drained his glass and disappeared in the direction of the engine-room. Bond glanced at Ariadne. The girl's light-brown eyes were veiled and the firm Grecian mouth drooped at the corners. He put his hand gently on the back of her neck.

'What is it, Ariadne?'

'Oh, darling, I'm so depressed. A big operation like this and they put that man in charge of Security, a fat little fairy, a ... a monster of complacency. At least they were competent before. What's happened?'

'I could read you a lecture about bureaucracy and how promoting people for political reasons means not getting the best people, but I'll spare you that. Forget it. Rely on Niko and me. And yourself. We'll do what Arenski couldn't.'

Ariadne nestled against him. Bond grinned to himself. Not the least oddity of this adventure was finding himself promising a Soviet agent that Soviet interests would be safeguarded. If M ever heard about that, he would—

The engine caught and Bond's mind shut down.

*   *   *

The main harbour of Vrakonisi, though comparatively small, is one of the best in the southern Aegean, safe and comfortable in any weather except a southerly gale, which is uncommon in these waters. Most volcanic islands rise too steeply out of the sea to afford decent anchorages – the bay of Santorini, for instance, is over a thousand feet deep, and you must tie up to the shore or to a communal buoy – but a primeval disturbance of the sea-bed has tilted part of Vrakonisi northward, reducing the angle of its cliffs and providing a shallow strip up to eighty yards or so from the shore. This area is bounded by two short moles, the western one visibly dating back to Venetian times. Here, after refuelling, the *Altair* moored.

Bond stood on the mole in the brilliant sunshine, waiting for the others to join him and looking about. There was plenty to see. The basin to his right was full of small craft: yachts, fishing-boats, transport vessels (most of Vrakonisi's needs have to be supplied by water), and a fleet of the little twenty- and thirty-footers necessary to an island where roads are few and bad and many inhabited places are virtually inaccessible except from the sea. Ahead, a row of small buildings lined the waterfront. At the near end were whitewashed cottages with blue or tan shutters and doors, then a grocery, a ship's supplier, harbour offices, a *tavérna* with a faded green awning. No neon, no cars, no souvenir shops. Not yet.

Litsas and Ariadne came ashore and the three moved off towards the bustle of the little port. From behind it the faltering zigzag of a dirt road led to the dazzling white scatter of the town, built on and around half a dozen minor crests at four or five hundred feet. And everywhere – apart from the slopes of an isolated limestone peak standing against the sky, older even than the volcano itself – ran the fantastic horizontal bands of igneous rock, black lava, porous white and yellow tufa, harder, more violently coloured strata of crimson, royal purple, seaweed-green. Vrakonisi is an unforgettable sight, but strange, even disturbing, rather than beautiful, in some way out of key with human habitation. The legend Bond had heard from Ariadne came irrepressibly to his mind. It struck him now as in one sense truer than any geological chronicle could be, in that it expressed the almost supernatural awe which any serious attempt to visualize so gigantic an upheaval must inspire.

They had a late lunch of fish soup made with plenty of lemon-juice, and half a dozen each of the admirable little quail-sized birds that fall to the gun all over Greece at this time of the year, accompanied by a sensible modicum of retsina. Litsas refused coffee and took himself off, explaining he must visit the harbourmaster's office, not merely to stay within the law by presenting the *Altair*'s papers there, but to keep his ears open and drop a few carefully-framed questions in that centre of island gossip.

He was back within the hour. The brown eyes were snapping and the mouth compressed in a kind of mirthless downward smile. One glance at him showed that he had news.

With a flourish he sat down, called for coffee now, and leant forward over interlaced fingers. 'Two points,' he said in a lowered voice. 'I believe I have traced von Richter. A mysterious Dutchman who's calling himself Vanderveld and says he's studying rocks has taken a cottage near the eastern tip of the island. He has with him another man, a young one, also supposed to study rocks. It wasn't difficult to find this out. Von Richter hasn't tried very much to hide himself. He dined at this *tavérna* last evening. Of course, he didn't think he could be recognized. I think he was never within a hundred miles of here during the Occupation. We've had good luck.'

Bond frowned. 'Niko – forgive me, but how do we know we have the right man? A description can't really—'

'My dear chap, I have some sense. Von Richter had a special mark. He has got a blast from a gun in the face. The gases from the muzzle have given him a bad burn on the left side of the head. That ear was damaged, and the skin near it, and he lost some hair for always. Our friend the Dutchman who likes rocks had the same thing. Enough?'

'I'm prepared to go along with it, yes.' Although he spoke coolly, Bond felt a surge of excitement. All day his restlessness at the lack of action had been sharpened by the fear that the right way to action might never be found, that the three of them might be ignominiously and hopelessly reduced to spending the crucial night in the offing of the islet, ready to pit the *Altair* and a rifle and tommy-gun against whatever mass-assassination weapon the Chinese had in store. Now at any rate they had a meaningful next step. But there was something else first. 'What was the second point?'

'Oh yes.' Litsas drained his coffee and chased it with ice-water. 'It would be useless to ask at the hospital. Our man walked out of it as soon as they'd bandaged him. On his way down into the town he met a farmer on a mule and he made him tie his shoes up. The farmer offered him a ride on the mule, but he said he would walk. Some people in the town asked him to stop and rest, but he wouldn't. Everybody's talking about it and saying the farmer should have made the man go back to the hospital. Anyway, the thing is that when last seen, this chap was walking to the west. Where the Russians are having their meeting on the islet. The opposite direction to von Richter's hide-out. What do you make from that?'

'Two hide-outs,' said Bond, gazing at the scrubbed boards of the table. A memory was stirring, pushing feebly at the threshold of his consciousness. Something small, something recent. To grope for it was no good, he knew; to thrust it away might double its pressure, force it in the end to break through. He went on, 'They'll join forces soon. Tonight; they can't leave it any later. The business end of the operation is presumably in the western part of the island rather than the east, so it must be von Richter who'll be making a move. The question is how. This house he's taken, Niko: is there a road to it or a path or anything, do you know?'

'Above the house there are some vine-terraces, but you must climb a cliff to reach them. Not impossible, but very hard. I think we can forget that. He'll move by water.'

'So we watch the place from the *Altair* and follow him when he comes out,' said Ariadne briskly. 'Obvious.'

Litsas made a face. 'That will be damn tricky, my dear. If we're near enough to see we're near enough to be seen. I can't see how to help that. We're somebody who just happens to be passing? Then he waits until we pass. Very very tricky indeed.'

'So we dowse our lights.'

'The moon'll be up.'

'I saw him!' said Bond suddenly. They looked at him. 'Not von Richter, the man from the hospital. This morning, while we were waiting for you to come back, Ariadne. He was scrambling down the hillside in a clumsy sort of way, as if he were injured. From where he was he might have been making for any one of half a dozen houses along that shore. But we know the area now.'

'How can you know he was that chap?' asked Litsas.

'I'd bet anything you like. I remember asking myself what could be so urgent that it would make an obviously handicapped man undertake a bloody awful ordeal like that. It was him all right, going to report to his lords and masters.'

'But that's the northern shore.' Litsas still seemed dissatisfied. 'You can't even see the islet from there.'

'And they can't see you. We've no hope of understanding that part of it at this stage. What we have got is what to do next. We go off now and sail past that part of the coast at a discreet distance and find somewhere to . . .'

Litsas's expression changed and his body grew rigid. His hand on Bond's forearm felt like heavy metal. He said in a strangled undertone, 'He's here. Herr Hauptmann Ludwig von Richter. To your right. James. Coming out of the grocer's. You can look at him. They still stare at the foreigners in these parts.'

Bond turned his head casually and at once caught sight of the German about twenty yards away. In sports shirt and shorts, a bulging shopping-bag in his hand, the man was looking over his shoulder and laughing, sharing some joke with the grocer. His companion, a fair-haired youngster carrying a wine-jar, grinned amiably. Between them they made an attractive picture of holiday high spirits, innocence, relaxation. Then von Richter faced his front and Bond saw the livid patch of skin round the ear and the dark hairless region above it. Chatting light-heartedly, the pair turned away and moved off along the quay.

'Going home,' said Litsas. 'I'll just stroll along and have a look at their boat. Might help us later.'

He left. Ariadne said, 'James, one thing puzzles me. With plenty of others. Why do they want this guy along? He always might be recognized. What's so special about him that they must have him?'

'A good point. I suppose he might have done some work for

them before. Then he's an ex-army man. That could have its uses all right.'

Ariadne nodded thoughtfully. 'Then you're thinking of some sort of gun. A gun on the land more likely than the sea ?'

'Oh God, there's no knowing at this stage. Land diversion, sea attack, the other way round. Anything.'

Another thoughtful nod, but one that suggested a private train of reasoning being pursued. 'There are millions of ex-army men. This one's an atrocity expert. That's what's special about him. But why must they have one ? And that gun still bothers me. How could you get anything big enough up that slope ? And how was it brought here ? Perhaps there's a sort of gun that—'

'Atomics,' said Bond grimly. 'Close-support type. That would be portable enough. At the moment I can't think of any feasible alternative.'

The thought silenced them both until Litsas returned.

'A biggish dinghy thing with an outboard motor,' he reported. 'They're casting off now – we'll give 'em five minutes.'

'There's a matter we can settle in those five minutes,' said Bond. 'Yanni.'

'What about him ?'

'Well, we've got to pay him off now, haven't we ? We shan't get another chance.'

Litsas considered. 'I know we said we'd do that, but must we, the way things have turned out ? He's good with the knife. And he's jolly useful on board. He can stay out of the really bad part.'

'Look, Niko.' Bond faced the other man squarely. 'Yanni is going. Right away. The kid's got a family, I suppose, parents ? Well, how's anybody going to face them if Yanni's damaged or killed ? And there are other ways of being damaged than just physically. Enough has happened to Yanni already on this trip.'

'I didn't think of that,' said Litsas, looking crestfallen and self-reproachful now. 'Of course you're right. There's a chap I know just along there who will go to Piraeus late this evening. I'll fix it up with him.'

Ten minutes later, after a brisk exchange of handshakes, Yanni had been dropped and the *Altair* was standing out from the port. In one of those mental film-clips that the memory sometimes records at such moments, Bond registered everything around him in all its hard-edged clarity.

Astern were the gay variegated tints of the harbour, sails, awnings, flags of a dozen nations and freshly-painted hulls showing among a dense thicket of masts, and above all this the natural colours of Vrakonisi itself, no less diverse, but grim and ancient, giant washes and scribblings on a raw pile of rock with a life-span measured in millions of years. To Bond's right Litsas was at the wheel, dark eyes narrowed, brown hands easing the bows round to starboard; to the left Ariadne stood poised like a statue, clothed marble, fine tendrils of tawny hair blowing forward above her ears in the evening breeze. And ahead, the sun going down like a fat incandescent orange and a hint of lead entering the steely brightness of the enormous sea.

Chapter 15

'Walk, Mister Bond'

BOND SAT on the moonlit hillside two hundred feet above
water-level and longed for a cigarette. He had found a
lump of granite the size of a golf-hut which gave him shadow
and something to lean his back against. It was not a perfect
observation post but it was the best that could have been hoped
for after a hurried visual reconnaissance from the deck of the
Altair just before the daylight went. Stationed at a roughly
central point above and behind the five scattered houses
marked down earlier as possible headquarters of the enemy,
he had a direct view of two, could see a third by moving fifty
yards to his left, and had a clear enough grasp of the positions
of the fourth and fifth to make it impossible for von Richter's
boat, even if it approached unlit, to put people ashore without
giving away their destination.

For the moment all seemed in order. While sailing past they
had spotted a tiny beach no bigger than a billiard-table, with
what was evidently a climbable outlet to the steep slopes above.
Down there, after a lot of grumbling, Litsas had agreed to
remain and watch developments from a lower angle, the dinghy
hauled up behind a tongue of rock that would, by night at any
rate, mask it from seaward observation. The *Altair*, with an
even more rebellious Ariadne on board, was a mile and half
away on the southern coast, tied up at the quay of a fishing
village among a dozen other boats of similar build, the best
camouflage available.

Though most of the time the silence was immense, it was
not altogether unbroken. Until an hour before, a wireless or
gramophone in the nearest house had been playing snatches
of *bouzouki* music, that curious amalgam of conventional

Western harmonies and Slav, Turkish and Arab rhythms and turns of phrase, a style in which the best singers, with their broken, complaining intonation, can blend together harshness, sexual excitement and desolate sorrow. Now the exotic melodies had faded and the house they came from was in darkness, but its neighbour was still lit up and an occasional snatch of talk or laughter drifted up to Bond on the warm air. Once or twice he had heard the wavering, chilly call of an owl from the crags above him and, immeasurably far off in the direction of the town, the clink of a goat-bell. Otherwise nothing.

Bond peered at the luminous dial of the Rolex Oyster Chronometer on his wrist. Three ten. He had no doubt that his basic reasoning was correct and that von Richter would come. When he would come was another question. First light was favourable, but arrival at some other time could not be ruled out, even possibly well on into the following morning with everything out in the open, von Richter and his companion welcomed as house guests. That would almost certainly put paid to any reasonable hopes of effective counter-measures. Typically, Bond did not allow himself to pursue this train of thought, but he was coldly aware that this operation was becoming more and more of a slippery slope, on which not merely a false step, but miscalculation of any detail of the lay-out could be fatal.

Then he heard the boat.

It was approaching from the west, coming round the corner where the islet was. In a couple of minutes it puttered into view, carrying navigation lights and a rather dim white one for'ard. When it had completed its rounding movement it ran parallel with the shore for perhaps a quarter of a mile, then turned in and began to make straight towards the farther of the two houses Bond could see from his post, the one whose lights were still burning. No fuss, no elaborate concealment, no double-bluff blaze of publicity either. Bond nodded to himself and got to his feet. He must get down for a closer look.

Losing lateral distance but gaining time, he began by moving back down the way he had come, a zigzagging trough at about ten degrees from the vertical between two banks of granite slabs. Next, an all-fours scramble across a larger, smoother expanse canted like the deck of a foundering stone ship, a drop of eight feet on to bare soil, a piece of straightforward rock-climbing down a cliff-face pocked and knobbed with erosion – the last and most exposed stretch protected from upward view by a bulging overhang. This first leg of the descent had taken care of about half the height he needed to lose, but had brought him a hundred yards or so too far to the east. Here was a handy left turn, a natural terrace running parallel to the shore-line for almost the length of a football-pitch, the first half of it at least in the visual lee of the overhang, and level going. Underfoot was rich springy turf like the green of a well-kept English golf-course. When had he been at Sunningdale? Tuesday afternoon. And this was Friday night, or rather the small hours of Saturday. A fairly strenuous three days.

At the point where the ground began to fall away to his right Bond dropped to his knees and looked down. The boat was coming in at reduced speed. Part of an anchorage was in view but the house itself was still hidden. Further lateral and downward movement needed. He hurried to the end of the terrace-like formation, bending low to use the dark background of a straggle of stunted thorn-bushes. Now, in bright moonlight, a wide bare slope of whitish rock littered with loose stones, the mouth of a narrow gully downhill at its far side. There was no time for a detour. Bond walked slowly and deliberately across the exposed slope, his eyes on the ground. He would be seen only by somebody who happened to be looking in his direction; if he dislodged a stone he would make his presence obvious to anyone with ears. The boat's engine had been cut and he could hear voices. He listened with held breath for the sudden urgency in their tones which would show he had been spotted. They murmured levelly on.

He reached the gully. It was an irregular fissure in the granite, twisting this way and that but leading him down in the general direction of the house, its floor smooth and over-grown with tall coarse grasses, such that it might have been a dried-up stream if watercourses of any sort had existed in the island. Twice he had to push his way into and through the clinging, ripping embrace of bushes that filled his path from wall to wall. Then a swing to the left, a bad moment when those walls leaned towards each other and he had to crawl for five yards or more, a rapid drop eased by a sort of straggling banister on the seaward side, another corner, and he was there, very much there, dangerously near.

Cover first. He glided into the protective shadow of a slab shaped like the gable end of a farmhouse that lay across the lip of the gully as if it had fallen there yesterday, though it must have reached its present position before Vrakonisi was on any map. The nearest angle of the house was less than thirty yards away, its flat roof on a level with where he crouched; that could wait. A little farther off at about ninety degrees, von Richter was just stepping on to a miniature stone quay. Bond caught the shiny, hairless patch of skin above the left ear. A short heavy man with a round head, who had been making fast at the bow of the boat, now moved amidships and, with the help of von Richter's blond assistant, heaved ashore what looked like a large sports-bag. Bond craned forward. The bag bulged oddly and was clearly awkward and heavy. There followed perhaps a dozen boxes about eight inches square, of dark-painted metal as far as could be made out in the illumination of the one light on the boat and another, not much stronger, on a bracket at the corner of the house. The boxes too seemed heavy for their size. Then, incongruously, came two smart tartan-panelled, plastic-covered suitcases. So far, the unloading had proceeded more or less in silence. Now a voice spoke.

The speaker was somewhere at the front of the house and out of view. His voice was pitched at a conversational level, in key with the casual, non-furtive atmosphere of the whole landing procedure. The man addressed von Richter by name and welcomed him to the house in the most ordinary terms. Unexpectedly, he spoke in English, but much more striking were his odd pronunciation, as if instead of learning the language he had had it fed into him mechanically, and, through a thin veneer of pleasantness, the unmistakable ring of authority in his tone. Bond knew that he had heard the enemy leader speaking. He waited as patiently as he could for a sight of the man.

For the moment, evidently, he was to be denied this. Von Richter, calling a greeting in return, moved across to the front of the house, extending his right hand just as he went out of sight. There was more talk (indistinguishable), a laugh or two, and the voices faded as if the speakers had gone indoors. The light on the boat was dowsed. The stocky man and the fair-haired lad picked up the sports-bag between them, carried it past Bond's hiding-place and in at a side door. They returned and made a series of journeys with the boxes, then the suit-cases. The door shut with an air of finality. The light at the angle of the house went out. Silence fell, except for a mutter of talk and the occasional faint slap of water under the hull of the moored boat.

Bond stretched himself full length in the darkness and prepared to wait out the chance of something left on board being remembered and returned for. To assume that he had just had a view of the assassination weapon and its ammu-nition seemed irresistible – part of that weapon, at least: the mounting must be elsewhere, brought here separately. Even so, surely the bloody thing was far too *small*. Nothing that size, with its inevitably puny muzzle-velocity, could do more than bounce a shell off the walls of the house on the islet, stoutly built of local stone. The dismal thought suggested itself that his first guess had been right, that this was to be the centre for a diversion and that the real attack was to come by sea, launched from somewhere there would be no chance of finding. Then he thrust this away. The leaders were here; it was here that mattered.

He hung on for another twenty minutes. No change. He moved.

It took him something over an hour to make a slow, careful circuit of the house and the possible approaches. At the end of that time he had satisfied himself that there were no trip-wires or similar alarm systems, that no sort of access from the sea was both physically practicable and free of a strong risk of immediate detection, and that, in addition to the gully he had used tonight, a good alternative route led directly down the hillside to within ten seconds' dash of a terrace at the back of the house. The terrace was a difficult but possible climb for one man, no problem for two.

Back in his shelter under the horizontal slab, Bond weighed chances and times. At the moment, with the moon down, the darkness was entire, relieved only by starlight, but the first signs of dawn could be expected within fifteen minutes. He must be off soon. But a glimpse of the internal lay-out of the house would be invaluable. He walked briskly down the final slope and across rough stone flags to the side door of the house. Without hesitation he lifted it against its hinges by the shank of the knob and turned slowly, producing a single, almost inaudible squeal of metal. Then, still lifting, alert for the first beginnings of a creak, he pushed. The door yielded. A millimetre at a time now.

In five minutes or so he had an aperture a foot wide. He took in the staircase in profile ahead of him, the beginning of steps on the left that must lead to the rear terrace, a dimly-lit corridor with rooms opening off it. At once, as if activated by his glance, the door of one of these rooms opened and somebody started to come out.

What saved Bond for the moment was that whoever was emerging paused at the threshold as if to exchange a word with another person inside the room. Bond shut the side door in an agonized conflict of care and speed, turned and ran. Before he was halfway up the slope the external light flicked on. He dived into his refuge and was facing the house, Walther in hand, without an instant's conscious thought.

This was a justified precaution. The side door opened and von Richter came out. He glanced around for a moment or two, then walked purposefully up the slope straight for where Bond was lying. Bond took aim at the German's chest. The man came on until he was a bare five yards away. Abruptly he turned aside and passed out of view. Bond waited two minutes, three minutes. He could hear nothing, assumed that von Richter had halted somewhere close by. Waiting for something, for somebody. Now another man came out of the side door and Bond had his first sight of Colonel Sun Liang-tan.

He stared hard at the tall spare figure as it approached, the shoulders and hips loosely jointed, rolling easily, the yellow face set in a faint smile, presumably in the direction of von Richter, but not altering its basic impassivity. Movements and expression gave an air of vast careless power. This was a man who would do anything. Bond was considerably impressed, but he grinned savagely to himself at this confirmation of another guess. All the way from China, by God!

The man followed the direction von Richter had taken. Ten to fifteen yards away, and slightly above Bond's position the two began to talk.

'Is this place suitable for your purposes?' asked the first voice in English, the same English as Bond had heard earlier from the front of the house.

'Yes, Colonel, I'm sure it will do admirably.' An unexpected light drawl, accented but agreeable. 'Not on the rock, of course. I may have to water the soil a little, but I can experiment with that later. So. Quite satisfactory. Perhaps we could have the light off now.'

'Certainly.' The Chinese raised his voice. 'Evgeny! The light, please.'

Evgeny: a Russian. That would be the stocky man.

'Now we shall see exact operating conditions,' the curious tones went on. 'I think you'll find we've timed it correctly.'

The light went out.

'We shall have to wait a little while to recover our full vision,' said von Richter, 'but it looks to me already all right.'

All right indeed! Bond bit his lip. Ten seconds was enough to show him that dawn was already on the way. The first faint tinges of colour were beginning to steal into his surroundings, the rocks, the vegetation, the side of the house. How long were these two going to continue their parley?

Infuriatingly, neither spoke for several minutes. Then the German said, 'There! You see him?'

'Ah yes. Excellent.'

'We're using a simple colour code which we've brought to

something near perfection this last month. As I told you, we had every facility. Enjoyable work. And the necessary *research*' – von Richter put a special emphasis on this word; Bond imagined an accompanying grimace or gesture – 'was fascinating.'

'And conclusive, I hope.'

'Yes, yes. It'll look right and be right. Ballistically and medically. You can be positive on that point.'

The Chinese muttered something polite and silence fell again.

Bond was sweating. He had just made up his mind to shoot both men in the back as they returned to the house and count on surprise to deal with Evgeny and the blond boy and whoever else was about. He wiped his right hand on the torn knee of his slacks and settled himself more firmly.

'Well, I think we've seen enough for now,' said von Richter. 'Willi and I will line up after breakfast.'

'Very good. This Willi – how did a boy like that take to the research?'

'Remarkably well. He's had rather an interesting history, young Willi. His father was one of Himmler's men; the Americans hanged him at Nuremberg – you know, the usual war-crimes fantasy. Willi was a baby in arms then . . .'

There was more, but Bond stopped listening. The voices were retreating in the direction of the anchorage. He brought his gun up and waited. Perversely, the two did not cross diagonally from where they had been standing, but evidently walked straight to the water's edge. When they finally came into sight they were between seventy and eighty feet away. Bond dismissed it at once as not worth trying: the light was still poor and the chances of an effective left-and-right negligible. Unless they turned back. . . . But no; awkwardly bunched from his point of view, they strolled past the upperworks of the boat and disappeared behind the front of the house. So much for that.

Poor the light might have been for an aimed shot, but it was already uncomfortably good enough for movement to be spotted, and increasing as if a screened lamp-wick were being turned up. Bond spent a minimal three minutes listening for any sign of the return of the German and the Chinese, then came out of his shelter and started up the gully. But going up was slower than coming down, and by the time he reached the upper end the sun was showing signs of appearing. He paused here to breathe and consider; the stony slope looked horribly exposed; still, there it was, a naked streak of hillside he would have to climb a hundred feet to get round. So . . . He got to his feet, squared his shoulders and walked steadily over to the far side. Up on to the level stretch, walking as before – no point in using the thorn-bushes as background in this light – and into the shelter of the overhang. On to where the flat pathway ended.

Ahead of him now, and below, lay an extraordinary geological formation, or rather hundreds of these: a great jumble of squarish and near-rectangular stone blocks twenty and thirty feet high and stretching for half a mile, piled next to and upon and across one another so haphazardly that gaining ten yards in the desired direction meant climbing and descending twice as many. Above and below were cliffs. On Bond's outward journey it had taken him fifty minutes to cross this dump of outsize nursery bricks; even now he could not hope to do it in less than thirty. Still, once past it there was a short rise to a level platform of rock, and after that an easy descent to the beach and the boat. On with it, then.

In the event it took him well over the half-hour. He was moving up on to the rock platform when a man on the far side of it got up and levelled a revolver at him.

He was a tall man in a cheap dark suit, now crumpled and torn. Binoculars in a green plastic case were slung across his shoulder. He said in a thick Russian accent, 'Good morning, Mister Shems Bond,' and sniggered.

Bond stood stock still and waited.

'I see you from . . . up,' the man went on in a tone of good-humoured explanation. 'Now . . . we go up.' He pointed to the hillside with his left hand.

Bond made no move.

'No? Then ... shoot you. Not too bad.' The Russian slapped his leg. 'Friend of me ... up.' He made hoisting and carrying motions, but the revolver never wavered. 'Is difficult. You fall maybe. Me ... that's all right.' Another snigger.

It was plain enough. The only hope was to wait for a chance of finding a moment's cover from the revolver during the proposed climb and before the absent friend made his appearance. Bond nodded.

'Good boy.' A gold-toothed grin. 'Come to here.' The left hand indicated a point on the platform well beyond rushing distance. Bond went to it.

'Now ... gun of you. Slow, please. Slow slow.'

The revolver pointed steadily at Bond's breast-bone. Nobody can aim and fire faster than a man already on aim can fire. Helplessly, Bond took the Walther from his hip pocket and held it out in the palm of his hand.

'Intelligent. Throw ... away.'

Another chance gone. Bond tossed his automatic aside and heard it land on rock.

'Friend of you' – a gesture towards the beach – 'no good, eh? Now ... walk, Mister Bond. Slow slow.'

Bond was on the point of obeying when the other lurched abruptly as if slapped hard on the back and the unmistakable sharp bang of a medium-calibre cartridge came apparently from beneath their feet, immediately followed by the sound, thin but clear, of a rifle-bolt being pulled back and returned. There was one echo of the shot, distant and delayed.

The man's gun-arm had dropped. His eyes held Bond's with a dreadful look of puzzlement, of pleading to be told how this thing could have happened. Bond said hoarsely, 'You've been shot with a rifle, from the beach.' His heart was thumping. He never knew if his message was understood. The Russian had half turned to look behind him when a second shot flung him off balance. He went down the slope in a sort of slack-limbed dive and finished with his face in a heap of small stones. There was a patch of blood on one shoulder-blade and another above the hip.

After scooping up the Walther Bond made it to the beach

in two minutes. Litsas had the dinghy already in the water, pushed off at once and grabbed the oars.

'Good shooting, Niko,' said Bond at length.

'Not bad, eh? Uphill too, but fighting in Greece makes you used to that. Anyhow, not more than two hundred yards. I dropped a Jerry staff-sergeant once at six hundred with that little beauty.' He gave the Lee Enfield, now lying across Bond's lap, an affectionate nod. 'These fellows today forget all about the rifle. If they see nothing for fifty feet all round they think they're safe. Eh, I bet our friend up there had a very big shock when I hit him.'

'He did,' said Bond in a hard voice, remembering the look on the man's face.

'I was watching jolly carefully but I had no idea he was there until he popped up at you. Didn't give me much time.'

'He saw you all right. He said as much.'

'Oh, really? Then he had no excuse at all to show himself to me like that and to stay exposed while he waved his gun at you. Who was he, anyhow?'

'One of Arenski's men. He saw me while he was patrolling the hillside and came down to cut me off.'

'I'm afraid we make the brave general very angry. Let's hope he doesn't try to interfere with our plans for tonight.'

Chapter 16

The Temporary Captain

AT NOON that day the *Altair* was five miles due south of the port of Vrakonisi, running north-westwards. Visibility was excellent, promising fair weather to come, but the sea had again got up a little since the early morning, and the caique, moving diagonally across the direction of the waves, lurched clumsily from time to time. More clumsily, in fact, than an experienced hand at the wheel would have permitted.

George Ionides was relatively inexperienced with boats of this sort, though he was an expert handler of his own little coastal runabout, the twenty-four-foot *Cynthia*. He hoped the weather would not get any worse before it got better, not for his own sake – his next few hours' sailing would be mostly in the protection of one island or another – but for the sake of the *Cynthia* and, to a less extent, of the people now on board her. What did they want with her and where were they making for?

First things first. With a satisfied grin, George brought the head of the *Altair* round just far enough to take an extra steep sea squarely under the bow and so forestall any tendency to roll. He was learning fast; he always had. It was a matter of instinct, of being a natural sailor. His grandfather had often said. . . . But forget that. Those people. They were up to something illegal, no doubt of it. The two Greeks, the man and the girl, had been smooth and plausible enough, but the other man, the hard-faced Englishman, was undoubtedly a desperate type. George Ionides had seen that immediately. It had been no surprise to him at all when, an hour previously, the men had taken aboard the *Cynthia* two objects wrapped in sacking that were clearly guns of some sort. George had politely turned his back, of course, and pretended to study the weather. It was not for nothing that he was a native of Cephalonia in the Ionian islands. That was the Cephalonian way of handling things: use your head, use your eyes, keep your mouth shut.

So, except to agree to everything proposed to him, George had kept his mouth shut when this Athenian approached him at the harbour and suggested that, for a consideration of three thousand drachmas (half now, half later), he might be willing to exchange boats for thirty-six hours or so. He had merely nodded his head, as if such things happened every day, when the Athenian stipulated that the hand-over should take place, not here at the anchorage, but at a sea rendezvous to the south, and that he should let half an hour go by before making any move to set off. He had shown no surprise, let alone resistance, when the Athenian told him very forcefully that, as soon as the transfer was complete, he must head straight on south to Ios and stay there until the two parties rejoined contact to-morrow afternoon or evening. Cheerfully and readily, he had sailed south at a good eight knots until the *Cynthia* was below the horizon. Then he had simply turned and headed north-west.

For George had never had any intention of going to Ios. Not today, anyway. By six o'clock that evening at the latest he would be moored in the port of Paros. Anything like an early start in the morning would give him a nice comfortable southward run, with the weather behind him, down to Ios in plenty of time to be sitting innocently drinking coffee outside one of the harbour *tavérnas* when the *Cynthia* arrived. He grinned to himself, then shouted to his cousin, a boy of fourteen who crewed the *Cynthia* for him and at the moment was idling in the sun on the *Altair*'s cabin-top. When he came running up, George said a few words to him, pointed briefly, and strode for'ard to the saloon, leaving the boy at the wheel. The sea had moderated as they came into the shelter of Vrakonisi, and there were no shoals off this corner of the island.

Obeying instructions to help himself to whatever he fancied, he poured a glass of *kitró* and settled down on one of the benches. He sipped luxuriously at the delicious drink – native to Naxos and obtainable only there, on Ios and on Vrakonisi –

and reflected that it was perhaps a little early, but he was on holiday. The deceptively weak-tasting liquor, bland and viscous, with the bitter tang of the lemon rind in it as well as the sugared-down sharpness of the flesh, relaxed him.

Lighting a cigarette, he glanced idly out of the window. They were passing, at a distance of about a hundred yards, the islet at the south-western tip and, on it, the grand house where a very rich foreigner was known to be staying and amusing himself with the local boyhood. These people seemed to think they could do as they liked in the islands! George made a spitting grimace. Then he noticed somebody in a dark suit, perhaps the foreigner himself, standing on the terrace of the house and apparently looking straight at him. As George watched, screwing up his eyes against the glare, the man hurried indoors, returning after a quarter of a minute with another. The new arrival examined the *Altair* for a longer period through binoculars, which he then passed to his companion. More examination. A third man now came bustling out and joined the first two. All three seemed very interested in the passing boat. George could not imagine why. He got up, strolled out to the rail and gave a friendly wave.

The effect, in a small way, was extraordinary. The three figures straightened abruptly, looked at one another and then back at the *Altair* with exactly the demeanour of a trio of priests taken off guard by some unseemly act. George waved again. This time there was a response, half-hearted at first, then suddenly enthusiastic – priests deciding to show they were men like anyone else. George laughed aloud and went back into the saloon. It was quite true, the old Greek saying that all foreigners were mad! But these were certainly rich enough, he decided a minute later, catching sight of a big grey-painted motor-boat lolling gently at the anchorage below the house. Rich. And mad. It crossed his mind uncomfortably that perhaps the cause of the recent excitement was that the *Altair* had been recognized as a stolen craft or as belonging to wanted criminals. Both these possibilities had already occurred to him. But then foreigners, tourists, took no account of such matters. He dismissed the idea.

As, half an hour later, he and the boy were finishing their bread and cheese, olives and beer on the after-deck, George's thoughts returned to Paros. The point about Paros, as far as he was concerned, was that Maria lived there. He had been engaged to her for three years, and marriage was in sight at last, but it was no use pretending that everything was as it should be. Although her parents liked him and knew he was honest, they pretty clearly did not think he had come as far in the world as, at twenty-seven, he ought to have done. Tonight he was going to show them how wrong they were. First, he would invite them all on board – Maria, her father and mother and younger sister – and show them round, offer them drinks in the saloon, explain casually that one of his friends from Athens had put the little tub at his disposal for a couple of days so that he could thoroughly try her out and see what he thought of her. Then he would take them all out to a lobster dinner, and finally buy them each a good present at one of the expensive tourist shops that lined the alleys of the town.

By way of immediate return for these efforts, George would be entitled to talk to Maria, to hold her hand and above all to look at her. He would not, of course, expect to spend much time with her alone. That had always been part of the system, the way life was arranged. George was tall and well-built and dark-eyed, and working in the tourist trade brought him plenty of sexual opportunities. He took them. Nobody minded that, but a great many people would have minded a great deal if he had started trying to treat his affianced bride in public like a German or English office-girl on holiday. He knew that some of the younger people made a mock of the system, but it suited him well enough. (It had never occurred to George to wonder what Maria thought of the system.)

However, at times when he was picturing Maria in his mind, as now, he would find himself trying to imagine in detail what lay beneath her spotless white dress, what that swelling bosom would be like to see and touch, what she would do when he . . . George pulled himself together. Such thoughts were useless as well as disturbing – if he had been backward and provincial, instead of modern and sophisticated, he would have called them sinful.

They left his mind for good when he glanced astern. A shape rapidly overhauling them soon identified itself as the motor-boat he had seen moored at the islet. This was puzzling, and a little frightening. George Ionides examined his conscience and, as best he could, his legal standing. The paperwork position might be irregular, but he had done nothing against the law by temporarily swapping boats with a man whose good faith he had had no specific reason to doubt. George held to his course.

The motor-boat came up, matched its speed to the *Altair*'s and stayed parallel with it. The three men George had seen by the house watched him again. He waited, maintaining speed. Half a mile off, a fishing-boat chugged past in the opposite direction and, on the horizon, a streak of smoke showed where one of the big passenger steamers was making its way down to Sikinos.

Presently a hail came in Greek.

—What ship are you?

—*Altair*, Piraeus. What ship are you? George added with a boldness he had not consciously intended.

This was ignored. —Who are you?

—George Ionides, temporary captain.

—Who is with you?

—Only my cousin, this boy here.

There was discussion in the motor-boat. Then:

—We will come aboard you.

—By what right?

—That of the Royal Hellenic Coastguard Authority.

George knew of no such body, but this time he had the sense to keep his mouth shut in the Cephalonian way. It was obvious now that he had landed himself in trouble of some magnitude, and there was no point in worsening matters by futile argument. Powerful people, such as these clearly were, whichever side of the law they might be on, were notoriously touchy. An ill-advised word might put paid to his chances of getting to Paros at all. He cut back the motor and said to his cousin,

—This is a nuisance, little one, but nothing to worry about. I expect they're looking for some big criminal from Athens. They want to make sure we're not carrying him. It's what they call routine. Now, as soon as they've come aboard, you take the wheel so that I can talk to them.

A little later, the three men completed their fruitless search of the *Altair* and confronted George on the afterdeck. Two of the party were foreigners, disagreeable-looking fellows with tight mouths; the third was fat and soft and looked like the worst sort of Greek, perhaps a Salonikan. One of the foreigners spoke in a language that sounded to George like a form of Bulgarian. The fat man translated.

—Where is the man Bond?

—I know nobody of that name.

—You are lying. He was on this ship a few hours ago.

George shrugged. The fat man went on translating.

—There was an Englishman on board this morning, wasn't there?

—Yes. He didn't tell me his name. We had no dealings with each other.

—Where is he now?

—I have no idea. He did not confide in me.

—You are lying, you lump of excrement. Where did you last see this man? And this time see that you speak the truth.

—About fifteen miles away. At sea, south of Vrakonisi. He and his friends took over my boat and I theirs.

—Where were they bound for?

—I have already answered that. I don't know.

Before the fat man had had time to translate this, one of the foreigners shoved himself forward, caught George by the front of his shirt and shook him to and fro. At the same time he shouted his horrible language into George's face.

This was a mistake. Coming on top of the abuse, the false accusations of lying made in what was for the time being his own territory, and accompanied as they were by an odour of rotting potatoes, these ravings had the effect of making George forget that he was a Cephalonian and reminding him that he was a Greek. For the moment, it seemed to him that he could pick up these three tricksters one by one and drop them over the side. He brought his muscular forearm down hard on the foreigner's wrists and gave him a push that sent him staggering against the mast. With all the dignity he could muster, George said,

—Unless you produce your documents immediately I must order you to leave my ship.

This was a much more serious mistake. The words were hardly out of his mouth before, slammed in the belly and pistol-whipped behind the ear, George was grovelling half-conscious on the deck. He heard his cousin cry out in protest, then in pain. The fat man spoke.

—Where is Bond?

—I don't know. I'd tell you if I did. I don't know.

There was a pause. Somebody gave an order. More pause. George, in the act of trying to get up on his hands and knees, was flung on to his back. His ankles were grasped and held wide apart. Then there exploded at his right knee a pain such as he would never have believed possible, a pain that instantly flooded up his thigh and into the whole right-hand side of his pelvis and through his guts. A pain compared with which all other pain was a mere discomfort, an itch, a tickle.

George had been struck with the heel of a shoe on the medial condyle of the femur, the boss of bone at the inside of the knee. This is the most immediately devastating assault that can be inflicted on the human frame. It triggers off vomiting in the strongest and bravest of subjects. George vomited.

—Now. Where is Bond?

—. . . I don't know. He didn't tell me. I think they turned east. I didn't notice.

Some discussion.

—Very well. Give the name of your boat and describe it fully.

George did as he was told; this was not a situation in which you kept your mouth shut. He gave a very full description of the *Cynthia*. He was still adding details when there was another explosion, inside his head this time, and the sun went out.

Chapter 17

In the Drink

GEORGE IONIDES had been right in his impression that Bond and his companions had moved off east after parting company with him, but his questioners would not have found it helpful to follow this up. As pre-arranged, no sooner had the *Altair* disappeared to the south than Litsas had made a U-turn and headed straight back to Vrakonisi. By three o'clock the *Cynthia* was anchored in a small bay on the southern coast of the island and almost at its eastern tip, a full eight miles by sea from the islet. A dozen small craft lay near by and there were groups of figures on shore.

The place was more a jagged hole bitten into the coastline than a bay in any full sense. In one corner a granite shelf just above the water-line, narrow but level, made landing comparatively easy. Next to this, a dozen yards of sloping shingle constituted as much of a beach as nine-tenths of all island bays provide. A succession of weird rock-formations ran along the other arm of the inlet, weird in their very regularity – cave-mouths and arches square-set enough to have formed part of a ruined Homeric palace, rectangular tower-shaped structures, tall isolated stacks like the piles of a vanished bridge, all coloured in delicate gradations between tan and olive-green. The land above was less precipitous than elsewhere in Vrakonisi, with vine-terraces and clumps of evergreens: myrtle, arbutus, and oleander.

With a gesture of finality, Litsas let down the tattered side-awning, screening the three of them from view as well as from the sun.

'We'll be safe here,' he said. 'Parties come all the time to bathe, God help them, and there's a piece of a temple up on the hill. It's mostly pavement, but the island has nothing else like this, and you don't know how small it is until you get there. Anyhow, nobody will notice a small boat of this type. I'm worried about our fuel, though. We've enough left for only about thirty miles. Shall we call quickly at the port after it's dark?'

'No.' Bond's voice was decisive. 'If, as we assumed, they do have a man at the harbour, they'll have two on tonight. We'd be risking blowing our cover. And tomorrow ... we can get all the gas we want.'

The unspoken 'if' behind this statement silenced all three for an instant. Then Litsas sprang up and lifted the rust-pocked lid of the cooler.

'I'm going to have a beer,' he grunted. 'Let's finish that too. Anybody else?'

Ariadne, sitting on the deck with her knees drawn up and her gaze lowered, shook her head. Bond also declined. He had had enough of the thin, soapy local brew.

Litsas leant the neck of the bottle against the cooler lid and banged the cap off with the end of his fist. He seemed to pour the beer straight down without swallowing.

'Now,' he said, wiping his mouth, 'again the battle-plan, James, if you please. We can't have it too many times.'

'I agree.' Bond spread open on the deck the sketch-plan he had roughed out on the back of a chart. 'We leave here at eight PM and go round by the north coast. Taking it easy, we should get to that little beach about ten ...'

More thoughtfully than before, Ariadne shook her head. 'I still say it's too early. Everybody will be awake and watching.'

'They'll be that all night tonight. They won't be expecting us then. We don't know what their time-table is, so we daren't leave it until late. And at ten o'clock there'll be plenty of other boats around, so there'll be nothing special about us.'

'That's logical,' said Ariadne in her brisk student's tone. 'Go on, James.'

'Good. We drive the *Cynthia*'s bows up on to the beach and moor her. Now, are you sure that's possible, Niko?'

'It must be, mustn't it? We can't fool about with anchor-chains then. Anyhow, leave it to me. No problem.'

'Then we climb the cliff. Not nearly as difficult as it sounds. But we'll need a sling for the tommy-gun – must have both hands free.'

Litsas nodded. 'My department. Easy.'

'Now here' – Bond put his forefinger on the sketch-map – 'there's this shelf of rock where Niko shot the Russian. Then the troublesome part I told you about; just troublesome; not difficult or dangerous. After that . . .'

Bond took over ten minutes to describe minutely the route to the enemy's house and the surrounding terrain 'We halt here,' he said finally, pointing to the last bend in the rocky gully that led down to the house. 'Niko and I move uphill and round until we're in position to make a run for the rear terrace. That move'll be easy going, comparatively. Should take us about fifteen minutes to get to our assault station. As soon as we're there, we go in together. By that time, Ariadne, you'll have moved down the gully to the cover of that slab of stone I mentioned. You'll hear us make contact all right. From then on, this is what you do. As soon as the shooting starts you begin counting slowly. If you see anybody, shoot him and go straight in at the side door. Go to the foot of the stairs and cover the rooms opening off the passage. We'll join you there. Blaze away at any stranger you see – they won't be letting my chief run about the house, you can be sure.

'Alternatively, if you *don't* see anybody early on, count on to thirty. Then you go in by the side door. But not unless there's shooting still going on inside the house. No shooting will mean that our assault has failed. In that event, go back the way you came, and get away in the *Cynthia* – Niko will make it easy for you to cast off and he'll show you how to start the motor. Then disappear. Steer well clear of the islet. It won't be a healthy place to be if these people have anything to do with it. The rest of it will be up to you. I'll give you a letter which I'd like you to take to the British Embassy in Athens.

'Any questions? Then let's all get what rest we can. We're going to need it.'

Bond's sleep, by Ariadne's side on an improvised bed of seat-cushions, was fitful and haunted. A formless being, a shape too fantastic to be identified, pursued him through his dreams. He fled from it across a perfectly smooth plain of marble. At the far side of this were geometrical rows of trees, all identical, all of formalized shape, like representations in an architect's drawing. As he ran between them, one after another exploded silently into a puff of flame, leaving nothing behind. When he looked back to see what was doing this, he found himself face to face with a brick wall constructed in a strange way, such that the bands of mortar were as broad as the bricks themselves. A distant humming roar became audible and the wall began to tilt towards him. Before it could collapse, Bond had forced himself out of sleep, but the steady humming continued. With a strong sense, even in his half-awakened state, of the illogic of the action, Bond got up, twitched aside a corner of the awning and peered out.

What he saw was, to him, disappointingly irrelevant. With the vague but oppressive memory of his dream upon him, Bond gazed lethargically at a large, expensive-looking grey motor-boat which was just throttling down in the bay. A rich party, no doubt, in search of a bathing spot. Idly, he ran his eyes over the decks of the new arrival. Nothing special was to be seen there. No movement or figure presented itself. It was as if the thing were controlled from afar by wireless.

Still drowsy, Bond dropped the awning and returned to sleep. He did not hear the muted roar of the motor-boat's engines as, its obscure mission completed, it backed away from the shore and moved slowly out of the anchorage. And, obviously, he could not have known of its arrival in the smaller inlet that lay a couple of hundred yards to the east, nor of the installation of an observer among the curious volcanic arches in the coloured rocks lining that side of the bay.

When Bond awoke finally, the light had taken on that faintest and most melancholy hint of dullness that, in Greece as nowhere else, makes late afternoon so oddly indistinguishable from early morning. Ariadne progressed in a second from deep childlike sleep to wary wakefulness. Blinking slowly, she looked at Bond.

'What do we do now?'

'What we do I don't know,' he said, kissing her. 'I only know what I do. And what I do is swim.'

'It's what I do, too.'

While Litsas slept on, they stripped to the skin and within seconds were side by side in the unbelievably clear water. Bond turned and grinned at Ariadne.

'This is rather daring of you, isn't it?' he asked. 'I thought Greek girls would die rather than be seen naked in public.'

She laughed. 'That shows how little you understand. It isn't modesty or shame, it's social respectability. Nobody around here knows who I am and they're all too far away to see anything very intimate. There's just you, and it's kind of late to begin to worry about what you see, isn't it?'

As she talked, she had been moving away from the boat and now took off towards the open sea, using a steady and unexpectedly powerful breast-stroke that looked properly economical of energy. Bond was impressed. At every turn this girl showed herself to be fine material. He followed her in the same style and found, not to his surprise, that he had to exert himself to catch up. When they were level he kept to her speed and they swam out side by side for perhaps a hundred yards. The water slid like silk along their bodies and limbs. Beneath, it was dark and dense; Bond guessed that they were already at a great depth. As they paused, he felt on his cheek a tiny breath of chilly air, a first reminder that the summer which coloured everything around them was not endless after all.

By unspoken consent, they turned and made their way back towards the boat. They had wanted to refresh and relax themselves, not take hard exercise. After a while the sea-bottom glimmered into view and Bond felt a sudden longing to dive towards it, to enter again the twilight rocky groves of the subaqueous world he loved. But not now. Another time . . .

Litsas helped them back on board. He ran an appraising

and rather obviously expert eye over Ariadne as she stepped down to the deck.

'I know I shouldn't be looking,' he said blandly. 'Because it makes me feel very non-something. What's the word that means "like an uncle"?'

'Avuncular?'

'That's it. Avuncular is how I'm not feeling. You're a lucky chap, James. Now, Ariadne, you must dry and dress quickly. I want to show you the Thompson again before the light has gone. These bike-lamps of Ionides' are perfectly bloody hopeless.'

Just before eight o'clock, Ariadne had finished her weapon-training (including the vital point of changing magazines by feel), Bond had again taken them carefully over his battle-plan, all three had swallowed a scratch meal of sausage, vegetables, and fruit, and Litsas had got the anchor up. With his hand on the shift lever, he caught Ariadne's eye.

'*Thée mou, voíthisse mas!*' he muttered, and she bowed her head. 'Sorry about that,' he went on conversationally, slipping into gear and moving the throttle up a notch. 'A little prayer. It makes us feel better. You must forgive our superstition.'

'I don't feel like that about it,' said Bond in some discomfort, wishing dully that there was somebody or something he could appeal to at a time like this.

The operation had begun on schedule. Afterwards the whole first phase became concertina-ed in Bond's memory: the move out of the dark, silent bay, the turning northward, then westward, the long eventless run under the moon past stretches of vast mountainous blackness relieved here and there by the lights of a hamlet, a tiny anchorage, a single house, the occasional passing of a small boat like their own, the monotonous vibrating hum of the little Diesel, the watery noise of the *Cynthia*'s progress and the dim whiteness spreading from her bow. Everything inevitable and apparently changeless until Litsas looked up from his seat at the tiller and said, 'I'm sorry, but I think somebody's following us. It's not easy to be sure. There. Six or seven hundred yards back.' He pointed and Bond peered along his arm. 'Somebody quite big. I don't know how long he's been there. Annoying.'

The dark shape, unlit except for its running lights, was obvious enough. There were no other craft in the offing now. The enemy, if enemy he was, had bided his time. Bond looked at his watch, then at the coast.

'Turn inshore and get all the speed you can out of this scow,' he told Litsas. 'I reckon we're about two miles from our landing-point. We'll stand a better chance ashore than afloat.'

'If we ever get there. It's a long swim.'

'He's turning with us,' said Ariadne over her shoulder. 'That proves it. Coming up fast now.'

'Take the tiller, Ariadne,' said Litsas. 'James, can I put the lights on? Good. I'm going to take the governor off this thing.' He lifted off the engine-cover and rummaged in the tool tray.

Bond gazed over the stern at their pursuer, now not much more than a furlong distant and closing rapidly. He drove his finger-nails into his palms. The prospect before them seemed virtually hopeless. The open deck gave them no cover at all and they had no cards up their sleeve. He wondered furiously how they had been identified. Perhaps Ionides had . . .

The sound of the engine rose abruptly to a shuddering whine and the *Cynthia* seemed to lean forward into the water. Litsas doused the deck lights and made his way aft.

'That engine will be scrap-iron in an hour or two. But we shan't be needing it that long, I think. Well, what do we do, captain? Sell our lives dearly?'

He had taken the Lee Enfield out of its wrapping and Bond heard him open the breech, slam a clip of .303 into the magazine and thrust the bolt home. By pure reflex, Bond touched the butt of the Walther behind his hip. He had no plan, but his despair had passed.

'It's all a matter of what these people want,' he said. 'If they're just out to obliterate us then there's nothing we can do. If they want us alive we may be able to stave them off for a bit.'

Litsas grunted. 'Well, we'll soon find out which. They can—'

He broke off as, with a kind of silent explosion, everything around them leapt into hard, glaring radiance. He felt cruelly exposed and quite defenceless. The moral effect of a one-million candle-power searchlight at under a hundred yards is tremendous, and the enemy must have known this, since the unbearable illumination continued in silence for a full quarter of a minute. Bond fought the effect for all he was worth, shutting his eyes tight, feeling for the Thompson and bringing it into the ready position. Then an amplified voice spoke in English across the water.

'Halt! Halt immediately or you will be killed!'

'Want me to put that light out, James?' said Litsas's voice.

'Save it for now and get down. You too, Ariadne. Let them decide on the next move.'

Another quarter of a minute or so went by while the *Cynthia* strained her way towards the land. Then there was the abrupt, smacking boom of a light gun and a heavy thump from the water ahead of them.

'Well, no mystery about who we're dealing with after that – General Arenski's men. Von Richter and his friends wouldn't dare to come out in the open like this hereabouts.' Bond knew what to do now. He spoke at top speed. 'We have a little time. They'll hesitate before they fire into us – their orders must be to get us alive if possible. We hang on here as long as we can. Then we have only one chance. We lash the tiller, go quietly over the side and swim for it. At the moment we must be about a mile and a half out. Could you manage that, Niko?'

'Yes. Eventually.'

'We'll wait for you. Get your rifle ready.'

'It's ready.'

The amplified voice spoke again. 'Halt at once or the next shot will hit you!'

'I'll stall them,' said Bond. He hung on as long as he dared, then called, 'Very well. I am ready to surrender to you. But on condition that you release the girl who is with me. She has no part in this affair.'

A pause. Bond counted the precious seconds. Then, 'No condition. You will surrender immediately.'

'I demand that you release the girl.'

A much shorter pause, ended by, 'You have ten seconds to switch off your engine. If you do not, we will fire into you!'

'Count to five, Niko. Ariadne, helm hard over when he hits.'

Bond held his breath and half-opened one eye. The light bored into his skull. At the first slam of the rifle beside him he opened up with the Thompson, in no hope of hitting anything, only of throwing the gunners off. Litsas fired again and the light vanished utterly. The *Cynthia* lurched wildly as the tiller came across. After an interval that seemed no longer than that between two heartbeats there came the boom of the gun and at once a dreadful tearing thud only feet away and water drenched Bond's head and shoulders. He realized he was still holding his breath and let it out with a gasp.

Laughing with triumph, Litsas was tearing off the navigation lights and flinging them one after the other over the side. 'They'll be as blind as bats for some minutes now. The trouble is they can still hear us, if anyone thinks of cutting the motor. Let's use this time. Back and across our previous course. That's it.'

Twice more the gun sounded, but the bursts were fifty and sixty yards away.

'Just angry. Here, James. I know you don't think much of it, but it feels just the same as cognac when you're in the water.'

Bond took a good swig from the proffered brandy-bottle and passed it to Ariadne. The spreading fire of the drink was physically comforting, but when he spoke his tone was bitter.

'So we're disarmed. As regards doing anything at all on shore. We might as well throw our guns into the sea now. Our only useful weapon is my knife.'

'Now quit that, James.' Ariadne had laid her hand on his shoulder. 'Our job for the moment is just getting to shore. That's quite enough to handle, isn't it?'

'It is,' said Litsas grimly. 'And I hope they can't fix that searchlight soon. We'll be for it if they can.' He gazed into the darkness. 'Ah. Making for land on the wrong course. Wait, though . . . I think they must be slowing. Yes. They've cut their engine. Time we were off. Not together. Best swimmer first.'

'Vital point,' said Bond abruptly. 'Bring your shoes. You'd be helpless without them.' He took off his espadrilles and tucked them into his waist-belt. 'Right. I'm away.'

'Then Ariadne, then me. I'll describe to her the bay. You get off, James. See you on shore.'

'Yes, Niko. Good luck.' Bond shook Litsas's hand and kissed Ariadne. He drew the Walther from his hip and dropped it over the side. Then he lowered himself into the water.

There was a mile to go, or a little less. Bond set off at the fastest speed he thought prudent; he must overtake Ariadne somewhere inshore so as to guide her to the beach. The sea was flat calm and there was no current against him. The *Cynthia* receded and he saw her no more. He had made perhaps two hundred yards when he became aware of the motor-boat crossing his front at speed. At least once he caught the flash of its gun. Soon its wash reached him and when he emerged there was nothing to be seen before him. Only the island. He breast-stroked steadily towards the notch in the skyline he had fixed on as his mark, looking to neither right nor left, deliberately postponing thought, driving his limbs with all his strength to distract him from the sick sense of defeat.

After twenty minutes he was approaching the edge of the shadow of Vrakonisi cast by the moon, and thought he saw a swimmer almost dead ahead cross into it. Here anybody in the water would be practically invisible, even if the motor-boat passed within yards. He paused and looked westward, but could see nothing. On again, into the shadow, the beach coming into view only a little to the left, a change of course, the last hundred yards. But no sign of Ariadne. She must have found the beach unassisted and be lying down to rest. A few yards of shallows; Bond swam as near the water's edge as he could to avoid sea-urchins. He pulled himself upright; he was ashore. Ariadne was nowhere to be seen. He whirled round.

He had only begun a desperate visual search of the black waters when something that was brighter than the searchlight flashed in his brain and he felt himself start to fall.

Chapter 18

The Dragon's Claws

'EXCELLENT. EXCELLENT. Mr Bond is with us at last.'
Bond's consciousness had returned as quickly and fully as if he had been awakened from a natural sleep. He was half-lying back in a comfortable low chair in a medium-sized, high-ceilinged, well-lighted room. A number of people were looking at him with varying degrees of interest. Two girls, both strikingly attractive, were sitting together on a day-bed. They were strangers to Bond. But all five of the men present he had seen before. The man standing with his back to what was evidently a terrace was the black-haired gunman he had encountered at Quarterdeck. The doctor who had been there was putting a hypodermic away in a black leather case. By the door stood the stocky Russian servant-type from the previous night. Bond could not immediately place the rough-looking local with the bandaged left arm. The tall Chinese, however, leaning down towards him now with an air of kindly solicitude, was unforgettable.

Bond spoke sharply. 'Where's the girl who was with me?'

'A very natural question.' The Chinese smiled his approval. 'You needn't worry about her. She has not been harmed, nor will she be for the moment. Now let me introduce you. Miss Madan and Miss Tartini, two of my female helpers. Mr De Graaf I think you know, and Dr Lohmann from the same occasion. You've met Mr Aris before, too, though only at a distance, as it were, during one of your more successful sea-borne operations. He took a lot of trouble to bring me news of you. My servant Evgeny' – ludicrously, like a well-trained butler, the Russian made a slight, respectful bow – 'and myself.

Sun's the name, Colonel Sun Liang-tan of the Chinese People's Army.'

During this speech, Bond had prevented himself from inquiring after Litsas, whose continued absence was the only factor making for any sort of hope – if he were not already shot or drowned. Pausing for a moment, the Chinese settled himself on a padded olive-wood stool a couple of feet away. His smile turned thoughtful and sympathetic.

'Bad luck has been a marked feature of this whole affair,' he said in his curious accent. 'You've certainly had your full share of it tonight, Mr Bond. Not even you could have predicted that our mutual friends the Russians would have advertised your approach so spectacularly – a real *son et lumière* effort, so to speak.' Sun chuckled briefly at his own wit. 'And then again you were unfortunate in being forced to swim ashore and thus allowing me ample time to get my little boatload of men along to your only possible landing-point. But then, that's life, isn't it?

'Anyway, a most hearty welcome from us all. Some of my colleagues, I know, are feeling very relieved as well as grateful at your arrival. They were in some doubt whether it would take place at all. I was not. I had faith. Thus I was unmoved by Mr De Graaf's opinion that not enough positive action was being taken to secure your services. My fears were that, on the contrary, some over-zealous person would kill you prematurely. I always knew that you would come here of your own accord while you still lived. It was inevitable. As you'll come to realize, you and I are destined for each other.'

Here Colonel Sun allowed another pause, the smile fixed on his face, his metallic eyes trained unblinking on Bond. Then he became solicitous again.

'But forgive me – I'm being careless and unfeeling. How is your head? I hope it's not troubling you unduly?'

'Thank you, just a slight throbbing. Nothing to speak of.' Bond forced himself to match Sun's polite conversational tone. To remain calm, to give no sign of rage or despair, was all that could be done for the moment.

'Excellent; Dr Lohmann's little local anaesthetic has been

effective, then. And Evgeny is an artist with the bludgeon. I hope further that you're suffering no ill effects from your long swim. As you'll have gathered, we took the liberty of drying your garments while you were unconscious. And of removing the knife strapped to your leg.'

'You've been most thoughtful,' said Bond easily. 'I've no complaints. I would like a little whisky if you have it.'

'Of course, my dear fellow, a pleasure. I've been keeping a bottle of Haig specially for this occasion. With ice and water?'

'I think neat, please.'

Sun nodded at Evgeny, taking his eyes from Bond for the first time. They soon returned to him. 'Then apart from some minor discomfort and fatigue your present physical state is satisfactory, it seems.'

'Perfectly.' Bond concealed his growing anger at the continuance of this absurd charade.

'I'm most relieved. The fatigue will be nothing to one of your physique and general condition. I am most relieved.'

The whisky appeared, a generous measure. Bond accepted it gratefully and took a sizeable draught of the honey-coloured fire. Sun watched. There was perhaps a slight edge to his tone when he next spoke.

'It's essential to my purposes, you see, that you cooperate with me to the fullest extent of which you are capable. At any rate for the next . . .' – the colonel consulted a wristwatch which had clearly not originated in People's China – 'five hours or so. After that time you will be incapable of cooperation.'

'There's no question of my co-operating with you for any of your *purposes*,' said Bond scornfully. 'Whatever they may be, I promise you I'll resist them as long as I'm physically able.'

'Bravely spoken, Mr Bond. But – quite naturally – you misunderstand me. Your resistance *is* your co-operation. Hence my concern for your unimpaired power to resist. However, we can defer a full explanation of this question until later. For the moment, I'll explain my purposes' – here a tight grin was switched on and off – 'in the clearest terms. It's essential, absolutely essential, that you learn now just what lies ahead of you.

'Quite soon you'll be taken to the cellar that lies beneath the kitchen of this house. There, using the most sophisticated of the interrogation techniques I've been privileged to be able to develop, I shall torture you to the point of death. But you must realize that this won't be an interrogation in the more common sense of the word, i.e. no questions will be asked of you and whatever information you may volunteer, whatever promises you may make, anything of that kind will have no effect at all on the inexorable progress of the interrogation. Is that clear, Mr Bond?'

'Perfectly.'

'Good. I don't mind admitting, before the present company, that in this respect I'm exceeding my orders a trifle. Or – why not be honest? – actually disobeying them. I was instructed to obtain as much as possible of the specialized knowledge at your disposal before killing you. This was a most unimaginative requirement, typical of the sterile thinking of officialdom with its insistence on routine methods, standard procedures and the like. I imagine that all of us, in our different ways, have come up against the limitations of the bureaucratic mind. In this case, I'm just going to use my own initiative; I'm sure that, as an Englishman, you'll approve of that, Mr Bond. And, being like me an executive, and thus used to outwitting administrators, you'll understand that I'll experience no great difficulty in hoodwinking my masters by pleading that, in view of your well-known courage and the short time which the incompetence of others had allowed for my efforts, I can't be blamed for having failed to break you down. In fact, of course, if I wanted information from you, I could induce you or anyone else to start giving it in a matter of minutes. But, as before, a man of your experience will know how desirable it can be to allow one's bosses to underestimate one.'

It was hideously plain that the Chinese meant every word he said, that he spoke without irony and, in an odd way, without pleasure in his total power over his prisoner. Such an attitude would have suggested madness in a Western mind, but Bond had heard and read enough of the thought-processes of oriental Communism, with its sincere indifference to human suffering and its habit of regarding men and women as objects, statistics, scientific abstractions – enough to see that Sun might be, in a clinical sense, entirely sane. That made him more formidable.

Was there the thinnest, most fanciful hope that any of the others present might be feeling a stir of revolt at the idea of torture for its own sake, so much as a flicker of sympathy? He glanced stealthily at the two girls. The slim dark one had turned her head away, out of indifference, probably, rather than disgust. Her heavy-breasted companion was looking at him with blank dark-brown eyes; a frenzied performer in bed, he guessed, but as sluggish as a cow outside it. The Greek was openly bored, the Russian quite indifferent. By the doors to the terrace, the man called De Graaf stood watching Sun with a grin on his face, half contemptuous, half admiring. Only the doctor, who was sweating and biting his lip, showed signs of disquiet, and his support would be worthless.

'Anyway,' – Sun had impatiently swept his own digression aside – 'it will be my part to see to it that you undergo the worst possible pain, consistent with your remaining alive, until dawn. A delicate task, a severe challenge to my skill. And to your fortitude, Mr Bond. Then at the proper moment I shall cause your death by a method that has never, as far as I know, been tried before. It consists, firstly, of breaking all twelve of the main bones of your limbs, and, secondly, of injecting you with a drug that will send you into convulsions. Perhaps you can form some sort of mental image of the agony that will be yours when your muscles pass out of control and your shattered arms and legs begin to heave and twist and thrash about of their own accord. You will be dead of shock in a few minutes. At this point you will cease to be of direct concern to me. Under the supervision of one of my colleagues, your body, together with that of your chief, will become vital instruments in an ingenious political scheme aimed, roughly, at inflicting serious damage on the prestige of your country and of another power hostile to us. Please come with me. Unless you have any questions so far?'

Bond drained his whisky and gave the appearance of considering. 'No, I don't think so,' he said with deliberation. 'It all seems quite clear.'

'Excellent. Let us be going, then. I'll lead the way.'

As Bond rose to his feet he was desperately contemplating some outburst of violence, some assertion of the will to resist that could never succeed, but would win back the initiative for even a few seconds. He had hardly measured the distance to that yellow throat when his right arm was seized from behind by De Graaf and shoved up behind his shoulder-blade in a vicious hammer-lock. For a moment he was helpless with pain, and in that moment Evgeny had him by the left arm.

'We'll take it slowly, Bond,' said De Graaf's businesslike voice. 'If you try anything at all, I'll break your arm in one second. We weren't allowed to use that sort of method back at your boss's place. This time it's different. That arm's going to get broken anyway in a few hours. Now.' The pressure relaxed a little. 'Walk. Like I said, we'll take it slowly.'

They moved out of the room and across the low hall with its festoons of climbing plants. Bond's mind seemed frozen, totally absorbed in his own bodily movements as he mounted the stairs. At the stairhead they turned right along a short uncarpeted passage. Sun threw aside high and low bolts – recently fitted, by the look of them – on the door at the end and went in. Bond was hustled across the threshold after him.

M stood stiffly with his hands behind his back. He was pale and gaunt and looked as if he had neither eaten nor slept during his four days in enemy hands. But he held himself as upright as ever, and his eyes, puffed and bloodshot as they were, had never been steadier. He smiled faintly, frostily.

'Good evening, James.'

'Hallo, sir,' said Bond awkwardly.

Sun's face split in a cordial smile. 'You gentlemen will have much to say to each other. It would be unfair to embarrass you by our continued presence, so we'll withdraw. I give you my word that you will not be eavesdropped upon. Don't waste your time on the window, by the way; it's quite secure. Is there anything you want?'

'Get out if you're going.' M's voice was hoarse.

'Certainly, Admiral,' said Sun with mock deference. Immediately and instinctively Bond lashed back with his heel at De Graaf's shin, but a heel reinforced merely by canvas and a rope sole is just not a weapon, and the only result was an agonizing momentary push at his doubled-back right arm. The two held on to him until Sun reached the doorway. At the last moment Bond saw him glance at his watch and give a small frown. However minutely, the time-table was being disturbed in some way.

The door shut and the bolts slammed home. Bond turned to M.

'I'm afraid I haven't been much use to you, sir.'

With an air of total weariness, M shook his head. 'I know that nobody could have done more. You can spare me the details. Is there any chance at all of our getting out of here?'

'Very little at the moment. I've counted five able-bodied men round the place, plus one who's injured but could still shoot. Are there any more, do you know, sir?'

'No, I don't know. They've kept me in here all the time. Apart from that Chinese lunatic, I only see the servant fellow who brings me my food and takes me to the lavatory. I can't be any help at all.'

This last was said in a defeated tone that Bond had never expected to hear from M, who now sat himself carefully down on the unmade bed. Bond heard him give an abrupt gasp.

'Has he been torturing you?'

'A little, James, yes. Chiefly burns. Only superficial. He got that doctor to dress them. I was forgetting a moment ago; that makes three people I've seen. It's rather curious about these bits of torture. Earlier on, Sun was trying all sorts of threats. He was going to make me pray to be dead and so forth. Nothing on that scale has materialized. My impression is that you're his main target.'

'That's my impression too,' said Bond flatly.

M nodded in silence. Then he said, 'What's the object of all this flapdoodle, anyway? They wouldn't have gone to these lengths just to try out their new torturing methods. Is it ransom or what? I haven't been told anything.'

'Just the other side of the hill from here the Russians are holding a secret conference. These chaps are going to launch some sort of armed assault on it. When the smoke clears, there are you and I. Dead but identifiable.'

There was silence while M digested the implications of this. 'We'll have to prevent that,' he said eventually. 'And listen. If there's the slightest chance of your escaping, you're to take it and leave me here. I'd slow you down fatally and I'd be no good in a fight. That's an order, 007.'

'I'm sorry, sir,' said Bond at once, 'but in that event I should have to disobey you. You and I leave here together or not at all. And, to be quite frank, there's somebody else I've got to take care of too. A girl.'

M looked up grimly from the bed. 'I might have known. So that was how you got yourself into this mess. Very chivalrous of you, I must say.'

'It wasn't like that, sir. She's been working with me and we were captured within a few minutes of each other. If you knew the full story you'd realize how important she's been. She's brave and tough and she's stuck with me all through this business. She's . . .'

'Very well, very well,' muttered M. His mood had changed suddenly, become abstracted. His hands clenched and unclenched a couple of times. Bond heard him swallow. Then he said, 'I must ask you. It's been so much on my mind. What happened to the Hammonds, James?'

'Dead, sir, both of them. Shot. An expert job, fortunately. I don't think Mrs Hammond can even have known what had happened.'

At Bond's first word M had flung up a hand in an odd and touching gesture, as if to ward off a blow. He said without discernible emotion. 'Another reason. For stopping these people.'

Again silence fell, broken by footfalls on the stairs, along the passage to the door. The bolts clicked aside and Sun came in. His manner was brisk and confident now.

'You must excuse the interruption, gentlemen, but it's time we proceeded to the next stage. There has been a minor delay arising from the need to neutralize Mr Bond's other associate, the man. This has now been accomplished.'

'What have you done with him?' From the sudden lurch in his stomach at this news, Bond recognized that, despite himself, he had still been holding on to a fragment of hope. That fragment had now disintegrated.

'He put up a fight and suffered damage. Nothing severe. He's here now, under sedation. Some use for him may be found. Forget him. Come, both of you.'

Perhaps through fatigue, Bond found some of his experiences that night taking on the blurred rapidity of a dream. De Graaf and Evgeny appeared beside him; Litsas, skein of blood descending from his scalp, was being hustled into the room next to M's; they were downstairs again and von Richter was ceremoniously handing a drink to the blond youth called Willi. The girls had gone. Sun was speaking.

'. . . for my purposes. This exact knowledge is better conveyed to you by my colleague, Major von Richter. I can allow you just five minutes, Ludwig.'

The ex-SS man leaned back in his chair with an intent expression, as if conscientiously marshalling his thoughts. The scar tissue at the side of his head glistened in the strong light. He spoke without hurry in his curiously attractive drawl.

'The technical problem was how to penetrate a strong stone building by means of an inconspicuous weapon that should have very clear associations with the British. An investigation of the structure of the building on the islet provided an immediate answer. All such houses possess very thick walls, such as even a field-gun might not at once penetrate. But the roof is not so thick. It is also flat, so that a projectile arriving from above would not glance off. Only one weapon of convenient size satisfied these requirements, besides being not merely inconspicuous but, to anybody in the target area, potentially invisible.'

'A trench mortar.' Bond was hardly conscious that it was he who had spoken the words. Even at this moment he was filled with a kind of triumph and an unearthly sense of wonder, as if he had solved an ancient riddle. Four apparently unconnected facts had revealed themselves all at once as disguised pointers to the truth: the detail in the legend about the dragon who could attack his victims from behind a mountain; Ariadne's speculations about guns the previous evening, bringing her within half a sentence of the solution; the sports-bag with the heavy and oddly-shaped contents he had himself watched being brought ashore here; the pun in his nightmare six hours or so ago, when he had noticed the thickness of the mortar in the wall that had been about to fall on him. The last of these had not really been a clue at all, but an answer to the problem, brought up from the depths of his unconscious mind while his consciousness was still struggling with logic, figures, practical possibilities. If only he had seen the true significance of that wall! But, even if he had, what then?

'Ha! Ten marks! *Er ist ja schlau, der Willi, was?*' Von Richter, like Sun, was showing the excessive and nervous geniality Bond had seen in war among men about to go into action with the odds on their side. 'Yes, Mr Bond. To be precise, the heavy Stokes mortar, three-inch calibre. We obtained our example of it from the neo-Nazi armoury at Augsburg. Much captured weaponry of the second war is there, and very much ammunition. We were fortunate. The Stokes is an admirable weapon. Typically British. Ideal as pocket-size close-support light artillery that can search behind cover. The height of its trajectory is such that an example positioned outside this house can with great ease send its bombs over the hill and on to the islet. Since the piece has no trigger, merely a firing-pin at the base of the barrel which detonates the cartridge of each bomb as it slides down from the muzzle, a quite staggering rate of fire can be attained. An expert will place twenty rounds in the air at once. Every tenth round we shall fire will be smoke. You can imagine the confusion among our friends when the attack begins. Also the loss of life. It will be considerable.

'There is the question of accuracy. Here practice is important. I have accustomed myself to our example of the mortar during ten days in Albania recently. I understand now its peculiarities. You will realize that, when the firer cannot see his target, as in our case, he must employ an observer. This is the job of Willi here. The Albanian government kindly placed at our disposal a piece of ground very similar to this terrain. Willi and I have worked out our procedure. He will climb to the hillcrest, to the point we have established as being on a straight line between our firing-point and the target. Just below the crest he will install a light. This will be my aiming mark and will give me direction. I already have a precise knowledge of the range. Almost no wind is expected at the chosen time. We have practised a code of signals so that I shall be guided on to the target. Our proficiency has become so that within a minute three bombs out of four will hit the house or the area immediately surrounding it. This will prove sufficient.

'The bombardment will commence at dawn. Upon its conclusion, you and your chief will enter the story. Or rather, your corpses will. Investigators will discover your remains on the firing-point. One of you has been careless with the ammunition and an explosion has resulted. This is quite plausible, since the detonation cap at the nose of the bomb is sensitive. To drop one on to rock from chest height would be fatal. Needless to say, the true course of events will be different. From behind cover I shall simply toss a bomb on to the firing-point, where you and your chief will be lying disabled. This step has required some preliminary research. It would not do to damage your frame so superficially, Mr Bond, that evidence remained of your having been tortured before being killed, nor must you be rendered unrecognizable. Therefore I had to conduct experiments while in Albania. They were carried out with corpses. Very largely with corpses. There is a good supply of fresh examples of these in that country.' Von Richter laughed heartily at this stroke, then became official. 'That concludes my exposition of the military aspect of this operation.' Without looking at his watch he added, 'Just under five minutes, Colonel.'

Bond's mind had become preoccupied with the thought that Ariadne had again asked a highly relevant question: what there was about this project that required a man with experience of atrocities. The answer was plain enough now. Its implications were horrible.

'Thank you, Herr Major. Now, do either of you gentlemen require further information?'

M spoke up. 'You'll have prepared your fake documents, I presume?'

'Very well taken, Admiral! Yes, a full operation order for your act of flagrant aggression has been run up in our Albanian office. Its remains will be found on your corpse. Your government will denounce it as a forgery, naturally, but what else could they do if it were genuine? Rest assured that their complicity will be proved. The injury to Russian prestige is straightforward enough not to need such artificial aids.'

Bond said, 'How did your people find out about this conference in such detail?'

'Oh, one of the minor people concerned with it in Moscow became momentarily indiscreet, quite unintentionally, in the hearing of one of our operatives there. We made arrangements to interview this man and I was able to induce him to be indiscreet at great length, intentionally. And to convince him that we would know, and react most unfavourably, if he revealed his indiscretion to his superiors. But now, please let us have done with such affairs and move on to something more interesting. Are there any further questions?'

Silence, because no words were any good. And absence of movement, because no action was any good. Powerlessness. Hopelessness.

'I recommend that you say goodbye to your chief now, Mr Bond. You will probably not be able to when you see him again.'

Chapter 19

The Theory and Practice of Torture

THE CELLAR was small, not more than ten feet by twelve feet by six and a half feet high. The floor bulged and sloped, and an irregular column of living rock leaned across one corner. Whatever had been left here by previous occupants was here no longer; the place was bare, swept, and scrubbed. A stout wooden ladder led to a trap-door in the ceiling. Along one wall lay a schoolroom bench; by another a small collapsible table and a kitchen chair had been placed. An unshaded but rather murky bulb burned in a bracket on a third wall.

Resist as he might, Bond had been unable to prevent himself being bound securely into a heavy, old-fashioned dining-chair set in the corner opposite the tongue of rock. The material used to tie his wrists and ankles was strips of towelling; as he struggled with De Graaf, Evgeny, and Willi, Bond had half-heard parts of a careful explanation from Sun about ropes causing chafing and the undesirability of pain not deliberately inflicted. Chains running from ring-bolts cemented into walls and floor would keep the chair stable however much its occupant might throw himself about.

Left alone for the moment, Bond sat and waited for Sun. More than anything he longed for a cigarette. A jumble of images circled in his brain: the delicate moulding and coloration of Ariadne's face — M's firm handclasp of ten minutes earlier — the wordless plea Gordienko had made in his last seconds — the blood on Litsas's head — the game of golf with Bill Tanner, half a century ago — the terrible bewilderment on the face of the Russian as the rifle-bullet struck him — von Richter's amusement as he remembered his 'experiments' in Albania — the sprawled bodies of the Hammonds in the kitchen at Quarterdeck – Ariadne again. Then the figure of Sun, the loose powerful movements, the metal-coloured eyes, the sloping teeth, the dark lips. The man who was going to start him on an agonizing road to death. Bond found he was sweating with fear.

Footfalls sounded overhead. Bond forced himself to begin taking some deep breaths. The trap-door was pulled back and Evgeny came down the ladder. He was carrying a wooden tray which he put down on the small table. Without glancing at Bond he went back to the ladder and ascended. Bond studied the objects on the tray: two metal meat-skewers of different sizes and a wooden one, a bottle of colourless liquid, a funnel about the size of a coffee-cup, what looked like a bunch of bristles from a broom, a knife with a six-inch blade in the shape of a slim right-angled triangle, several boxes of matches. His breathing became heavy.

After a dreadful minute of utter silence, Sun arrived. He smiled and nodded at Bond, like somebody greeting a favourite acquaintance, and sat quietly down next to the table.

'Before you start, Sun,' said Bond in a level tone, 'I want to ask you a favour.'

'Ask away, my dear Bond. You know I'll do anything I can.'

'The girl. What's happening to her?'

'I believe De Graaf is with her now. Or perhaps Evgeny. Or even both of them. The other girls may be participating too. On a night like tonight I suppose a certain amount of licence is to be expected'

Bond tried to ignore this. 'In the morning, let her go. Drop her off somewhere. Whatever she says afterwards she can't threaten the success of your project, and you and all your team will be safely out of the way.'

'I'm sorry,' said Sun, shaking his head and sighing. 'Believe me, I wish I could help you, but it's impossible. You must see that. What would those unimaginative bosses of mine have to say if I allowed any sort of witness to survive after an operation on this scale? The rule-book says that must never happen. So I'm afraid she'll have to die.'

'Then could you have it done quickly? Cleanly?' Bond

hardly noticed the abject appeal in his voice. 'There's nothing against that, is there?'

'Of course not. I am no barbarian, Mr Bond, whatever you may think. I've always opposed needless suffering. I'll see to it that De Graaf, who's an expert in these matters, shoots her in the back of the head. She'll know nothing about it. I'll supervise the whole thing personally. You need have no fears on that score.'

'Thank you for that.' Bond believed him and was grateful. Then rage and loathing filled him. 'Now get on with your squalid sadistic charade. Have yourself your messy little kicks. Enjoy them while you can.'

'It seems, Mr Bond,' said Sun judicially, 'that your ideas on the nature of sadism are in an unformed state. You said—'

'Never mind the state of my ideas. Bring out your thumb-screws and your hot irons. They can't be much more painful than having to sit here listening to you.'

The colonel did his smile. 'Your defiance does you credit. But you've no conception of what you're defying. In a short while you'll be wishing with all your heart and soul that you'd encouraged me to delay your pain by just a few seconds, just one little remark about the weather.

'Now, James. . . .' Sun got up and paced the tiny area of floor in front of Bond's chair. 'I hope you don't mind if I call you James. I feel I know you so well.'

'There's nothing I can do about it, is there?'

'No, there isn't, is there, James? Anyway, it's appropriate, don't you think? Sets the right tone of intimacy.'

'I was wondering when we'd get to that,' said Bond with revulsion. 'I suppose people who look like you can't find any willing partners, so they have to tie someone up and—'

'Oh, no, no, no.' Sun sounded genuinely distressed. 'I knew you were on the wrong track there. True sadism has nothing whatever to do with sex. The intimacy I was referring to is moral and spiritual, the union of two souls in a rather mystical way. In the divine Marquis de Sade's great work *Justine* there's a character who says to his victim: "Heaven has decreed that it is your part to endure these sufferings, just as it is my part to inflict them." That's the kind of relationship you and I are entering into, James.'

Sun went on pacing the floor, frowning in concentration, a passionately serious thinker intent on finding the precise words to impart his ideas. After a while he shrugged, as if finding the struggle for expression on the highest level beyond him.

'You must understand that I'm not the slightest bit interested in studying resistance to pain or any such pseudo-scientific claptrap. I just want to torture people. But – this is the point – not for any selfish reason, unless you call a saint or a martyr selfish. As de Sade explains in *The Philosopher in the Boudoir*, through cruelty one rises to heights of superhuman awareness, of sensitivity to new modes of being, that can't be attained by any other method. And the victim – you too, James, will be spiritually illuminated in the way so many Christian authorities describe as uplifting to the soul: through suffering. Side by side you and I will explore the heights.'

As if flushed with excitement or some deeper emotion, Sun's cheeks seemed to have turned a darker yellow. His broad chest rose and fell under the white tee-shirt. Reversing an earlier judgement, Bond said critically, 'You're boring me, Sun. Because of your mental condition. There's nothing more totally uninteresting than a madman.'

Sun chuckled. Suddenly his manner speeded up. His arms moved jerkily. 'Predictable reaction, my dear chap. Let's get on, shall we? Here we are, James, the two of us, in a cellar on a Greek island. Not a very lavish scene, I'm afraid, such as some of your earlier opponents have provided. But then you and I aren't opponents, are we? We're collaborators. Right, then. What shall I do to you? Whereabouts in your body shall I attack you? And with what?

'First, the apparatus. Electricity can provide some of the most exquisite anguish known, if applied in the right place. But that's too easy. No scope for finesse. And, let's face it, here in Eastern Europe the supply isn't too reliable. No, I feel strongly that any self-respecting security officer ought to be able to make do with what the average kitchen provides –

knives, skewers, broom-straws, such as you've no doubt noticed on this tray. I'm going to have to cheat a little when I give you the final injection that will send you into convulsions. The chemical isn't found in any average kitchen. But it is derived from a mushroom that grows in China, so one might semi-legitimately say that it's possible to imagine a kitchen that contains this particular essence.

'Now, the all-important question of where I'm to locate my assault. The obvious, all-too-obvious place is the genital organs. I'm sure experience has taught you that tremendous pain can be inflicted on them, plus the very valuable psychological side-effect whereby the victim fears for, then laments over, the loss of his manhood. But that won't affect you very much. I trust I've convinced you, James, that it's not your manhood I'm going to deprive you of, but your life. And the whole idea of a genital assault is so . . . unsophisticated.'

A pause. The blood thudded in Bond's ears. From his slacks Sun brought out a red tin of Benson & Hedges and offered them.

'No thank you.'

'Are you sure? It'll be your last smoke.'

'I said no thank you.' Bond had almost forgotten his nicotine-hunger. And the thought of those yellow fingers putting the cigarette in his mouth, helpfully removing it to shake off the ash, as he could so clearly imagine them doing, was not to be borne.

'As you wish.' Sun operated a leather-bound Ronson and puffed out smoke. 'So, then. Where? Where does a man live? Where's the inmost part of a man, his soul, his being, his identity?

'One can do very unpleasant things to a man's fingernails, for example. Or to his genitals, as we were saying. The knee-joint is a neural focus and the most surprising results can be obtained by interference with it. But all this happens, so to speak, somewhere else. A man can watch himself being disem-bowelled and derive great horror, as well as pain, from the experience. But it's going on at a distance. It isn't taking place . . . where he is.'

Sun came over and knelt beside Bond's chair. He spoke in a half-whisper. His throat was trembling. 'A man lives inside his head. That's where the seat of his soul is. And this is true objectively as well as subjectively. I was present once – I wasn't directly concerned – when an American prisoner in Korea was deprived of his eyes. And the most astonishing thing happened. He wasn't there any more. He'd gone, though he was still alive. There was nobody inside his skull. Most odd, I promise you.

'So, James, I am going to penetrate to where you are, to the inside of your head. We'll make our first approach via the ear.' Sun got up and went over to the table. 'I take this skewer and I insert it into your skull.' The thin length of metal gleamed in the muddy light. 'You won't feel anything at first. In fact, in the true sense you won't *feel* anything at all. The tympanic membrane, which I'm about to stimulate, has no touch receptors, only pain ones. So the first you'll know will be when . . . well, I leave it to you to put a name to your experience. If you can.'

Crushing out his cigarette beneath his heel, Sun gazed over at Bond with a sort of compassion. 'Just one more thing, James. This cellar is well on the way to being sound-proof, down here in the rock. And blankets and rugs have been laid on the floor overhead to seal it even further. Our tests showed that virtually nothing can be heard at a hundred yards. So you may scream all you wish.'

'God damn you to hell.'

'He can't do that, James. He can't reach me. It's I who am damning you to hell.'

Then, with the brisk stride of a man anxious not to be late for an important engagement, Colonel Sun came over to the chair. With ferocious efficiency he seized Bond's head in a clamp formed by his powerful left arm and his chest. Bond strained away with all his strength, but to no purpose. In a couple of seconds he felt the tip of the skewer probing delicately at the orifice of his left ear. Teeth clenched, he waited.

It came without warning, the first dazzling concussion of

agony, as instantaneously violent as the discharge of a gun. He heard himself whimper faintly. There was an interval just long enough for the thought that the cessation of pain was an infinitely more exquisite sensual thrill than the wildest spasms of love. After that, pain in bursts and thrusts and sheets and floods, drenching and blazing pain, pain as inexhaustible as the sea or the sands of the desert. Another interval, another thought: this is as bad as it can get. Immediately, worse and worse pain. Breathe in; whimper. Breathe in; whimper. Breathe in . . .

The scream ceased. Sun felt Bond go limp and released him. The head, running with sweat at every pore, fell forward on to the labouring chest. With a gesture like that of an adult to an engaging child, Sun ruffled the saturated hair. He turned away abruptly, climbed the ladder and pushed hard at the trap-door. It rose a few inches.

At once a muffled voice spoke. 'Yes, sir?'

'You may come down now, Lohmann.'

'Right away, sir.'

The doctor, carrying his black leather case, appeared and descended. He was followed by von Richter and Willi.

'I hope you don't mind our joining you, Colonel.'

'Of course not, my dear Ludwig, I appreciate your interest. As you see, provision has been made for spectators. Do please sit down.'

'This . . .' The doctor cleared his throat and started again. 'This man is unconscious, sir.'

'I'm glad you agree with me. Now sit down and prepare to observe closely. This is good training for you. If you want to be of further service to our movement you must allow your inhibitions to be broken down. You appreciate that?'

Dr Lohmann hesitated, nodded, and took his seat on the bench next to Willi.

'Well, what have you in store for us, Sun?' Von Richter drawled the question. 'We expect great things of you, you know. Everybody tells me that Peking leads the world in this field.'

Sun tilted his head, pleased at the compliment, but anxious

to be strictly fair. 'Good work is also being done in Vietnam. Some of Ho Chi-minh's men have learnt their job with remarkable speed, considering the comparative backwardness of that part of the world. Very promising. Ah . . .'

He stepped over and lifted Bond's chin. The blue-grey eyes fluttered open, cleared, and steadied. 'Damn you, Sun,' said a thin voice.

'Excellent. We can proceed. I'm working on his head, Ludwig, as I described earlier. He's taken it well so far, but this is only the beginning. Eventually he'll scream when he merely sees me advancing on him to continue the treatment.

'I now propose to stimulate the septum, the strip of bone and cartilage that divides the nasal cavity. Can you see, all of you? Good.'

More pain, different at first from the other, then indistinguishable. Bond tried to build a place in his mind where the pain was not all that there was, where there were thoughts, as he had been able to do under the hands of other torturers and so to some degree hold out against them. But the pain was fast becoming all that there was. The only thought that he could find and keep in place was that he would not scream yet, not this time. Or this time. Or this time . . .

It was later and the pain had receded for the moment. He was somewhere. That was all he knew. But there must be other things. Screaming. Had he screamed? Forgotten. But still try not to.

People were talking. He recognized some of the words through a sound like a fast-running river. Danger. Shock. Injection. A tiny pricking in his arm, ridiculously tiny.

More pain. It was all that there was. There were no thoughts anywhere in the world.

It was much later and he was back. There were thoughts again. Or rather one big thought that filled everything and was everything. It weighed down on him like an impossibly thick blanket, it came oozing up round him like the cold slime of the sea-bed. Bond had never experienced it before, but he knew quite soon what it was. It was despair, the terminal state of life, the foretaste of death. In comparison, the blood in his nose and mouth, the ferociously throbbing ache within his head – all this was nothing.

Bond opened his eyes. He found he could see reasonably well. Sun's face was a foot away. But something had happened to it since he last saw it. Something had dried it so that the skin looked like paper out of an old book, the eyes were red and dull, the open lips had shrivelled. The man's breathing was shallow and noisy, and he swallowed constantly. He seemed in the grip of an exhaustion as profound as Bond's. This was puzzling, but it did not matter. Nothing mattered now.

Somebody was coming down the ladder. Bond looked up automatically without interest. It was one of the girls in the team, the dark one. She glanced at Bond, then quickly away again. Her small features expressed faint repulsion and great fear. Sun straightened up slowly and turned to her.

She caught her breath. 'You ill, sir?'

'No. No. It's my experiences. They have an effect.' The voice too had changed. It had become harsh and cracked, with a monotonous quality that suggested the recitation of a lesson not perfectly understood. After a long time the man added, 'They cause a change in one.'

'Oh. What you wish, sir?'

Sun gestured spasmodically towards Bond. 'This man . . . is near his death. During his life his greatest pleasure has been love and sex with women. With your assistance, I intend to bring home to him the bitterness of being deprived of this love for ever.'

Sun had spoken entirely without conviction. He paused awkwardly, as if turning over a page in his mind. Then the dried-up voice toiled on. 'James Bond must be in the proper spiritual state to meet the death I shall give him. The deepest pitch of hopelessness and grief and misery a man can attain.'

He fell silent. The girl stared at him. 'What you wish, sir?'

'Strip yourself naked and stand before him,' said Sun as if he were dictating a message. 'Show him your body. Caress him very lasciviously.'

The girl still stared, but now her face showed outrage and

rebellion as well as fear. 'No!' She struggled for more words. 'Cannot do this. Is . . . wrong.'

'You can and you will. If you want to be of further service to our movement you must allow your inhibitions to be broken down. Do as I say.'

'Will not!'

A ghost of animation returned to Sun's voice when he said, 'If you disobey me I'll have your throat cut and your body thrown overboard as soon as we're at sea.'

The silence roared and rustled and rang in Bond's ears. The girl's face changed again and suddenly, for no reason he could have specified, he became alert. He found himself watching with intense concentration.

'Okay,' said the girl at last, her eyes flickering round the room. 'But please . . . not look.'

'Certainly not. You need feel no embarrassment. Our friend Lohmann is a doctor. Not that he seems likely to look at you either.'

Lohmann sat alone on the bench, huddled up with his face in his hands. On the floor in front of him were the remains of a cleared-up pool of vomit. Bond glanced briefly at him, then back at the other two. He saw the girl, a trim figure in her long-sleeved turquoise jacket and green slacks, walk over towards the table and halt in front of it. Saw Sun turn towards him and study his face. Through half-closed lids, saw the girl look hastily over her shoulder, then make some movement at the table. Saw her turn and begin to speak.

'I have good idea. First I will kiss him some. Then strip.'

'Very well. You understand these matters. What you do doesn't concern me. All that is important to me is the results.'

Bond saw the girl walk up to him, her right arm moving in an unnatural way. Saw her face come down towards him – saw, at the same instant, Colonel Sun's shrivelled mouth twitch in distaste, saw him turn his back. Saw the girl glance over her shoulder again. Felt a movement in the area round his right wrist.

It was a few seconds before he identified this movement as that of a sharp knife shearing through the towelling that bound that wrist to the arm of the chair.

Chapter 20

'Goodbye, James'

'SOMETHING WRONG here, sir. I think this man . . . dead.'
The girl was intelligent. She had quickly re-wrapped the severed towelling round Bond's wrist so that it would fool a casual glance. The knife was clenched in his hand, hidden from above. Taking his cue, he dropped his head on to his chest, but kept his eyes open in a fixed stare.

'But that's impossible! He can't be dead!' There was nothing of the sleepwalker about Sun now. He hurried over to the chair. The girl moved aside, well out of the way. Sun's body bent forward over Bond. He began to say something. Then, with all his remaining strength, Bond brought the knife up and round and into Sun's back behind and just above the left hip. The man grunted and flung up an arm, made as if to throw himself clear, but his feet slipped on the irregular floor and he came down on one knee, half-leaning across Bond's left forearm. Now, with more weight behind it, the knife went in again, thumping up to the hilt this time, close to the shoulder-blade. Sun gave a moan of great weariness and gazed into Bond's face for a moment. The pewter-coloured eyes seemed full of accusation. The moment passed, the whites of the eyes rolled up, and Sun, the knife still in his back, fell over sideways and did not move.

The girl was sobbing, her hands pressed tightly over her mouth, her body bent at the waist. Lohmann, trembling all over, had got to his feet. Bond looked from one to the other.

'Give me the knife,' he said. His voice was thick and choked but it was his own.

Violently shaking her head, the girl turned away, groped towards the chair by the table and collapsed into it, her face hidden. Lohmann hesitated, then hurried forward and pulled out the knife from the middle of the spreading stain in Sun's tee-shirt. After wiping it he began fumblingly to cut through the towelling at Bond's left wrist. As he worked, he talked in a jerky babble.

'I wanted to help you earlier but I couldn't think of anything. He's a devil. He made me watch what he was doing to you. When he couldn't make me look he threatened me. Terrible things. I didn't know it was going to be like this. Just medical supervision, they said. Keeping people tranquillized. Easy. And this girl. I knew something would happen there eventually. He let her guess what she was in for, you see.'

Free at last, Bond stood up shakily, swayed and held on to the chair. His head hummed and swam. He had to force himself to speak. 'What's the time?'

'You've got about half an hour before they start shooting that thing off.' The doctor had stopped trembling. He became practical, even brisk. 'Willi's on his way up the hillside. Von Richter's at the firing-point, setting up.'

'What about the other people?'

Lohmann did not answer. He had been feeling Bond's pulse and looking him over. 'You won't be able to do anything strenuous as you are at the moment,' he said. 'I'll give you something to pull you round.' He went over and opened his bag.

'Why should I trust you?'

'If I hadn't made up my mind to change sides I'd have gone for help while you were still three-quarters tied up in that chair. Don't think I'm doing it out of love for you. He was going to have me killed as soon as the job was done. I'm sure of that. Here.' A hypodermic came up. 'Now this will give you a lift for about an hour. Then you'll collapse. But by that time you'll be either safe or dead. You asked me about the other people. Your friend, the man they brought in, is under sedation in the room next to your chief's, the one that was booked for you. He's not badly hurt. No key needed. Just the bolts.'

'What about the sedative?'

'It's quite light. A shot of this will bring him round. You'll have to take it with you. I'm not leaving this cellar until you come and tell me it's safe. I'm no good at fighting. There you are.' Lohmann handed over the loaded hypodermic in a card-board box. 'It doesn't matter where you give it to him, as long as the point's well into the skin. All right?'

'Yes,' said Bond. Perhaps it was no more than imagination, or the joy of being free again, but already energy seemed to be returning to him and his head clearing. 'Where's my girl?'

'She's in a room in the passage on the other side of the landing, first door on the left.'

'De Graaf?'

'He was there too when I went up to fetch Luisa here,' said the doctor stonily. 'So was the other Albanian girl. I don't know where Evgeny is. But you'd better get a move on, Bond. He and De Graaf are due down here in ten minutes to carry you out to the firing-point.'

'Right. The other man – the Greek with the bandaged arm – where's he?'

'Opposite your chief. Sedated to the eyes. No problem.'

'Which of these people are armed?'

'De Graaf always carries a gun in his right hip-pocket. I don't think Evgeny has anything. Von Richter I don't know about.'

'Willi?'

Lohmann hesitated oddly. 'Again I don't know,' he said. 'But you've no need to worry about him. He's out of the way.'

'Maybe. Hadn't you better have a look at Sun?'

'That second blow of yours must have finished him. But one can't be too careful, I agree.' Lohmann knelt down by the motionless form of the Chinese. After a moment he said: 'He's still alive – theoretically. He'll never move again. What do you want to do? Do you feel like finishing him? I can show you a certain spot.'

Bond had the knife in his hand. He glanced down at it and shuddered. 'No. We'll leave him. I'll be off, then. Look after the girl. I'll be back.'

'Yes. All right. I'll bolt us in. Good luck.'

There was nothing friendly to be said to the man who, until five minutes ago, had played an indispensable part in Sun's monstrous conspiracy, so Bond said nothing. But, short of time though he was, he could not pass by the girl who had saved his life at such dreadful risk. He put a hand on the slumped shoulder and she looked up, her face still dull with shock, but no longer weeping.

'Thank you, Luisa,' said Bond gently. 'What made you do it?'

'He . . .' – she pointed without looking – 'kill me. You . . . help . . .' Her gesture, oddly touching, apologized for her bad English.

Bond kissed her cold cheek, then made for the ladder. There was a bad moment when he pushed at the trap-door and it failed to budge. If some heavy object had been moved on top of it he was finished before he started. Then he remembered what Sun had said about piling it with rugs and such to muffle sound. He pushed harder; it began to yield. The effort brought a surge of pain, but the pain was beginning to be different. Without exactly decreasing, it seemed to matter less.

The kitchen was empty. Its window showed a rocky slope beginning to turn the colour of elephant-hide. If Lohmann had been accurate, there were perhaps twenty minutes to go before the bombardment. Enough. If no snags developed. And provided he could be out of this area before De Graaf and Evgeny converged on it to collect him.

The passage outside the kitchen was also empty and unlit, though the hall at its farther end was illuminated. Knife in hand, Bond crept along to the corner and peered round.

Evgeny was standing with his hands on his hips in the open doorway at the side of the house. His back was turned almost squarely to Bond as, presumably, he watched or stood ready to assist von Richter at the firing-point. Off his guard the Russian might be, but the chances of disposing of him silently in this situation were too thin to be considered. Bond measured with his eye the distance from his corner to the foot of the staircase. Eighteen paces. Say twenty.

Bond had taken three paces into the brightly-lit hall when he saw Evgeny glance at his watch. He was back in the passage before the man could have read the time. The hand went back on to the hip. Bond walked quickly across the hall to the stairs.

A single small bulb burned on the deserted landing. Bond unhesitatingly turned right and halted at the last door but one. The bolts were easy. The door made no noise. The sleeper's breathing was a guide. Bond's left hand went across the mouth while his right stayed ready with the knife; there was still just a possibility. . . . He whispered urgently into the ear. 'Niko. Niko, it's James. James Bond.'

There had been a jerk and a grunt and a momentary struggle, then relaxation. Bond cautiously withdrew his hand an inch.

'James,' the familiar voice whispered back. 'I'm afraid they got me. As you understand.'

'How do you feel?'

'Bloody awful headache and very sleepy.'

'I've brought you something that'll take care of the drowsiness at least. An injection. Give me your arm.' Bond went rapidly on as he brought out the hypodermic. 'The Chinese gentleman is out of action. There are two others in the house we must deal with separately. The first one's in a bedroom on the other side of this floor.'

Litsas winced as the needle went in. 'You would be a very bad doctor, James. Go on.'

'He's expecting to be called soon. I'll knock. When he comes out, as I hope to God he does, your job is to see he doesn't call out; if he does, we're cooked. Then I'll deal with him.'

'What have you got?'

'A knife. Nothing for you at the moment. Now in the room with him there's Ariadne and an Albanian girl. Some sort of rape-cum-orgy seems to have been going on. Never mind that for now. We've got to keep the Albanian girl quiet. That may be tricky. We'll have to see how it goes.'

'All right,' said Litsas shortly.

'Has that stuff made any difference yet?'

'A bit. Moving about will perhaps help. I'm ready.'

They sidled out along the passage to the stairhead. Bond looked down and saw nobody, listened and heard nothing. At the door mentioned by Lohmann they took up positions close to the wall on each side. Bond knocked gently.

'All right, who is it?' called a man's sleepy voice.

'Lohmann,' said Bond in a grunt.

The length of the ensuing silence made him bite his lip. Then, 'Hold on, I'm coming.'

Within, a bed-spring twanged. The heel of a shoe scraped the floor. A female voice muttered something indistinguishable. The man yawned deeply. There was silence for half a minute. Then footfalls approached the door, a key turned in the lock, light flooded into the passage and De Graaf, buttoning his shirt, marched confidently out.

Bond just had time to notice the deep parallel scratches on the gunman's left cheek before Litsas grabbed him and clapped a large hand over his mouth. Bond stepped forward and looked into the dilated eyes. 'This is for the Hammonds,' he hissed, and drove the knife in. De Graaf's body gave one great throe, as if he had touched a live terminal, then went totally limp. Bond turned aside at once and stepped into the room.

Ariadne, under a thin coverlet on the floor, jerked to a sitting position and stared at him, but Bond's attention was all on the swarthy blonde in the bed. She too had sat up, showing herself to be naked to the waist at least. Bond hardly saw. He gazed into her bewildered dark eyes and brought his bloodstained knife forward as he approached.

'If you make a sound I'll kill you,' he told her.

'Not ... no, I stay quiet.' The hand she held out palm foremost was trembling. With the other she pulled the sheet over her breasts.

Bond stood near her at the head of the bed. Ariadne, wearing brassière and panties, got up and came over to him. Their hands touched, then gripped.

'Are you all right?' she asked. 'Your voice sounds funny.'

'I'm all right.' There were a thousand things he longed to say and he could not get any of them said. 'What about you?'

'I don't mind anything now you're here. We must gag this bitch, I suppose. If it were my decision I'd shut her up for always. How are you, Niko? I thought you were dead.'

'A bit better than that.' Litsas had dumped De Graaf's body in a corner of the room. He now held a revolver, a sawn-off Smith & Wesson Centennial Airweight. 'We should get – ' He broke off abruptly.

They all heard distant footsteps crossing the stone-paved hall and beginning to mount the stairs.

'That's our second man,' said Bond.

As he stood for a moment irresolute, Ariadne sprang into action. She swung her fist and cracked Doni Madan hard under the jaw. Doni's head jerked back and hit the headboard of the bed. Within five seconds Ariadne was under her coverlet again. Litsas had put himself out of view beside a battered wardrobe and Bond had slipped behind the door.

Evgeny had no chance at all. He crossed the threshold, caught sight of De Graaf's body, exclaimed, began to move forward and took the knife under the fifth rib, his mouth muffled by Bond's left forearm.

'Great – but too quick and clean,' said Ariadne, looking down at the bodies. 'Anyway, I hope it hurt like hell for both of them – the bastards!'

Bond caught her hand again. 'Forget about them,' he said. 'Now listen. The house is clear for the moment. I'm going to get my chief along here. Where's the key of this room?'

'It'll be in the pocket of the tall one.'

'You and my chief are to lock yourselves in and stay till I come for you. No,' – as Ariadne started to protest – 'we've only one gun and one knife and we're two to one already. Niko will explain. Gag that girl and tie her up.'

'It'll be a pleasure.'

When Bond returned with M, Doni Madan, still senseless from Ariadne's blow, had been dealt with and a sheet thrown over the two bodies. M was clearly dazed with strain and a sleepless night. He had obeyed Bond's summons and followed him along the passages in total silence. He sat slumped on the edge of the bed, a nerve jumping in his neck. Bond looked anxiously at him.

Ariadne caught the look. 'He'll be all right, I promise you.' She put her arms round Bond and kissed him. 'Now go finish them.'

'What now?' asked Litsas as they moved off.

'Trench mortar operated by von Richter. His boy-friend on the hill spotting for him.'

'Clever, eh? But easy to miss.'

'They've trained a lot. Look, there.'

A window on the landing gave a view of the firing-point. By now there was enough light to make out the stubby shape of the trench mortar, two and a half feet of canted-over stove-pipe clamped to the rectangular base-plate. There was a movement in the shadows that must have been von Richter.

The possible plans were few. Bond picked the quickest one. 'Take the gun, Niko, go out by the terrace at the back of the house and work your way round above him. You'll be able to get a shot at him from there. I'll come at him from the sea end. If I can't get close enough to rush him I can certainly distract his attention from you.'

'Be careful. I'll have to be close with this bloody sawn-off barrel, or I might hit you. Has he got a gun?'

'Don't know.'

'Give me five minutes.'

'No more – the timing's tight.'

In the hall they shook hands in silence and parted. Bond walked quickly through the sitting-room where he had first regained consciousness, out on to the terrace and along to the west corner of the house. From here he took a careful look.

Von Richter was in the act of opening a box of ammunition on the firing-point. This, on its raised natural platform, was about twenty yards away, across mainly broken ground but not so much so as to give any cover for a direct approach. The only possibility was to move parallel with the sea into the shelter of the edge of the cliff, which would mean crossing the open in full view of anyone facing that way. At the moment, von Richter's position was such that the tail of his eye might just pick up this manoeuvre. But soon, surely, he must turn his back to look out for Willi at the hillcrest. The man seemed in no hurry. A minute went by while he laid out a row of bombs on the ground, took the canvas cover off the mouth of the mortar, straightened up and lit a cigarette. At last he swung round and began studying the skyline. Bond moved.

Before he had covered more than a third of the distance to the corner of the cliff his foot struck a loose chip of stone and immediately the German wheeled and saw him. Bond changed direction and made straight for the firing-point. With his feet stumbling and slipping on the smooth hummocks of rock, he expected a bullet at any moment. What he had not expected were the immense shuddering explosions from the mortar, driving into his ears: one – two – three. . . . Then von Richter turned and waited for him, arms extended, with all the advantages of a higher and more secure foothold. But Bond caught him out of position by going for the mortar, not the man. He flung himself forward and brought barrel and base-plate and all toppling over sideways, ruining any immediate prospect of further aimed shots. The pain lunged at him. He was half-way to his feet when his head seemed to dissolve and everything stopped.

Litsas was there. His voice came through an invisible wall. 'James. Come on. We've work to do.'

'How long . . . ?'

'A minute. He kicked you and was looking round for a rock to drop on your head, so I fired at him. The range was too much, but I must have been close. He forgot you and ran into the house. Can you manage?'

On his feet again, Bond steadied himself. 'Yes. Let's go and get him. Together this time.'

'But with me first. Don't forget he's mine, James.'

They went in by the side door. The rooms opening off the passage there were empty. They made for the stairs, then stopped dead as a motor started up in the anchorage.

Litsas was in front when they burst on to the terrace and ran to the edge of the tiny quay. The dinghy with the outboard was swinging away, but the inexpert hand on the tiller brought the stern and its crouching occupant almost under their feet, and Litsas had no trouble in dropping lightly into the boat. He spoke without looking up. The Smith & Wesson was levelled at von Richter's chest.

'The major and I will have a little sail, James. We're in not much hurry now. There's the major's boy-friend to deal with, but he's got some way to travel. I'll be back to help you dispose of him.'

Von Richter cut back the throttle and turned his head. In the grey light, the patch of damaged skin looked ghastly, the product of some loathsome disease. 'This man means to kill me, it appears,' he drawled. 'I'm quite helpless, as you can see. You're an Englishman, Mr Bond. Do you approve?'

'You're beyond any law, von Richter,' said Bond slowly. 'After what you did at Kapoudzona.'

'Clearly, argument is useless. Emotion has taken over.' The man gave a faint shrug. 'Very well. Let us go for our sail.'

The boat began to move away. Abstractedly, Bond watched it receding for a couple of minutes, then sauntered back into the house. He had reached the hall before he noticed the blood-spots.

There was a group of them at the corner of the passage, as if somebody had rested there for a moment, and another near the side door. Bond turned in his tracks and rushed to the kitchen.

The trap-door had been flung aside. Below, Luisa lay on her back with her eyes open, a metal meat-skewer through her heart. Dr Lohmann was sitting on the floor against the wall, his knees drawn up. Beside him was his black case and a shattered hypodermic. There was no colour at all in his face. He opened his eyes and spoke in a slurred voice.

'He forgot,' he said. 'He forgot that morphia can do quite a lot for a man with holes in his guts. It never occurred to him.'

Amazement as much as horror had tied Bond's tongue. 'But how did he . . . do all this? According to you he was as good as dead twenty minutes ago.'

'Any ordinary man with those wounds would never have

been able to get up off the floor, let alone spring at me like . . .'
Lohmann shuddered and gasped. 'Supernormal vitality. There
are cases in medical jurisprudence. . . . Even so, after so much
blood-loss . . . He's not human.'

'Is there anything I can do for you?' asked Bond with
unwilling compassion.

'No. He pierced my intestine ten or twelve times with one
of those skewer things. I've only got a few more minutes.
Thanks to the morphia it's not intolerable. He wouldn't like
to know that, would he? . . . Tell me . . . I suppose you've
killed everybody else?'

'All but Willi are as good as dead.'

'Willi's as good as dead too. Sun's orders, agreed to by
von Richter. They worked out it would take Willi over twenty
minutes to get down that hill to the boat. Too long, they
thought. So they got me to give him a pep pill before he took
off. A capsule of one of the organo-phosphorus compounds.
The first symptoms should have come on by now. I told you
not to worry about him. So you see you needn't feel sorry for
me.'

Bond said nothing. Awkwardly, he laid his hand on Lohmann's shoulder for a moment and hurried away up the
ladder.

Beyond the side door the trail of blood was easy to follow.
It led across the firing-point and into the twisting gully Bond
had made his way down just over twenty-four hours ago. He
pushed on as silently as he could, eyes alert, ears straining to
reach through the woolly barrier in them that constantly
thickened and thinned, knife-hand at waist level. The light
paled every moment and progress was not difficult. He came
to one of the sections where the walls leaned in on each other,
the landward one rising, the seaward falling away, turned a
corner and found Sun not ten feet off.

The Chinese had propped himself against a granite buttress
to Bond's right. He looked shrunken, physically drained, and,
judging by the pool of blood on the dusty rock at his feet and
the half-coagulated stream that stretched from his mouth to
his waist, that was what he must have been. His right hand

was behind him, no doubt pressed against the wound he could reach. A sort of smile twisted the gory lips.

'My reasoning was correct, then.' Unbelievably, the voice was firm and full. 'In fact I knew you'd come, James. You must be feeling pretty pleased with yourself. I take it you've killed everyone?' he asked, in grotesque unconscious repetition of Lohmann's question.

'They've all been dealt with.'

'Excellent. Then it's back to you and me again. Under conditions very much more favourable to you than those obtaining in that cellar, you may think. But you'd be wrong.'

Colonel Sun brought his right hand into view. It gripped a mortar bomb.

'You see? I am in control still. I need hardly tell you, James, that if you move suddenly, or even if I happen to drop this contrivance by accident, I shall kill us both. I'm dying anyway. So, in a sense, are you. Because very soon I shall dash the nose of this against the rock at my side. Our fates really were linked, weren't they? Can't you feel that now?'

'What do you want, Sun?' Bond was calculating distances in feet and split seconds, trying to visualize the shape of the corner behind him, estimating the possibility of leaping the lower wall to his left.

'Admit that in me you have found your master, who in an equal contest, without the intervention of treachery, would have broken your spirit as finally and irresistibly as your limbs. Admit it, I say!'

'Never! It wouldn't be true! You had the numbers and the initiative and the planning on your side from the start. And what have you done with all that? Got yourself killed!'

Sun's stained teeth showed. 'I insist! I order you to—' Then the eyes flickered and blood pulsed from the mouth and Bond vaulted the seaward wall of the gully, dropped on all fours into a bowl of scrubby grass only five feet below, scrambled to a stump of rock like an eroded tombstone, swung himself to the far side of it. The rumbling in his ears pulsated on. Sun's voice, feeble now, came through from above and half right.

'Where are you, James? But that's a question only a fool would answer. I should have dropped this thing a moment ago, shouldn't I? But the desire to hear you acknowledge defeat must have taken charge of my fingers. What am I to do with it now? That's easy. I'll explode it next to me. Go out with a bang. That's the way my world will end.

'I want to tell you now that what I said to you earlier was quite wrong. De Sade misled me. Or I didn't read him properly. I didn't feel like a god when I was torturing you back there. I felt sick and guilty and ashamed. I behaved in an evil and childish way. It's ridiculous and meaningless, but I want to apologize. Can you forgive me?'

Bond never remembered what he was going to say, only that he bit back the saying of it at the last millisecond. The roaring silence went on. Then, full-throated again, the voice crying 'Damn you, Bond,' the oscillating dart-shape of the bomb thrown at random, the muffled, almost boxy explosion from the fissure where it landed, and more loud silence.

Sun had slipped to his knees against the wall of the gully. The extraordinary eyes were open. They fixed on the knife Bond still grasped and their expression became one of appeal.

Bond knelt, placed the point of the knife over Sun's heart, and pushed. Even then, in the last moment of that inhuman vitality, the bloodied lips stirred and mumbled 'Goodbye, James.' The moment was whisked away. Sun had turned into a life-sized doll.

Now the dream came back. But this time Bond himself was the formless creature he had fled from earlier, not knowing what it was he pursued, everything dissolving into puffs of flame as he passed it. Litsas was somewhere, and Litsas was crying. Ariadne was near. Then there was nobody.

Chapter 22

A Man from Moscow

'I HAD a devil of a job this morning, squaring things with the local authorities,' said Sir Ranald Rideout fretfully. 'Sticklers for form and their own dignity, as always. A lot of talk about the honour of Greece and of the Athens police department. Mind you, I can see their point in a way. A gun-fight in the streets, four dead, two of them foreigners and one of those a diplomat of sorts. No evidence at all, but the Commissioner fellow I saw had his guesses all right. Ah, thank you.'

Sir Ranald took a tomato juice from the white-coated waiter, set it down untasted on a table topped with marble, and went on at full speed.

'Then this business on Sunday. Half a dozen corpses, two German tourists missing, mysterious explosions, goodness knows what else, and who have they got in the way of witnesses and/or suspects? A half-witted Albanian girl who won't or can't talk, and a Greek thug with a lot of burns who says he doesn't know anything about it either, except that a man called James Bond killed one of his friends and tried to kill him and blew up his boat. I must say, Bond – speaking quite off the record, you understand – I can't altogether see why you didn't square things off by getting rid of that fellow too while you were about it – he was only small fry, wasn't he? After all, according to your report you'd put paid to three of the opposition already that morning. Surely one more wouldn't have—'

The air-conditioning in the upstairs banqueting room at the Grande Bretagne was not working properly and there was a good deal of noise, especially from the Russian group by the drinks table. But, encouraged by a nod from M at his side, Bond exerted himself to reply.

'It would have been a killing in cold blood, sir. By that time I'd had enough, and there was nobody I could or would have asked to do it for me. I'm sorry if it's inconvenienced you, but an unsupported accusation doesn't carry much weight, does it?'

'I see, I see,' Sir Ranald had begun to mutter before Bond had finished. 'Yes, I suppose knifing people one after the other can become a strain, even for someone like you. Someone who's been trained in that kind of work, I mean.' The Minister's feelings about the infliction of death seemed to have abruptly gone into reverse. He now stared at Bond with slight distaste.

M broke in. 'What happened finally, sir?'

'Oh yes. Well, I was able to convince them they'd be wiser to take no action. Their Home Office chap agreed with me. He was on my side as soon as I mentioned this Nazi character, von Richter. Seems the man was quite a legend. And then the fellow with the burns, Aris or whatever his name is – they'd been after him for some time for theft and crimes of violence. He won't embarrass us. They were a bit huffy about our having conducted our quarrels on Greek soil, but I pointed out that it wasn't our choice. I managed to smooth them down in the end. I think the PM will be satisfied.'

'Well, that's certainly a great relief.' M's eye, frosty as ever, was on Bond.

'Yes, yes. And it's a relief to have you back with us, too, both of you. Now. That Greek friend of yours, Bond – Litsas, isn't it? I wonder if I ought just to have a word with him before I catch my plane.'

'I'm sure he'd appreciate it, sir,' said Bond. 'And I think he does deserve something in the way of thanks, after voluntarily risking his life on behalf of England. Don't you?'

'Yes. Yes, of course I do. Excuse me a moment.'

Bond grinned sardonically at the Minister's retreating back. M gave a faint snort.

'Difficult not to think hardly of a man like that, James. But I suppose politicians are necessary animals. Anyway, we can afford to feel tolerant about them this evening. I must say our hosts have exerted themselves. Special representative from Moscow and so on. They seem quite pleased with us. No more than they ought to be, of course. Occasion for rejoicing, after all. Except for one thing – the absence of Head of Station G. You won't see your friend Stuart Thomas again.'

'Is that certain, sir?'

'Pretty well, I'm afraid, after this time. My private bet is that he got himself killed rather than be used for whatever the Chinese party wanted him for. Better forget all that. Let me ask you a question, James. Your report. I'm curious to know why you didn't just sit back and let that Prussian blaze away at the people on the islet. They were no friends of yours, after all.'

Bond nodded. 'I've asked myself that. I must have just got caught up – I wasn't thinking. The three of us had combined to smash the lot of them and the job had to be finished. But I hope you agree it was the right thing to do anyway.'

'I do. Very strongly. Quite against the cards, we've pulled off something that's going to have a favourable effect on the world balance of power. Or rather you have. The Russians realize that all right. Notably this delegate fellow. Who evidently wants a word with you.'

An elegant young Russian with high Tartar cheekbones had made his way over. 'Excuse me, Admiral, sir. Our Mr Yermolov from Moscow would like to have a talk with you, Mr Bond. Would you come, please?'

The man from Moscow was tall, stout, red-faced, with small authoritative eyes. Bond put him down as a veteran Bolshevik, old enough, probably, to have seen some service as a youth in the Wars of Intervention, working his way up through the Stalin machine, coming to real power since the fall of Khrushchev. He looked quick-witted and determined; he would have had to be both these things to be still alive.

Wasting no time on preliminaries, Yermolov led Bond to a pair of ornate pseudo-Empire chairs that had been placed, obviously with the present purpose in mind, near the marble fireplace.

'You have enough to drink, Mr Bond? Good. I shall not detain you long. I want to say first that you have done my country a considerable service and that we are properly grateful. Comrade Kosygin himself has of course been fully informed of your role in this affair, and he has asked me to convey to you his personal thanks and congratulations. But more of that later.

'Besides our gratitude, it's also suitable that we offer you our apologies. For certain specific failures of judgement on our part. I have to admit to you that our security apparatus in this area had been allowed to fall into disrepair. This was not the fault of the late Major Gordienko, a capable enough officer who—'

'One moment, Mr Yermolov, if I may.' Bond had grown tired of the official jargon he had had to talk and listen to and write for so much of the last three days – in being formally interviewed by Sir Ranald, in a six-hour session alongside Ariadne at the Russian Embassy, in compiling his own report. 'Can we talk naturally? For instance, just to satisfy my curiosity, what happened to the traitor in your set-up here that Gordienko talked to me and Miss Alexandrou about?'

Yermolov breathed in slowly through his nose. His little eyes looked quizzically at Bond. Without shifting their gaze he produced a cigarette that had apparently been lying loose in his pocket, inserted it into a stained amber holder and lit it with a cheap metal lighter. He said abruptly: 'Yes. Why not? I'm sorry, I've been opening too many power-stations recently. That sort of thing doesn't encourage informality. Let's talk naturally, then. But that's not so easy, you know, for a Russian. I'll have to have a serious drink, and I insist that you join me. Vodka. We can offer you Stolichnaya, not the best there is, but perfectly wholesome.'

He snapped his fingers at the high-cheekboned young man and went on talking.

'Putting it naturally, then, the traitor, or rather the double agent, tried to escape when he found his bosses' plans had gone wrong. He's been dealt with.'

'Throat cut and dropped into the harbour, I suppose.'

'If you go on putting things as naturally as that, it's going to be a strain to keep up with you, Mr Bond, but I'll do my best. No. We're trying to avoid that sort of method these days. He'll be going to prison on a number of civil charges. Genuine ones. We like to have insurance cover on certain of our employees abroad. What happens to him when he comes out has still to be decided. Ah, good.' The drinks had arrived. 'My very best respects. Long live England.'

'Thank you.'

'Hm. Now as to General Arenski and his ill-advised scepticism about the story Miss Alexandrou told him. Arenski has ... had it. That's correct, isn't it? He was luckier than he deserved when the shells fired by that Nazi all exploded in the sea and did no more than give everybody a bad scare. It was lucky for us, too. I've had a strenuous day playing down the whole matter of the conference to the authorities here. I couldn't have managed that if they'd known who was involved. Which a few deaths would have given away unmistakably.'

'But surely ... no amount of playing-down would have concealed the fact that your people had been shipping in illegal immigrants by the boatload.'

'A good point.' Yermolov did another slow inhalation. 'To answer that I'm afraid I'll have to fall back on not being natural. Just for the moment. A richer Power can always find ways of conciliating a poorer one about what are really only technical matters. The conference was over anyway. Is that acceptable?'

Bond grinned. 'It'll have to be, I suppose. Go on about Arenski.'

'Well, of course he tried to blame the shells on you. But that won't stick. All the governments concerned are being circulated with a very full account of Chinese responsibility for this act of attempted terrorism. You and your bosses needn't worry about that. If you'll forgive me for saying so, it's much more important to us that the reputation damaged in these parts should be Peking's rather than London's. We've put some good men on it.'

Bond savoured the smooth ferocity of the vodka. 'What's going to happen to Arenski?'

'It's corrective training for him, I'm afraid. Reindoctrination with fundamental Socialist principles in Siberia. We still keep up that part of our traditions. In a more humane way than formerly. Rather more humane. Well ... I think that covers everything. Except ...'

Yermolov chewed at his lips. The noise of the party swelled in the background. Bond caught sight of Ariadne, beautiful and magnificently groomed in a lilac-coloured linen dress, the centre of a group of admiring Russians. The first really profound sense of relief swept through him. It was over. They had won. And more than that ...

The man from Moscow was speaking again. 'I'd like you to know that what you've done is extremely important. It's helped to show my bosses, not just who our real enemy is – we know much more about Chinese ambitions than your observers do – but who our future friends are. England. America. The West in general. This Vrakonisi business may lead to a great deal.

'And that means I've got to go back to being official for a moment. Sorry. My government wants you to accept the Order of the Red Banner for services to peace. So do I, Mr Bond. Will you?'

'It's very kind of them,' said Bond, smiling. 'And of you. But in my organization we're not allowed to be given medals of any kind. Not even by our own people.'

'I see.' Yermolov nodded sadly. 'I rather expected you to say that. I told Comrade Kosygin so. Well, there it is. It was an honest offer, expressing honest feeling. But, uh, you might not have found membership of the Order all that much of a distinction. Or an advantage. It wouldn't do you any good at all if you happened to come up against our counter-espionage forces in the future, as you've so often done in the past. As a matter of fact,' – here Yermolov leant forward confidentially – 'even Russian nationals who've been given it haven't noticed that it protected them very well – against anything. But, please, you must allow an old man his cynicism. Speaking naturally tends to go to one's head.'

He got up and held out his hand; Bond shook it. 'If there's

ever anything I can do for you, you must let me know, Mr
Bond. Is there any chance that you might come to Russia – I
mean as a visitor ?'

'Not at the moment. But I'll remember.'

'I'll remember too. Goodbye.'

Ariadne had extricated herself from the Russian circle
and was now talking to Litsas. Bond went over to them.

'Thank you for all you did, Niko. I've said it before, but
this seems another occasion for saying it.'

Litsas clapped him on the back. 'No thanks are needed.
I enjoyed it. I'd do all of it again. Except for one thing.'

'I know,' said Ariadne, looking grave.

'You won't remember, James, but I became rather silly
when I came back from ... taking von Richter for a sail. I
was like a baby. I couldn't make him understand, James.'
The brown eyes were at their saddest. 'He thought he'd
been quite all right at Kapoudzona. Reprisals against civilians
to punish guerrilla activity as laid down in orders. I asked
him about the children and he said it was ... unfortunate.
I wanted to make him *know what he'd done*. And feel bad
about it. He didn't. He never understood. He was thinking
I was a fool until I shot him. I intended to make an act of
justice, an execution. But I just killed him because I was
angry.'

'Not in cold blood, then,' said Bond, desperately trying to
offer comfort.

'That's true. I must think of that.' Now, with obvious effort,
Litsas grinned. 'Well, you've recovered in a good way. The
glamorous secret agent again. I suppose that suit is full of
little radios and concealed cameras and things.'

'Packed to the seams.' With mild surprise, Bond remembered for the first time since his return the devices installed
by Q Branch – the picklock, the hacksaw blades, the midget
transmitter. He had been right about their irrelevance, their
uselessness when the crunch came.

Litsas had swallowed his drink. 'I must go. I will let you
know about Ionides. I've asked everybody I know to keep a
look-out for him. He must have sold the *Altair* in Egypt or

somewhere and decided to hide for a bit. But it's funny. I could have sworn he was honest.'

'So could I,' said Ariadne.

'And I,' said Bond, remembering the guileless look and the proud upright carriage.

'Oh well. ... You're leaving in the morning? Come to Greece again, James. When the Chinese and the Russians aren't chasing you. There are many places I'd like you to see.'

'I'll be back. Goodbye, Niko.'

The two men shook hands. Litsas kissed Ariadne and was gone.

Bond looked into the strong, vivid face at his side. 'How are you, Ariadne?'

'I'm fine. Don't I look fine?'

'Yes, you do. But I meant ... after that night.'

She smiled. 'It wasn't so bad, you know. Oh, I hated it and I hated them. But I made it better by preventing them from enjoying it. I never let up on that. Finally they threw me out of bed and one of them went away and the other slept. So forget it, darling. Come on. I'll bet you're hungry, aren't you?'

'Very. Where shall we go?'

'Not Dionysos' place.' They both laughed. 'I'll find somewhere. By the way, I noticed you didn't thank me for all my help the way you thanked Niko.'

'Of course not. You were on duty. You're an agent of the GRU. Or you were.'

She gazed levelly at him. 'I still am. It's my work.'

'After all that? After Arenski and his stupidity?'

'Yes, after all that. It showed me how important the job is.'

'If that's how you feel, obviously you must stay with it.'

Ariadne put her hand on his shoulder. 'Let's not be serious tonight. We haven't got long. Must you leave tomorrow?'

'I must. But you do believe I don't want to, don't you?'

'Yes. Yes, darling. Let's go.'

As, five minutes later, they walked along the side of the square with the evening bustle of Athens around them Bond said, 'Come to London with me, Ariadne. Just for a little while. I know they'll give you leave.'

'I want to come with you, just as you don't want to go. But I can't. I knew you'd ask me and I was all set to say yes. Then I saw it somehow wouldn't be right. I think old Arenski was right about one thing, when he said I was bourgeois. I'm still stuck with my middle-class respectability. Does that sound silly?'

'No. But it makes me feel sad.'

'Me too. It all comes from our job. People think it must be wonderful and free and everything. But we're not free, are we?'

'No,' said Bond again. 'We're prisoners. But let's enjoy our captivity when we can.'

JAMES BOND
007

Sales in PAN of these outrageously enter-
taining thrillers by IAN FLEMING exceed
twenty-four million.

Thunderball	3/6
You Only Live Twice	3/6
The Man with the Golden Gun	3/6
The Spy Who Loved Me	3/6
Octopussy	3/6
Casino Royale	4/-
For Your Eyes Only	4/-
On Her Majesty's Secret Service	4/-
Moonraker	4/-
Live and Let Die	4/-
From Russia With Love	5/-
Goldfinger	5/-

* * * * * * * *

The Life of Ian Fleming

by John Pearson   illustrated 7/6

'I have nothing but praise for a book which engrossed
me for two days and a night'—Cyril Connelly,
Sunday Times.
'Pearson has uncovered interesting facts about Bond,
the whys and hows behind the plots, about Fleming
too'—Scotsman.

TRAVIS McGEE

JOHN D. MACDONALD

The tough, amoral and action crammed stories of the popular Travis McGee as he tangles with passionate women and violent men to uncover blackmail and corruption from California to Mexico.

First of the Travis McGee series now filming starring Rod Taylor.

All available at (20p) 4/- each

THE QUICK RED FOX
A DEADLY SHADE OF GOLD
BRIGHT ORANGE FOR THE SHROUD
THE DEEP BLUE GOODBYE
NIGHTMARE IN PINK
A PURPLE PLACE FOR DYING

GAVIN LYALL

'A complete master of
the suspense technique'
Liverpool Daily Post

SHOOTING SCRIPT
5/-
'The sky's the limit for this
fine suspense/adventure story'
Daily Mirror

MIDNIGHT PLUS ONE
5/-
'Grimly exciting...original
in concept, expertly written
and absolutely hair-raising'
New York Times

THE WRONG SIDE OF THE SKY
5/-
'One of the year's best
thrillers'
Daily Herald

'Thrillers on this level
are rare enough'
The Daily Telegraph